Her Stowed Bones

Chapter 1.

A swirling wind whipped down the road, lifting a choking haze of red dust. Constable Jenny Williams ducked her Akubra hat to protect her eyes, as the dust cloud passed. Sweat dripped down her spine as she lifted her gaze and squinted into the radar gun screen.

Flashing red numbers made her sigh and brace herself for another lecture on how she should be out catching *real* bad guys.

The fact speeding drivers killed themselves and others almost daily was rarely an argument worth having. Especially not today. In this heat.

She puffed out her cheeks, then strode out in front of the powder-blue rusted Chrysler ute. Waving, she indicated for the driver to pull over on the red dirt verge.

Barking extractors and a throbbing V8 motor painted one picture. The grey-haired driver with a torn truckie tank top, hanging out the open window scowling, told another.

'Oh, hell Jenny. I was barely out of third gear.' The woman's menopausal moustache was highlighted with a fine mist of white dust.

'Mrs Carson.' Jenny turned the radar gun to show the old miner. 'You were doing 10k's over the limit.'

A wrinkled, sun-spotted hand waved at the radar gun.

'Damn those fancy, fandangle bloody things. You should be catching criminals like that stupid woman who nearly ran me off the road a second ago. Pissed as a newt, if you ask me.'

'It's barely two in the afternoon, Mrs Carson.'

'Exactly. You should go and find *her*. Get the piss-pot off the road and leave me to get my supplies back to my place.'

Jenny knew she should ignore the old miner and write up the speeding ticket, but something about the idea of someone drink-driving erratically hit a nerve.

The memory of a mangled wreck and her brother's lifeless body made her chest tighten.

She glanced over the roof of Mrs Carson's Chrysler and peered down Kempel Road toward town. Undulating hills rimmed her view, dotted with white and ochre mullock mounds and the occasional mining rig. Spindly shrubs hung at the roadside as another mini tornado of red dirt traversed the outlying land and hurtled toward her.

She ducked her head so she could see Mrs Carson.

'Who and where?'

Mrs Carson lifted both hands from the steering wheel in mock-surrender.

'I don't know her bloody name Luv.'

Jenny sighed as she reached for her ticket book.

Mrs Carson wiped her perspiring top lip with the back of her hand.

'You sure you can't let me off with a warning? It's nearly Christmas after all.'

Jenny noticed the lonely piece of silver tinsel wrapped around the rearview mirror.

'Are you keeping your explosives locked up properly?' The woman nodded vigorously. 'With the warning signs?' Another quick nod, accompanied by a hopeful expression.

Jenny recalled how Mrs Carson's stolen explosives caused a mine cave-in, trapping her friend Penny below ground. The forensic tech was lucky to survive the blast. The woman might have learnt her lesson, but Jenny doubted it.

Shaking her head, she lifted her pen and began to write on the pad in her hand. Mrs Carson deflated.

'This is a warning Mrs Carson.' She began writing and hid her grin as the woman wiggled like an excited puppy. 'It's all about minimising accidents after all, not about revenue raising,' she reminded herself aloud as she tore off the ticket and handed it to the old miner.

The woman held out her hand to accept the warning.

'Thanks Luv.'

Screeching tyres and grinding metal made Jenny peer down the narrow road toward town.

'Sounds like duty calls.' She slapped the paper into Mrs Carson's hand and jogged to her police Landcruiser parked under the only tree to offer shade within a kilometre.

Mrs Carson hung her head out the open window.

'Told you she was pissed.'

Jenny shook her head as she reached her vehicle, tossed the radar gun into the passenger seat, slipped in and started the motor.

She was parked a few k's from town. Although the crash didn't sound like a high-speed impact, she knew people died in the strangest circumstances from collisions all the time. She revved the motor and spun the steering wheel. The Landcruiser drifted in the red dirt verge as she made a tight U-turn.

She reached the intersection of Seventeen Mile and Hutchison Roads and for a moment she sat in the police vehicle, staring out of the windscreen, stunned.

'You stupid old bitch!' A blonde woman in a striped boob-tube and cut off shorts thumped on the side window of Betty Farrell's BMW.

The older woman cowered behind the locked door. Her eyes wide and close to tears.

Jenny checked her weapon was secure and stepped out. 'Excuse me!'

She stalked toward the outraged woman, whose face grew redder as she continued to shout at Mrs Farrell, ignoring Jenny.

Jenny scanned the street and found a gold VW Passat covered in rust and dust in equal measure. The vehicle was spun in 180 degrees, indicating the driver likely never tried to slow for the *Give Way* sign.

'Get out and pay for my car, you stupid-old-cow!'

The woman's left arm waved and pointed frantically toward the VW while her other hand thumped the window once more.

Jenny reached Mrs Farrell's door as a State Emergency Services vehicle screeched to a halt nearby.

'Excuse me!' Jenny tried again to get the woman's attention. 'You need to stop...'

'What the hell!' The enraged woman spun around. Her eyes fell on Jenny's uniform. Stumbling back, the driver gave Jenny a chance to step between Mrs Farrell and her attacker.

Jenny lifted her hands, palms out in front of the woman.

'I need you to step away from the vehicle.'

She would have liked to use the woman's first name, but she didn't know it. Her partner, Constable Danny Phillips would have. He was a born and bred local, while Jenny was nearing the end of her second year in Coober Pedy.

Jenny gave the woman a moment to react. When she failed to comply, Jenny reached for her arm. The woman snatched it behind her back and scowled.

'Don't touch me!'

The strong stench of rum and cola hit Jenny in the face. It appeared Mrs Carson was correct.

'What's your name?' Jenny kept her tone conversational. The woman remained wary. 'Can you come with me and let the SES volunteers get access to the other driver?'

And undergo a breath test, she thought as she directed the woman toward the VW Passat. As they drew closer, a quiet sobbing made Jenny's skin tingle.

'Is there someone else in the car?'

She jogged toward the untouched rear of the vehicle, dragged the creaking back passenger's side door open and gasped.

The sobbing stopped. Wide eyes greeted her—peering out from wet, dirty, bloodied cheeks.

'You didn't…' Jenny turned to ask the woman why she failed to mention there was a baby in the back seat.

Vacant space greeted her.

She considered trying to find the woman, but an approaching siren assured her back up was on the way. She returned her focus to the dark brown bewildered eyes staring at her.

'Hey bub. What's your name?' She knew the infant was far too young to answer.

His arms weren't restrained correctly. Blood ran from a gash in his forehead where he was likely flung into the overly reclined driver's seat.

'I've got you.' She slid across the back seat and unclipped the maladjusted shoulder straps.

As soon as the clasp clicked open, the child flung himself at her. Blood soaked her shoulder instantly. She didn't care. The little boy wasn't crying anymore. He was safe.

How could the woman just leave the child in the car while she ranted and attempted to assault poor old Mrs Farrell?

Why didn't she instinctively check on her child first? Was she high, as well as drunk? Surely any mother in her right mind would check on her child before anything else.

Jenny backed out of the vehicle. The little boy clung to her like a chimpanzee.

Phillips strode toward her. A deep furrow covered his brow.

'Is he alright?' He rubbed the boy's back reassuringly.

The action seemed to soothe her partner, more than the child. Danny and his wife Dianna spent months in the city while their son Tommy underwent treatment for leukemia. It was a scary time for everyone. Thinking about it, even now, made Jenny's eyes sting.

'He's alright. A bump on the head by the looks,' she reassured her partner. 'Is the ambulance on the way?'

'Yeah.' Her partner hesitated, as though he wanted to say more but focussed back on his job. 'Frank said the driver split a minute ago.'

'She did. I think she heard your siren, but it's weird. I was already here. Why run now?'

Phillips scowled.

'Beats me. Some people don't deserve kids.' Jenny said nothing as Phillips rounded the bonnet. 'Better secure the vehicle.' He opened the driver's side door and pulled a lever. The boot opened instead of the bonnet. 'Whoops.'

Phillips pulled another lever, and the bonnet popped. He left the driver's door open and lifted the bonnet to secure the battery. Jenny soothed the child as she approached the boot.

'Maybe we can get your nappy bag out the boot or a toy or something.'

She adjusted the little boy on her hip, then lifted the boot lid with one hand. A gasp escaped her lips before she could stop it. Letting the boot lid go, she pressed the child's face to her shoulder and staggered back. Her heart thudded in her chest. Her mind raced.

'I think I know why she ran,' she called to her partner.

The little boy wriggled, trying to see what the fuss was about. Jenny held him firmly as Phillips rushed to join them.

'Geez.' He reached for his lapel mic. 'We need some help.'

Jenny gaped at the crumpled figure, wrapped in thin, white plastic. Wisps of brunette hair, matted with blood, protruded at the side of the wrapping.

Pink painted toenails poked out the bottom edge.

Jenny absently cooed to the child and herself in equal measure. As she focussed on two petite hands, bound in thin wire, clasped together in prayer, begging her to find a killer, she realised all the calm words in the world weren't going to settle her nerves.

Chapter 2

The little boy's wide eyes darted around the ambulance interior as Jenny's roommate, and local paramedic Tim, waved a light in his eyes.

'Pupils are normal. I don't think he's concussed, but we'll let Nev check him more thoroughly back at the hospital.'

'What about his mum?'

Tim opened a cupboard above the bucket seat Jenny comforted the little boy on and pulled out a knitted blue teddy bear.

'Here you go little man.'

The toy was one of over a million hand-knitted bears donated by Red Cross volunteers since the inception of the Trauma Teddy program.

The boy's gaze narrowed at the small, soft toy. Turning his head, he regarded Jenny with questioning eyes.

'It's yours,' she reassured him.

The boy snatched the toy and hugged it under his chin.

'We'll keep him at the hospital for as long as it takes to get Children's Services in, or the mother turns up.'

Jenny gripped the child tighter.

'I know that look.' Tim waggled his finger in front of her. 'Don't even think about it.'

'But she ran off and abandoned...' She stopped herself from saying too much. The boy was likely not even two years old, but children were intuitive, and they heard and understood a lot before they could say a word.

'From what you've described, she was probably drunk. As soon as she thinks her alcohol limit is low enough, she'll rock up. I've seen it dozens of times.'

'You have?'

'Williams!'

Jenny didn't need to see the origin of the gruff voice to know her boss was going to peer inside the ambulance any second.

As Sergeant Mackenzie's head appeared, the little boy's bottom lip quivered. A shrill squeal escaped his lips a heartbeat later.

Jenny hugged him to her chest.

'Now look what you've done.'

The words were out of her mouth before she could stop herself.

Her boss's gaze narrowed, then softened as the toddler continued to fret.

'Sorry mate.' The sergeant waved his hands in front of his chest. 'I didn't mean to frighten you.'

'Hey Mikey.' A woman's voice made all heads turn. 'Whatcha doing in here? This place is pretty cool, hey.'

The little boy stopped sobbing, flung his head around and fixed his gaze on Nellie. The newest station constable squeezed past the sergeant, into the cramped ambulance interior.

'You know him?' Tim and Jenny asked in unison.

'Certainly do. This is Tanya Rothchild's son. Took the call for the accident. As soon as I recorded the vehicle description and heard bubba was left behind, I asked Sarge if I could join him.'

Mikey's pudgy little arms widened with the teddy still held tightly in one hand.

'Appears you've been replaced Williams.' Sarge kept his tone calm. 'We've got a scene to clear.'

Jenny reluctantly passed the toddler to Nellie and shimmied around her as they swapped positions.

'And I'll need to know what you know about the mother, as soon as you're done at the hospital Nellie,' Sarge ordered.

'You got it boss.'

Tim slid the ambulance side-door closed as soon as Jenny jumped out.

'Do we have any ID on the victim?' She watched the ambulance disappear as she spoke.

'Not yet. I don't want anyone touching anything until forensics get here. I've got Phillips documenting the accident scene. Once he's done, we'll tow the car to Ted's Garage. McGregor is on the way, but in this heat, we need to get the remains secure before it starts to puff up and stink.'

Jenny screwed up her nose. It wasn't a pleasant thought, but they couldn't remove the remains from the vehicle into refrigeration until the Adelaide forensic team finished collecting all the evidence.

'It's got to be a murder.'

'No kidding, Williams. I wasn't born yesterday. This isn't a dead body down a mine. This woman is wrapped up like a bloody Christmas turkey.' Her boss shook his head. 'That white plastic looks like one of those disposable paint drop-sheets. Find out if the local hardware store has sold any lately.'

'Will do.' Jenny watched as a State Emergency Service volunteer drove Mrs Farrell's vehicle from the accident scene then turned to Sergeant Mackenzie.

'I'll chase down the mother. I know the car is registered in her name, but despite her running off, I'm not sure she's our killer. Who leaves a body in the boot of their car in this heat? Then hangs around after an accident to assault the other driver?'

'Not every killer is smart Williams. We need to treat her as a suspect, but at the very least, she could know the victim. There must be a connection. Why else would the remains be in her car? We need to find her.'

'Tim said she'll likely turn up for Mikey once she's sobered up.'

Sergeant Mackenzie rubbed his stubbled chin and nodded.

'I'll inform the hospital to notify us as soon as she arrives. For now, run her background and if Nellie doesn't know where she lives, get it from the vehicle rego. We'll call by and see if she's there, but my guess is she'll be hunkered down somewhere trying to avoid an alcohol and drug test. Check if any of the local shops along this route have CCTV.'

They reached the rear of the VW Passat and examined the open boot in silence. One SES appliance blocked the crashed car from prying eyes, while a Country Fire Service vehicle parked up on the other side to provide more cover.

Ted's tow-truck waited expectantly beyond the scene. Jed, who now ran the garage since his father's retirement, leant against the door, puffing on a hand-rolled smoke.

Phillips drew up behind them and fixed his eyes on the body.

'Do you recognise her?' Sergeant Mackenzie asked her partner.

'Bit hard to tell all wrapped up like that, but I don't think so.' His tone was haunted.

'Not local then?' Sarge's voice was gentler than usual.

Phillips shook his head.

'I don't know. She looks young, about our age.' He waved between himself and Jenny. 'I can't be sure.'

'We'll know more when McGregor finishes with her. Maybe her prints are in the system?' Sarge pulled a glove from his pocket, slammed the boot closed, then gave the tow-truck the go ahead with a wave.

'As soon as Rothchild shows her face, I want her detained for questioning.'

Jenny's phone buzzed in her utility-vest top pocket. Retrieving it, she recognised Nev's mobile number. The local doctor was another of her housemates and one of the first people to befriend her when she moved to town.

'Hey Nev. Is Mikey alright?'

He chuckled.

'Tim said you were a bit clucky. We going to have a Nick and Jenny baby before the wedding?'

'No! I was not clucky. Just concerned.'

Nev wasn't the only one chuckling now. She glared at her partner. Phillips rolled his lips together as Nev continued.

'Mikey is fine. I'm running him through x-ray to be sure. His mother arrived a minute ago, and I'm not sure she'll take too kindly if I ask her to undergo a blood test. I'll need a little uniform support.'

'We're on the way.'

Chapter 3

The yellow bollards outside the Emergency Department were wrapped in bright red and green tinsel. The soft tunes of Michael Bublé singing *It's beginning to look a lot like Christmas* reminded Jenny she was yet to buy Nick a gift.

The triage nurse glanced up as they entered the Emergency Department. Her head nodded toward a row of rigid plastic chairs where Tanya Rothchild paced back and forth like a caged cat.

Jenny nodded for Phillips to wait by the exit while she approached. Tanya chewed her thumbnail, sat, then stood and began pacing again before she noticed Jenny crossing the waiting area.

Her eyes darted toward the exit. Phillips gave her a polite wave. She focussed back on Jenny, who reminded herself Tanya Rothchild could be unpredictable. They still didn't know if drugs were involved.

'Tanya. Sorry to bother you. I know you must be worried about Mikey.'

Maybe you should have hung around, she thought to herself.

'Can we ask you a few questions about the accident?'

A little girl around four, with round blue eyes and long pigtails, sat a few seats away. Jenny noticed her brow furrow as her eyes ran up and down Jenny's uniform. Without warning, she jumped to her feet, shoved her hands on her hips and opened her mouth.

Before she uttered a word, her mother whisked her from her feet, scurried across the room and put as much distance between them as she could.

'I don't want to speak with you. I—want—my—son!' Tanya didn't yell, but her tone made Jenny tense.

She lifted her hand and waved in a downward motion.

'I know you're worried. Mikey is with the doctor and won't be long.'

Jenny wondered over Tanya's quick arrival at hospital. Either she thought she was sober enough to submit to a blood test or the adrenalin from the accident wore off and she was worried about her son.

Jenny's instincts told her it was most likely the latter, which meant Tanya Rothchild was still over the limit. They had enough evidence to enforce her to submit to a blood test. But Tanya's demeanour right now wasn't going to make it easy.

Tanya turned abruptly and strode toward the triage desk.

'I'm not waiting any longer. He's my son. I want to see him, now!'

Jenny followed with a wave to the triage nurse, assuring her the situation was under control.

The Emergency Department was away from prying eyes. The perfect place to convince Tanya to take the blood test but also secluded enough to ask questions and hopefully get some answers.

'I'll show you through now.' Jenny reached out to guide the woman.

Tanya shied away with her arms held high.

'I told you not to touch me.' She spoke between gritted teeth.

Jenny scanned the exposed limbs for needle marks, raw sores or anything to indicate she was a drug user but found nothing.

'Okay, Ms Rothchild. I'll take you through. Please follow me.' Jenny led the way past the triage nurse, into the

Emergency Department. She glanced back to find her partner cautiously coming up behind them.

'Mikey should be in here.' Jenny continued to lead the way down the clean, white corridor toward the blue curtains, separating emergency beds.

'Mikey!' The woman called out, her voice wavering.

A pleated curtain swung aside to reveal Nev's broad smile, but tiny creases at the corners of his eyes gave away his tension.

'Ms Rothchild. Mikey is fine.' Nev stepped aside. Tanya rushed past, scooped up her son from the gurney and hugged him to her chest. Jenny noticed the knitted teddy squeezed between them.

'Wait up a minute,' Nev protested.

'You said he's fine. I'm taking him home.'

'The x-rays were all clear, but you can see the cut on his forehead needs attention. I was about to come and get you to sign the permission forms before I started.'

Jenny knew Nev was stalling. When a parent wasn't present, emergency care went ahead without parental consent.

'Well get me the bloody forms and I'll sign. I want to take him home.'

'Maybe pop Mikey back on the gurney,' Jenny pointed. 'Nev can get the forms organised and we can ask you a few questions while Mikey gets his stitches.'

'I'm not answering any questions.'

Jenny drew a slow breath, resisting the urge to puff out her cheeks. The last thing she wanted right now was for Tanya to go wild in front of her son. Keeping the woman calm was her top priority. The effects of alcohol were obviously wearing off, but an alcohol reading after an accident like this, was mandatory.

'It's your right not to answer the questions.' Jenny didn't point out how such a decision would likely result in them arresting her. 'But we need to collect a blood alcohol test before you leave.'

Tanya opened her mouth. Jenny raised her palm up in front of her.

'Hear me out.'

Tanya's lips pressed together. Her eyes darted to the faces in the cramped cubicle. Phillips guarded the exit with arms crossed and splayed legs. Nev held a clipboard in one hand, a pen in the other. His eyes searched the woman's face as she backed away with her son on one hip.

'How about I take that?' Jenny snatched the clipboard from Nev's hand, then reached for the pen. 'You two wait outside.'

Her partner's brow creased. Nev broke out in a white-toothed grin, turned and slapped Phillips on the shoulder.

'Let's go Danny. I could use a coffee.'

Her partner's frown deepened.

'I'll be out in a minute,' Jenny reassured him.

'A minute.' Phillips snapped the curtain aside. 'I'll be right outside.' He fixed his gaze on Tanya as he flicked the curtain closed behind him. 'Tanya. I don't know why you ran off, but we need to talk.' Jenny waved her hand for the woman to sit on the crisp white sheet. She remained standing.

Jenny shrugged, trying to appear casual.

'You have to make a choice.'

Tanya's eyes narrowed. She remained silent as she shifted Mikey to her other hip, guarding him behind her body.

'You were in a car accident. I'll need to get a statement, and you'll need to undergo a mandatory drug and alcohol blood test, but I think I can help you out.'

Tanya was frozen in situ, eyes drilling into Jenny's.

'I think you ran because you're on your last warning.' It wasn't a guess. Jenny ran Tanya's police record on the way to the hospital. 'A blood test right now is going to put you over the limit, and you'll be off to prison. Mikey will be put into foster care.'

Tanya's eyes narrowed.

'What do you want?'

The woman's tone ate into Jenny's resolve. Did everyone Tanya ever meet want something from her? Did they take it by force?

'My sergeant wanted me to bring you into the station, but if you cooperate and I get your full statement here, it will delay the test and save you a third strike DUI charge.'

'What about the reckless driving charges, and whatever else you have left up your sleeve?'

The woman was street savvy and dead right. The list of charges against Tanya Rothchild wasn't small. Reckless driving, failing to give way, assault, child endangerment, fleeing an accident scene…

'Tanya…' Jenny tongued her teeth and prepared for her next statement. 'The only charge you need to be worried about right now is murder.'

'Murder!' She held Mikey close to her chest as though hugging him would block out what Jenny was saying.

'Yes. Murder.' Jenny pointed to the gurney. 'Take a seat Ms Rothchild. I need to show you a photo.'

Usually, finding a body in someone's car was a clear indicator they were guilty, but the accident scene today told another story. And Sarge was right. They needed to know where her car was when the body was placed inside and they needed the victim's ID.

Jenny reached into her pocket and retrieved her phone. Tanya lowered herself cautiously to the gurney.

'After you left the accident, we found something in the boot of your vehicle.' Tanya's brow furrowed. 'Something with the potential to put you in prison for a very long time unless you help the police.'

'I don't understand. You found Mikey. He was the only thing in my car.'

'And you left him alone.'

'I… I wasn't thinking straight.'

Jenny opened the photo gallery on her phone and flicked to the image of their victim, curled up and jammed in the boot. There was no easy way to ID the body from the photo. Her face was shrouded. Even her clothing was wrapped in plastic.

'Is anything about this woman familiar?' Jenny turned the phone to Tanya, being careful not to let Mikey see.

Tanya's body stiffened. Her eyes grew wide before they shut tightly.

'That's… Oh my God. How did…'

'Just breathe Tanya. Take a moment. Tell me who is in this photo.'

As Tanya opened her eyes, Jenny noticed them glistening.

'It's Katie.' Her voice hitched as she spoke.

Jenny's palms sweated as she closed the camera app and opened the notepad app.

'Are you sure?' she asked, wondering how Tanya could positively ID a woman from a few strands of hair poking from the bloodied white plastic.

'Yes. She's wearing my nail…' She swallowed hard and cuddled her son. 'My nail polish and I put those purple spots on myself.'

Jenny nodded and made a note.

'What's Katie's last name?'

'Katie Montgomery. I work with her at…' Tanya shook her head. 'I need to get Mikey home. Where's the doctor?'

Tanya jumped from the gurney. Jenny placed her palm on the woman's chest.

'I need details Tanya, or I'll be enforcing a blood test, right now.'

'Go your hardest. I'm sober enough to pass your stupid test.'

'You're betting Mikey's future on that?'

Tanya clenched her jaw, drew back her shoulders and lifted her chin.

'I'll take my chances.'

Chapter 4

A rush of deliciously cool air flowed over Jenny as Phillips opened the station door and held it.

'Tanya must be more afraid of her employer than us if she was willing to lose Mikey.' Phillips let the door go and followed Jenny toward the high counter separating the foyer from the main open office area.

'Exactly. We'll need to run her tax file number to find her employer.'

'Already tried Williams.' Senior Constable O'Connell lifted a section of the counter for them to pass through. 'Tanya Rothchild is on a single parent payment. No employment records. If she's working, it's for cash.'

Sergeant Mackenzie strode from his office.

'And you might have gotten the victim's name, but I doubt it's her real one. We've found nothing on her. No licence, no registration, no electricity or phone bills.'

Jenny crossed to the bank of lockers near O'Connell's workstation. Each dented dark grey door was decorated with a cardboard cluster of bells, candy canes or Christmas trees. All with handwritten names on them.

Jenny smiled as she recalled her partner's son, Tommy and wife Dianna bringing them into the station. There was one for each officer, including O'Connell and Sarge.

She glanced over her shoulder, focussing back on her boss as she opened her locker and began undoing her utility-vest.

'That's not unusual out here.' She savoured the moment the compact vest lifted from her sweat-soaked shirt. 'Lots of people live in Coober Pedy to avoid unnecessary scrutiny. Maybe she shares a house and uses a pay-as-you-go phone.'

'Without a birth certificate, tax file or Medicare reference number? I don't think so Williams.' Sergeant Mackenzie crossed to the recently installed water cooler and refilled his mug. 'No. Our victim was using a fake name and according to forensics, we aren't going to get an ID from a picture.'

Jenny stilled her stomach, recalling the amount of blood in the matted brunette hair.

'Why?' she asked, already knowing the answer.

'Because as soon as your mate McGregor started her investigation, she extracted the victim from the boot, then called me. Whoever did this, smashed the poor woman's face in. I don't think they wanted us to identify her.'

'Or they were so enraged they couldn't stop hitting,' Jenny suggested with a shiver.

'Why didn't you bring Tanya Rothchild in for a formal interview? I'm sure those were my last words to you before you left. I want to know where her car was when the body was put into the boot and if she knows the victim, she likely has a less gruesome photo of her. And I want a list of other known associates.'

'There was no point,' Sergeant Mackenzie huffed, ready to argue. But Jenny rushed on. 'I tried to get more out of her Sarge. She wouldn't even tell me where she and Katie worked. Bringing her down here wasn't going to make her talk. She was terrified of something. So scared she chose to take the blood test, and risk a high alcohol, three-strike prison sentence and her son, instead of answering my questions.'

Sarge pursed his lips a moment, then nodded.

'Okay. Until forensics come back, we have no evidence to hold her anyway.'

The phone rang. O'Connell answered the call as Sergeant Mackenzie pointed to Jenny.

'Go help McGregor at Ted's Garage. See what she
needs. It's going to be a late one tonight, but I want that vehicle
searched from top to bottom.'

'Fun times.' Jenny re-fastened her damp utility-vest,
seriously considering changing her shirt but realising it would
be a waste of time because Ted's Garage wasn't
airconditioned. She closed her locker as O'Connell dropped the
phone receiver back into the cradle.

'That was old man Fergusson. The CFS just
extinguished a blaze in his haystack and Fergusson claims it
was dry as a bone. He reckons there's no way it was
spontaneous combustion.'

Sergeant Mackenzie frowned.

'It's hot enough to roast a duck out there. Could have
been started by a broken bottle.'

'He's adamant it's arson,' O'Connell offered.

Jenny's palms grew sweaty as she recalled last year's
investigation into the death of a real estate agent. The case was
linked to a pastoral and mining company with a rogue board
member found to be extorting landholders into selling.

Nick was one such landholder refusing to sell. Someone
cut the girth on his saddle and caused an accident. He could
have been killed. Jenny was sure that someone was Ben, Nick's
new assistant manager at the time. But there was no proof.

She begged Nick to fire Ben. He did the exact opposite.
When the murder case was closed, the corruption and extortion
investigation fell under federal police jurisdiction. The AFP
believed Ben could be a useful tool to expose the mining
company.

So Nick agreed to help them by keeping Ben on and
reporting back to the Feds. Jenny didn't like it one little bit, but
fortunately, everything had been quiet for months.

At least, that's what Nick told her.

'Fergusson is Nick and Mr Murphy's neighbour. It's been a year since we exposed the mining company extortion racket, but this could be linked.'

'We aren't privy to the AFP investigation Williams.' Sarge's tone held a warning to let it go.

'It can't be a coincidence though. I'll call Nick and see if Ben is at work today.' Jenny persisted.

Sarge pointed to the door. 'You go help McGregor. I'll get a hold of Nick and see if the AFP want to play nice and update us on the extortion investigation. But if we find a link with Fergusson's fire, the case will be out of our jurisdiction quick-smart. Whereas this woman's murder isn't. We need to focus on that.'

Jenny opened her mouth. Sarge's eyes narrowed. She pressed her lips together and nodded. 'I'll get going.'

Ten minutes later, Jenny slammed the door on the police Landcruiser with more force than intended. Jed glanced up with a bored expression, ran his fingers through his greasy hair then undid the lid on a bottle of cola. Leaning against the outside of the garage, he swallowed half the bottle in one swig.

Jenny's mouth watered as she approached.

'Stinks in there.' He lifted his half bottle of cola. 'How long you gonna be? I've got a business to run you know.'

'I'm sure SA Police will reimburse you for your down time.'

Jed scoffed. 'They're gonna have to pressure-wash the whole bloody place.' He hoicked his thumb at the side door.

Jenny opened her mouth to assure him they would get someone out, but as she drew closer to the access door, her eyes began to water. Despite it being after 6pm, the temperature outside was still hot enough to generate a heat haze from the metal building. Inside, with all the roller doors closed, it was going to be a furnace.

She forced herself to breathe through her mouth but stopped short of stepping inside.

'Hey Penny!' she called through the opening. 'You got some PPE for me?'

Something clattered to the concrete floor. The sound of fabric preceded the appearance of a tall, broad figure clad in disposable overalls, goggles, gloves, an N95 face mask and widely spread arms, ready for a hug.

Penny McGregor was one of Jenny's closest friends, despite the distance and infrequency of their visits. Under normal circumstances, Jenny would have dived into the embrace. Instead, she put her hands up in front of her face, palms out and hurried back out of reach.

'Sorry, but you really stink. Sarge sent me down to help. My uniform smells of sweat already, but that's way worse. I need some protective gear.'

Penny pulled down her face mask and greeted Jenny with a wide grin, which disappeared as the scent of decaying flesh, methane gas and who knew what else drifted into the forensic tech's nostrils.

'Yep, you're right. It's a bit ripe in here.' Penny disappeared inside, then returned a few moments later with overalls and all the necessary PPE.

'I'm not looking forward to this. I saw the body earlier. But now this heat.' Jenny shook her head at the thought of what she was likely to see.

'Remains are gone. I flew in on the SAPOL jet and they waited for the victim. She's on her way to Doc. He's put a rush on his report, but my preliminary findings will indicate she likely died from her head injuries.'

Jenny stepped into the overalls and zipped them up, then balanced from foot to foot to put her shoe protectors on.

'Can we open the roller door and let some of this stink out?'

Penny shook her head.

'No can do. There was enough contamination just bringing the vehicle in here. I don't need anymore.'

Jenny snapped her gloves on and pulled the goggles over her eyes, then stepped into the garage as she secured the face mask.

'What can I do?' Jenny's muffled voice made Penny giggle as she slipped her mask back in place.

They crossed the garage to the VW. Katie's matted hair and plastic-wrapped body flashed before Jenny's eyes as soon as she peered into the empty boot.

'I left the plastic on the victim. Doc will run it for any trace evidence. But check this out.'

Jenny followed Penny's finger to find something glinting in a spotlight.

'I was about to collect it when you got here.' Penny rummaged in her bag for a pair of tweezers and an evidence bag.

'Is that what I think it is?' Jenny glanced where her engagement ring often sat. Then patted her neck where she kept hers on a chain while working.

Penny rotated the dark blue sapphire and yellow gold ring as Jenny continued to speculate.

'Is there a chain anywhere? If it's an engagement ring, maybe she couldn't wear it at work.'

'Someone could have forcibly removed it. Doc will be able to confirm.' Penny dropped it into an evidence bag. 'It's not necessarily an engagement ring.'

'I guess, but either way, finding a ring in here probably takes robbery off the table as motive.

'Not my department.'

'I know. I know. You just find the evidence.'

'And you use it to catch the bad guys.'

'If only it were that easy,' Jenny sighed.

Penny snapped a series of photos, then turned to Jenny.

'At least it's a start.'

'Yep. One piece of the puzzle. Let's see if we can find some more.'

'Absolutely. The faster I get done here, the quicker I can get to the bar for a glass of wine.'

'And a catch up with Tim, no doubt.'

Penny's eyes smiled through her goggles. Tim and Penny met at university and hooked up from time to time when Penny was in town. Their relationship became challenging last year when they announced they were officially a couple. Tim had been chasing a transfer since.

'How's Tim's transfer going?'

Penny collected some fibres, placed them in an evidence bag, then added them to the evidence box with the ring.

'City placements are hard to get, especially close to where I live.' Penny's shoulders sagged. 'But he has another Skype interview this week.'

'Fingers crossed,' Jenny offered as she considered what might happen if she ever wanted to advance her own career. She'd already turned down an offer to train as a detective. Right now, Nick and their wedding were her focus.

Jenny used a torch to scan the boot interior through her sweat-fogged goggles. The light beam found obvious bloodstains and marks on the textured plastic side wall, but a strange pattern in a smear of blood made her stop.

'Penny. Look at this.' She flicked her torch beam back and forth over the smeared blood.

'Let's get the black light out.' Penny retrieved a torch from her kit bag and flicked the button until a purplish, blue light emanated.

As the beam passed over the interior wall of the boot, letters became clear. Jenny wiped her fogged goggles to be sure she was reading the name correctly.

'Here. Hold this.' Penny passed the torch to Jenny and delved into her leather bag once more.

Jenny studied the letters as the flash from Penny's SLR strobed over the scene. The name was clear. The letters smeared, faint but defined enough to be read under the blacklight. If this was the name of the woman's killer, things were going to get messy.

Chapter 5

The overworked station airconditioner struggled to keep up with the rising outside temperature. Jenny rolled her shoulders to ease the tension, then filled her cup with cool water from the new watercooler.

Sergeant Mackenzie joined her and did the same.

'It's only a name Williams. It could be her brother, the beginning of her last name, her boss. Just about anything. The fact the poor woman was alive when she was thrown into the boot with such horrific injuries is what really concerns me.'

'We don't know she was yet.' Penny balanced on the edge of Jenny's workstation.

Jenny plonked into her seat and watched Sergeant Mackenzie squint at the forensic tech.

'You think someone else wrote the name? Why would they do that?'

He drained his water.

Penny lifted her hands in the air.

'I'm only sharing a theory.'

Jenny suppressed a shudder as she considered a possible link between this latest victim, the attempt on Nick's life, and the lawyer who was blown up in a car-bomb during their last case. At the time, all indications pointed to one person. The same person whose name was written in blood beside their latest victim.

'But Sarge. Shouldn't we check to see where Ben Stokes has been?'

'McGregor is right. We don't know the victim even wrote the name, let alone the significance. Let's pick this up tomorrow.'

'I can call Nick now.'

Jenny ignored the desperation in her voice. She couldn't explain it, but her instincts were telling her Ben was mixed up in this, somehow.

'There's no tangible link between Ben Stokes and our victim and we don't even have a time of death yet Williams.'

Penny hopped up from the desk.

'I can probably help with that. It's only an estimate until Doc confirms. We can't use liver temp, because it was ambient when I checked. With daytime temps in the high 40 degrees, higher inside the boot, the body was well over 40, which is outside the average human temp of 37. But rigor was passed. The lack of body gases, even with the extreme heat…'

Sarge puffed out his cheeks.

'When you're ready McGregor. Let's have it.'

Penny's lips curled with satisfaction.

'I'd estimate between 36 and 48 hours.'

'Well, Ben's in the clear. I spoke with Nick earlier about the Fergusson's fire. He confirmed Ben hasn't left the property for the past two days. He also mentioned something about Ben being rostered on for another couple of days.'

It was true. Nick was due in town tonight. She couldn't wait to see him, but she couldn't help wondering about Ben. His arrival at the station and his link to their previous case were red flags. But she knew Nick was keeping a close eye on Ben for the federal police. If he said Ben was at William Creek Station, she was sure he must have been.

Penny patted Jenny's shoulder.

'Time to get showered and changed, because I know we both reek.'

Penny was right. Despite removing their overalls, putrefying flesh and sweat made a disgusting combo.

Jenny turned to her boss who spoke before she could protest.

'I know the extortion case still nags at you Williams. I've liaised with the AFP and as expected, we got stone-walled. We need to leave the arson case for the Country Fire Service. They'll bring in an expert, and we'll act on the report if needed. For now, we focus on our victim and discovering her ID.' Sarge waved the back of his hand toward Jenny. 'See you both at 7am sharp.'

Jenny didn't hide her disappointment.

'I'm not going to get any sleep. Can't I stay and run a few more leads? Has dental turned up anything?'

Penny shoved her toward her locker.

'Come on Jen. I need a drink, and you said Nick is coming into town tonight. I doubt his priority will be anything but his fiancé.'

'McGregor is right,' Sarge grinned. 'I was Nick's age once. The case can wait.'

Jenny glared at her boss as her cheeks reddened. Why did old people always have to go there?

Sarge smoothed his features.

'Go on Williams. Get out of here.' His gruff voice was back.

Jenny slipped from her vest, stowed her weapon and hurried from the station. Penny met her long gait as they crossed the sealed road between the station and the Opal Miner's Motel and Caravan Park.

Heat radiated from the bitumen, bounced off the high wall around the park and smacked Jenny in the face as the northerly wind stirred dust into the air and down the road.

By the time they reached the motel reception, Jenny's back was once more drenched. She tapped the doorway and poked her head inside the office. Marj glanced up over a rural romance novel, jumped to her feet and rounded the counter.

Her hair colour of choice this week matched her bright red lipstick smile perfectly.

'Oh. Just the woman I needed to see.'

Jenny cringed as Marj dragged her into a tight hug, then stepped back.

'Good lord, you're a little on the nose there, Luv.'

'Sorry.'

Jenny didn't bother explaining why. Marj likely already knew the details of their latest case. Nothing happened in town without attracting her attention.

'I heard about the dead body in the boot. A bit macabre, even for this outback mining town.'

'Can't talk about an ongoing case Marj.'

'Of course not Luv. But you *do* seem to attract more than your fair share.'

'Not you too Marj.' Jenny tried not to pout.

It was a sore spot for her. Nearly two years ago, fresh off the plane, she stumbled on her first wrongful death. The case turned out to be murder, committed by the former senior constable's wife and subsequently covered up by Les.

A few more suspicious deaths later, Phillips started calling her a murder magnet. The name stuck and now it seemed to have become contagious.

'Have you set the date for your wedding yet?'

Marj's change of subject wasn't any better. Everyone in town and her parents back home, seemed to ask about the wedding nearly every week. Thinking of her parents reminded her they were due in any day now, ready for Christmas.

Technically, she was rostered on for Christmas Day. They all were. But she hoped Coober Pedy residents were courteous enough to take the day off from crazy. It was a pipe dream. Being on call made choosing the location for the family Christmas dinner even more difficult.

If they went to Nick's property, and Jenny was called in to work, it would be a two-hour drive, or a chopper flight to get to town. It wasn't ideal.

Marj jabbed her playfully in the ribs.

'Well. Any date? You've been engaged more than a year.'

'Not yet Marj. And if everyone doesn't stop bugging us, I think we might elope.'

Marj pulled back and planted her hands on her ample hips.

'Over my dead body Jenny Williams.'

'Dead bodies are *my* business Marj.' Penny's ominous tone elicited a ripple of laughter from everyone.

'I'm sorry Luv. It's just that your wedding is probably going to be the biggest event in town for years.'

Jenny shuddered. The idea everyone was so interested in her life was an unpleasant thought.

Penny tapped Jenny on the shoulder.

'I desperately need a shower.' She turned to the motel owner. 'Can I grab my room key Marj?'

'Sure Luv. Is that smell what I think it is?'

And there she was, right back to the current case. Marj loved a bit of town gossip.

'You don't want to know.' Penny accepted the key, then turned to Jenny and pointed toward the front bar. 'I'll see you in 20.'

'You will.'

Jenny turned back to Marj.

'The body was a little ripe,' Jenny pinched her nose for emphasis.

Marj screwed up her face, but Jenny knew very little phased the former miner. She was tough as nails. The fact she wasn't shooing Jenny's tainted uniform from her office attested to her iron gut.

'Anyone I know?'

Jenny tried not to discuss cases in detail with the motel owner. Gossip in a small town could ruin an investigation, but local knowledge could be gold.

'I can't go into details.'

'I understand.' Marj leant in for details anyway.

'The victim hasn't been officially identified, but we've been given a name. The problem is, we don't believe it's her real name.'

'Oooh. Very clandestine.'

'We'll get to the bottom of it.'

'Yes, dental records, DNA and all that, but…'

Jenny grinned. Marj joined her.

'Maybe you know more about the woman?' Jenny spoke quietly.

'I might. I like to keep my ear to the ground.'

That was an understatement.

'The name we've been given is Katie Montgomery.'

Marj pursed her lips, then pressed her index finger to them and tapped thoughtfully.

'I've heard the name, but I don't think I've met the girl.'

Jenny deflated.

'That's alright. If you hear anything, let me know. Can I grab the room key?'

'No.'

'No?' Jenny frowned.

'Well yes. I'll let you know if I think of why I know Katie's name, but no, you can't have the key because Nick already has it.'

Jenny grinned, then spun on her heel.

'In that case, I'm out of here.'

'Wedding date!' Marj called as Jenny rushed from the office and waved without turning.

'After Christmas.'

'Ha, ha….' Marj kept talking, but Jenny didn't hear what she was saying as she jogged down the covered veranda to room number 12.

It was the room she stayed in for her first month in town. It was the same room Nick booked each Wednesday afternoon, for two nights to catch up with her in case she couldn't make it out to William Creek Station for the weekend.

She never expected to stay in Coober Pedy this long. She could have been pursuing a career in Adelaide, but life got in the way of her career plans. A distraction. An unscheduled, unplanned change of course.

She raised her hand to knock and licked her top lip. A smile crept across her face as the door opened. Standing in front of her, shirt off, crystal blue eyes sparkling, was the best kind of distraction.

'Oh geez.' Nick stepped back. 'What *is* that smell?' He waved his hand in front of his face.

Jenny cringed. 'Yeah. Sorry. Should have warned you. Work. Need a shower.'

Nick left the door open, vacated the narrow hallway next to the bathroom and reached for his shirt from the side table. 'You got that right. I think I'll meet you in the bar, if that's alright?'

Jenny stepped toward him. He backed away, stopping as his legs hit the bed.

'You sure you don't want a kiss first? Maybe a…' She tried unsuccessfully to keep the grin from her lips.

'Shower first.' Nick's expression now matched hers.

'Don't want to watch?'

Nick's eyes smiled. Her stomach did a little flip.

'Tempting.' He shook his head. 'I'll get you a beer. Don't be too long.' He reached for his wallet. Then turned back. 'On second thought. Take whatever time you need to get rid of that smell.'

Jenny stepped into the bathroom.

'I'll be quick. Penny is in town,' she called through the closed door.

'Guessed that from the smell. Tim and Nev joining us then?'

She thought she heard a hint of disappointment.

'Yep. Is that alright?'

'Sure. See you in a minute.'

Chapter 6

The sun hovered over the horizon as stars popped into existence, one by one. The sunset would usually signal a cool night, even in the middle of summer. Not tonight. The northernly wind continued to howl, promising more heat over the coming days and a drought on the horizon.

Jenny checked her watch, then quickened her step. It was after 8pm as she opened the glass door to the restaurant. Cool air wafting with the smell of beer and fried food dragged her in. Her stomach growled as she crossed the room, trying to find Nick amongst the sea of high-vis and dusty clothing.

It was Penny who caught her attention as she shimmied between burly bodies, hands holding a glass of wine and jug of beer above her head.

'Hey. About time you got here.' She nodded toward the back of the restaurant. 'We're around the corner. It's bedlam in here.'

'What's the crowd about?'

'Jag the Joker jackpot has hit 10k.'

'Really?' Jenny scanned the room as she followed Penny. 'No one ever wins that thing. I'm sure it's rigged. Still, I've never seen this many people in here for a game of chance. It must be something else.'

'Who cares?' Penny sipped her wine as she wiggled past two more tables. 'I'm starving.'

Jenny's stomach grumbled in agreement.

Penny laughed.

'Good thing Nick and I ordered for you.'

She didn't protest. In nearly two years, the restaurant menu hadn't changed. There were the occasional specials, but Nick and Penny knew her favourites.

'Perfect. The beer won't go straight to my head then.'

Nick reached over and pulled out a chair as she arrived.

'That's a shame. I was hoping to take advantage of you.'

Penny put the jug and her wine down and shoved her fingers in her ears.

'La, la, la. I don't need to hear that.'

'Why?' Jenny scanned the empty table. 'Tim working tonight?'

Penny plonked down next to her with an exaggerated sigh.

'Double shift. There was a chemical spill somewhere or something.'

Jenny frowned. 'Nothing reached the station, and a chemical spill should have.'

Nick filled an empty glass with beer, then topped his up. 'Off the clock Jen.'

She grinned and savoured her first mouthful. He was right. They agreed a while ago she needed to clock off when she wasn't on duty. It was hard at times, especially when murder was involved.

'Cheers to that.' Penny lifted her glass.

Jenny clinked it, then Nick's. 'So, Nev is on shift too?'

'Yep. Only the three of us unless Nellie takes me up on my invite.' Penny sipped her wine. 'But don't worry. I won't keep you two out late.' Penny flicked her thick long hair like a shampoo commercial. 'I need my beauty sleep.'

'What, no karaoke?' Nick's eyes smiled as he waited for Jenny to take the bait.

'I'll not dignify that with an answer.'

'You just did,' Penny teased.

Jenny's reputation for too much beer and very loud karaoke began with her first night in town. The photos still resurfaced from time to time. People in the outback had long memories.

The aroma of food filled Jenny's nostrils. She turned to see Marj balancing two plates on one arm, the other hand carrying a third.

'Here you go.' Marj placed a chicken schnitzel in front of Jenny. 'Steak for you Penny, and a large pizza for Nick.'

'Thanks Marj.' Jenny swallowed a mouthful of saliva and focussed back on the motel owner. 'What's with this crowd tonight?'

'No idea Luv. I hardly recognise most of these faces and there's a lot of workwear in here.' Marj nodded to the bar, three deep with fluorescent orange and yellow. 'Maybe the highway project site bar is out of grog.'

It was possible, but Jenny couldn't help wondering if there was another reason for the sudden influx. 'Did you hear about a chemical spill somewhere? With this many people here, it could have been a bar or something.'

Marj handed a slim paper-bag with a napkin and cutlery to Nick.

'Maybe that's it. Business has been quieter than usual this summer. The tourists always dry up when the heat hits the high 30's but this year has been the worst. Especially considering the highway re-construction project is only a few k's up the road. Maybe there's competition in town?'

Jenny couldn't think of a new motel, or bar, and no establishment was overly busy compared to the other. Either way, none of them should be able to avoid reporting a fire or chemical incident to police.

'Might have to do a little scoping around town tomorrow,' Jenny offered, knowing her motive wasn't purely a favour to Marj.

'You and me both.' Marj collected an empty wine glass next to Penny's half-full one.

Jenny lifted her knife and fork and turned toward Nick.

'I stumbled on something today. Do you think you can call Ben for me?'

She spotted two men in workwear shaking hands awkwardly as she popped food into her mouth. One was tall and lean, with tattoos visible above the collar of his fluoro shirt. The other rushed away too quickly for Jenny to get a good look.

'Ben.' Marj stopped, empty glass in hand. 'That's where I know the name from.'

'What do you mean?' Jenny swallowed hard.

'Ben grabbed some takeaway here last Friday. Couldn't stop talking about his girlfriend.' Marj shook the empty wineglass back and forth by the stem. 'No, fiancé. He said she was his fiancé and her name was Katie.'

'You're sure Marj?' Jenny forced the apprehension from her voice.

'Absolutely. Never met the girl, but that's what he said.'

Jenny reached up and squeezed Marj's hand.

'Thanks Marj. That's *really* helpful, and even more reason for me to talk with Ben.' She turned back to Nick. 'Did you know he was engaged?'

'I thought you weren't working.' His tone was flat.

Marj glanced from Nick to Jenny. 'I'll leave you to it.' She scurried away. Penny carved a slice of medium-rare steak and shoved it into her mouth as two men in workwear pressed by. Jenny recognised the tattooed one.

'Can we grab these two seats?'

'Sure.' Penny spoke with a full mouth and the wave of her knife.

Nick sulked. Jenny wasn't sure if it was because of her or the two table guests. She reached under the table and squeezed his thigh. He rubbed the back of her hand and smiled weakly.

Jenny let go, lifted her knife and fork and addressed the newcomers.

'The place is pumping tonight. What's up with that?' Her question was more curiosity than politeness.

Nick ripped a slice of pizza from his plate, shoved it into his mouth and tore off a chunk as his clear blue eyes studied the strangers.

The lean guy with the tattoos slipped into a seat with a schooner glass in hand. His eyes drifted to his bulky mate. A strange expression crossed their faces before the tattooed guy turned back to Jenny with a shrug.

'No idea!'

Jenny chewed a mouthful of schnitzel, swallowed and plastered a smile on her features. She didn't know these guys, but that wasn't new. No one considered her a local, but Nick didn't seem to know them either. Still not unusual. Her fiancé spent most of his time out on the property.

'You working locally? FIFO?'

The lean guy ran his hand through his thick brown hair. Jenny noted the slight tremor in his hand as he reached for his beer.

'Yeah.'

The one-word answer made it clear neither of these guys was into small talk. The cramping in Jenny's stomach no longer had anything to do with hunger.

'I guess you usually drink at the place where that chemical spill was today then?'

The tall guy drained his beer and tapped his stocky mate on the shoulder.

'Might grab a few for the road, hey Dave?'

His broad-shouldered friend skulled his beer and rose with his mate.

'Good idea.'

The two men sidled past Penny, who drained her wine and turned to Jenny.

'You sure know how to clear a room.'

Chapter 7

The front bar began to thin out as Jenny sat back and patted her tummy contentedly.

Penny slid her chair back.

'I'm going to see if I can catch Tim. I'm nearly done with the VW, so I'll likely be on my way tomorrow afternoon.'

Jenny slid her plate to the middle of the worn, wood veneered table.

'Oh, no fair. We've barely caught up.'

Penny shrugged, then grinned mischievously.

'You'll have to come visit me in Adelaide. Maybe I can host you for your hen's night.'

'I don't know about that.'

'We'll discuss it tomorrow,' Penny promised.

Jenny slid her chair back, then stopped. 'Actually, can you ask Tim where he picked up the chem spill patients?'

'Sure,' Penny grinned. 'Your Spidey senses tingling?'

'Just curious. I'll see you bright and early.' Jenny *was* curious, but she didn't want to harp on it and risk upsetting Nick again.

'Yep. See you at 7. Don't keep her up all night Nick,' Penny grinned.

Nick waved, but the creases around his eyes told her she might have killed the vibe earlier. They only saw each other a few times a week. Why did she always manage to let her work get in the way?

Condensation dripped to the cardboard coaster below Nick's beer glass as he ran his finger around the rim.

Jenny reached for his hand. 'You ready?'

His shoulders rose with an exaggerated sigh. 'I guess.'

'What does that mean?'

'Are *you* ready, is probably a better question.'

She forced a smile to her lips. 'For bed? Of course I am.' She squeezed his bicep to her chest and rose, attempting to drag him to his feet.

He eased his arm free. 'You know what I mean Jen.'

She didn't want to hear it. She didn't want to argue tonight. When she met Nick, they didn't exactly hit it off. He kept his emotions hidden, down deep beneath a permanent scowl. At least he shared his thoughts and smiled more, but now they argued more often. Jenny wasn't sure what the answer was.

Although she liked her work, she wasn't married to it. Usually, she switched off when not on duty, but murder was different. Cases like this tended to occupy every waking moment and sometimes invaded her dreams.

But Nick was right. She needed to try harder.

'Forget I asked about Ben. Sorry I let work get in the way again.'

She tried once more to pull him to his feet. He turned away, rising on the opposite side of the chair.

'You can head back to the dugout. I think I'll drive home tonight instead of staying in town.'

The last place she wanted to be right now was alone in the underground home she shared with Tim and Nev.

'Nick. What's going on?'

He strode toward the door. Jenny hurried to follow his retreating back. As they exited the building, she grabbed his hand and dragged him to a halt. 'Is this about Ben? Is he still under investigation with the AFP? Am I treading on their jurisdiction or something?'

He shook his hand free.

'Jenny, not everything is about catching bad guys. Ben has been working for me a year now and he hasn't stepped out of line even once.'

'That you know of.'

'You're being unfair.'

'Nick, it isn't a coincidence your saddle failed the week he started working for you, at the exact same time you refused to sell to the mining company he's linked with.'

'Through one lawyer. A dead lawyer. From a time in his youth that has nothing to do with mining and was during a tough time for him. What happened to Ben back then was outside his control.'

Jenny didn't point out how choices were always controllable. Deep down she knew the consequences of those choices often weren't. Ben grew up the hard way, but his brush with the law wasn't a misdemeanour. It was manslaughter and arson and as much as she wanted to believe his sister Trudy, no one could prove Ben was set up. Nick's reaction was her concern right now.

There was more to it than supporting one of his employees. Nick's upbringing wasn't easy. Taking on the farm at nineteen after his father's death and living without knowing why his mother disappeared, took a toll.

Was he relating to Ben because of his past?

'I'm sorry.' Her eyes began to burn. 'I know you've grown close to Ben, but Fergusson's fire is too much of a coincidence and now Ben is linked to the remains of a dead woman I found in the boot of an intoxicated single mum's car.'

Why was she being so emotional? This was just another dead woman. They weren't a rare sight anymore.

Nick stopped mid-stride and rounded on Jenny.

'That's a rough find.' He pulled her to his chest. 'I smelt the death earlier, but Jen, is it murder?' He spoke into her hair.

'Yes. And now Marj has linked Ben to the victim.' She didn't mention the bloodied letters from the vehicle.

He held her at arm's length. 'Why didn't you tell me?'

'You didn't ask and I know you hate me talking about work.'

'You don't seriously think Ben killed his fiancé?'

'If what you told Sergeant Mackenzie is true, he couldn't have. But I need to ask him about her. I thought a call from you might be easier on him.'

Nick hesitated a moment too long.

'You did tell Sarge the truth?'

Nick scratched the back of his head. A familiar crease spread across his brow.

'Nick, tell me you didn't cover for him.'

He strode across the artificial turf toward the veranda.

'Let's call him from the room.'

His long stride left Jenny standing open-mouthed. *Why would he cover for Ben?* She kept the question to herself and followed.

They were metres from Nick's room when the crash of glass made them stop.

'It's coming from the street.' Jenny reached the carpark in front of reception before Nick caught up.

'Wait up Jen. You're not armed.'

She grabbed at her empty waistline. Agitated voices grew louder. A light in the room alongside the office, switched on. Marj was likely calling the station. Nick was right. She should wait for back up.

A shiver ran down her spine as a shrill scream split the sweltering night. The following cry was all too familiar.

'Mikey!'

Her legs were pumping before she knew it. Nick overtook her as they ran across the motel carpark toward the main entrance and bottle shop. A streetlight illuminated a broad, dark figure with a long thin weapon in one hand and a screaming child tucked under the other arm.

Cowering below them was a petite figure, head bowed, with what appeared to be blood glistening on her fingertips.

'Stop! Police!' Jenny screamed instinctively. Hoping the assailant didn't realise she was unarmed.

The figure, shrouded in a dark hoodie, dropped the weapon, gripped Mikey with both arms and ran. The toddler howled at the top of his lungs as the assailant disappeared into the darkness. The side door of the motel reception opened as Jenny reached Tanya.

'Get Mikey!' Tanya screamed.

'I phoned the station. Ambulance is on the way,' Marj called as more room doors opened, and heads appeared.

Jenny hovered a split second, but when Marj's barman Stan rushed from the bottle shop, she made her decision.

'You stay with her,' she instructed Nick.

'Not on your life.'

There was no point arguing with him. Two people, wrapped in bathrobes, spilled into the carpark, asking if they could help.

Jenny sprinted toward the corner where the attacker was last seen, only to find the street deserted.

Chapter 8

Random streetlights did nothing to illuminate the shadows. Jenny scanned for a parked car. Listened for a motor. The only sounds were the commotion in front of the motel and Nick breathing heavily at her side.

'What now?' he asked.

Jenny sucked air in and held it, willing her heartrate to slow and her night-vision to start working. Peering down the road, she considered their options.

Two roads, plus a side street presented too many options. There was no way to know where the kidnapper went. Jenny tried to think clearly. Did the guy have a car nearby?

'Why take the kid?' Nick spoke into the darkness.

'Good question.' She studied the open dirt parking area either side of the roundabout.

'He's disappeared. There are too many options Jen.'

'I'm not giving up. He has Mikey.'

A gust of wind lifted dust from the dry, dirt carpark abutting the roundabout. Jenny shielded her face as it engulfed them and swirled past. The carpark adjoined the school oval on Paxton Street.

'He won't have parked his car on the main street. Too many cameras. Let's try this way.' She pointed toward the school road, crossed over the intersection and jogged toward the vacant carpark.

'If he parked around here, he could be long gone,' Nick offered as he easily kept pace with her.

The moon offered little light as Jenny scanned the darkened oval fenceline.

'Possibly, but I didn't hear a car. Did you?'

'What kind of person attacks a woman and takes a little kid from his mother?' She couldn't see Nick's features, but his tone shared his disbelief.

'Maybe someone who wants to keep her quiet about a dead woman.'

'Is she the woman whose car you found the body in?'

Jenny bit her lip. She'd said too much.

'Well, you can clear Ben. He's at William Creek and he isn't as big as that guy was.'

Jenny didn't argue. The man who snatched Mikey wasn't tall, but he was bulky and carried Mikey as though he weighed no more than a bag of groceries.

'I agree. I still need to speak with Ben, but right now, I want to find Mikey.'

Jenny wished she had a torch as she scanned the area. The moon and stars offered enough light to make out tall metal fences surrounding the few homes nearby. No dogs were barking. No porch lights were flashing on. Behind her, the motel and caravan park was fenced off by a high, inaccessible wall.

A single streetlamp illuminated a disused restaurant, accommodation and shop complex. The chain-link fence was covered with a mesh banner revealing what was planned for a future renovation.

Jenny pointed.

'Let's try over there.'

A siren wailed in the distance. Help was on the way. Jenny hesitated.

'Do you want to wait for them?' Nick was so close his words ruffled her hair.

'Maybe we should.'

The sound of grunting, and gravel crunching made her chest tighten. She jogged across the road toward the carpark at the rear of the renovation site. A heavy chain hung between thick posts, creating a perimeter around another dirt parking space. Jenny vaulted over it.

'Jenny. Wait up,' Nick called as he scrambled after her.

Jenny's heart pounded as she caught sight of an object lying in the dirt. Sliding to a stop, she studied it a moment before the object became clear. Reaching out, she lifted the soft knitted teddy and crushed it to her chest.

An ambulance siren wailed, then halted nearby, assuring her Tanya was getting the help she needed.

Jenny dreaded returning to the woman without her son. She needed to find Mikey. But she was out of uniform with no weapon, Taser or even a torch.

Headlights rounded the corner near the roundabout. Blue and red lights flashed, the siren now silent. As the spotlights silhouetted her, she waved to get their attention.

Gravel crunched under the tyres as the Landcruiser parked, and Phillips stepped out.

'Marj said someone took Mikey.' He slammed the door and jogged to join her.

'I didn't see which way they went, but this area is deserted.' Jenny lifted the bear. 'And we found this.'

Phillips' torchlight waved over the bear.

'Looks like you're on the right track.' He held something out to her. 'Here, take this. I'll check around the front of the building.'

She accepted his Taser.

'Thanks. I was feeling a bit naked.'

A nervous chuckle escaped her lips.

Phillips started toward the front of the worksite. She and Nick carried on across the carpark to the rear of the building. The smell of stale beer and body odour brought her to a halt.

'What's up?' Nick whispered over her shoulder.

'Ya lookin' for som'fin'?'

They jumped in unison.

Jenny grew instantly alert as the sound of fabric rustled, and a figure rose from the ground.

Her tension eased as soon as she realised it was a local, sleeping rough. The Coober Pedy climate made living out under the stars an option and if the landowner wasn't complaining, the police turned a blind eye.

Still, Jenny approached the barely visible canvas swag with caution.

'Did you see a man come through here, with a small boy?'

'Dat you Constable Williams?'

The moon and stars made it possible to see the outline of objects, but faces were impossible to distinguish. Instead, Jenny tried to place the voice but failed.

'It's Eric. Nev's brover.'

'Eric. This is urgent. Did you see a little boy?'

'Sure did.'

Jenny knew Eric battled substance abuse. He wasn't alone in his struggles. But he didn't sound drunk or high now. Why was he so casual, when Jenny was obviously stressed.

'Got 'im right here.'

Jenny blinked, wishing Phillips gave her his torch instead of the Taser.

'How?'

Eric moved closer, revealing Mikey, sleeping in his arms.

'White fella was running, tripped over me swag. Drop this bub in me lap and pissed off outa here.'

Jenny carefully extracted the apparently sleeping boy from Eric's embrace.

'He's unconscious. We need the ambulance.'

'I'll get Phillips.' Nick rushed away.

Eric watched him leave, then chuckled.

'He's just sleepin' Constable.'

'How do you know?'

Mikey snuggled into Jenny, reassuring her Eric was right.

'He was awake and scared silly when the fella run off. Poor little blighter. Must a been tuckered out. Fell asleep as soon as his eyes closed.'

'You should have taken him straight to the hospital or called us.'

'Nuffin' broken. It's dark and the cop shop's shut. No phone neiver.'

'Still. He's not your child. Didn't you think his mother would be worried?' Jenny knew she should be grateful Mikey was unharmed, but Eric's casual attitude disturbed her.

'Day all our kids in the bush. I got to be Uncle for a little bit. No 'arm in dat.'

Jenny forced herself to calm down and recall what little she knew about First Nations culture. Nev tried to explain it once. Something about indigenous children not belonging to their birth parents. How historically, they were cared for by whoever could provide food and shelter or wasn't out hunting or foraging for food.

'Thank you for taking care of him Eric. I need to get him back to his mum, but did you get a description of the guy who fell into you?'

'Nah. Too dark. Big bloke though. Real big bloke.' He returned to his bedding as Phillips came rushing across the carpark, torch beam flicking from side to side.

'I've called another ambulance.'

Mikey stirred in Jenny's arms. She pressed his teddy to his chest.

'You're okay now Mikey. Go back to sleep.'

Phillips shone his torchlight on the child, who rolled his face into Jenny's shoulder.

'Sorry.' The beam hit the ground.

'He's fine. Eric took good care of him. You can call the ambulance off. I'll take your cruiser and get him to his mum. Then I'll get changed into my uniform and be right back.'

Her partner spoke into his lapel mic as Jenny adjusted Mikey in her arms.

'Eric didn't see much, except he said the guy is big. I haven't heard a car take off from here, so he could still be around. Be a good idea to wait for backup before checking out the building.'

'Will do. Sarge, O'Connell and Nellie are all on the way.'

'Not much sleep coming our way tonight then.' Jenny glanced at Nick as she spoke. 'I'm sorry.'

Nick wrapped his arm around her shoulder and wordlessly led her to the police vehicle. There was no baby seat. Someone was going to have to hold Mikey and Nick wasn't allowed to drive the vehicle.

'Here, take him.'

Nick awkwardly wrapped his arms around Mikey and slid into the passenger seat. As Jenny started the car, she watched Nick in the dash lights. His features softened as his eyes studied the child, then turned to her.

'I'm sorry I gave you a hard time. I know this job means a lot to you.'

'You mean a lot to me, Nick. I'm trying to find a balance.'

He squeezed her thigh as she steered the vehicle through the roundabout and the ambulance came into view.

'We'll work it out. I'll call Ben later.'

Jenny rolled her lips and forced her emotions under control. She was back on duty. There was work to do.

Why would someone try and kidnap Tanya's son? A warning? Probably. How was she going to get the woman to talk now?

Chapter 9

Heat engulfed Jenny as soon as she opened the motel room door. Sunlight filtered over the horizon, highlighting the haze of red dust hanging in the air.

At least the wind was finally gone, Jenny thought as she opened the door to her vintage Dodge ute. An agonising creak filled the early morning silence.

It was after 1am when they finally called off the search for Mikey's abductor. The fencing around the building wasn't secure, but the building was locked up tight. They tried unsuccessfully to contact the owner for permission to enter the premises but a full search of the area turned up nothing.

There were too many vehicle tracks around the worksite to confirm whether the kidnapper used a car or not. Their only hope was if Tanya knew her attacker and was willing to tell them.

But Tanya was still in hospital. Her injuries weren't life-threatening, but Nev decided to keep her in overnight for observation.

The image of mother and son, curled up on the ward bed filled Jenny with mixed emotions. Tanya obviously loved her son deeply, but a blood test last night revealed she was once more intoxicated.

At least her car was still in police custody, or she may have been driving it, forcing Jenny to charge her with her third DUI offence.

She wondered again what life circumstances brought Tanya to this point. Then reminded herself last night was only a taste of the long hours to come. She needed a coffee. A *real* coffee. Although no one she knew considered her signature caramel latte *real* coffee.

She chuckled at the thought as she drove the short distance from the motel carpark, down Hutchison Street to Nikolic's Café.

She hopped up onto the concrete veranda and stopped. For nearly two years, a couple of old timers framed the screen door on Niko's café. Today, the space was empty. Jenny's gut clenched as the screen door slammed closed behind her.

'Where are your regulars?' She hoicked her thumb toward the front of the building, aware she didn't even know the two men by name.

Niko glanced up, his face lined with worry.

'Bob had a stroke.'

'Bob. Is he the guy with the pipe?'

'Yep. And Ad is the one who smokes the rollies. He went with Bob to Broken Hill.'

Jenny approached the counter, thankful for the Royal Flying Doctors Service.

'I hope Bob is alright.'

Living in a remote town like Coober Pedy without the RFDS would be fraught with danger.

'You have enough to worry about.' Niko busied himself pressing coffee into the portafilter. 'The usual?'

'Plus Penny's order.'

'Yes, I suspected so.'

The grinder whirred. The screen door slammed. Jenny spun to find Penny approaching.

'Heard your bucket of bolts roll out. Could have waited for me.'

Jenny chuckled. 'Do you want something to eat?'

Penny checked the clock on her mobile phone screen. 'Why not?'

Jenny turned to Niko as the first few coffees were done.

'Two egg and bacon wraps to go, thanks Niko.'

'You got it.'

The screen door opened once more. Jenny was about to joke to Niko about how it was busier than the Stuart Highway when the man entering baulked.

He recovered quickly, but Jenny was sure her uniform was the reason he appeared unsettled.

'I'll be with you in a moment,' Niko addressed the newcomer who nodded, then crossed the room to a table in the far corner.

His phone was in his hands as soon as he sat. Fingers texting wildly. The buzz of a phone receiving an SMS preceded the screen door opening again.

A familiar face appeared. His eyes widened as he glanced up from his phone to see Jenny. The first man met him by the door.

'Let's go.'

They disappeared through the screen door without another word.

Penny scoffed. 'What was that all about?'

'The second guy was one of the two men at our table last night.'

Penny frowned, then nodded. 'It was too. The one with the neck tatts.'

Jenny turned as Niko slid the coffee tray toward her, then added two white paper bags filled with baking paper and the aroma of bacon.

'Do you know either of those two?'

Niko frowned at the empty doorway. 'Not personally. Just workers from the Stuart Highway roadworks.'

Jenny nodded. Then smiled. 'Yeah. They've been in construction for nearly two years now.'

Penny lifted her food and a tray of coffee from the countertop. 'No wonder roads cost so much.'

Jenny reached for the remaining coffee, then headed for the door.

'Thanks Niko.'

'Have a good day,' he waved.

Jenny held the screen door as Penny passed through, then followed. As they reached her car, a white ute with orange decal and a yellow caution light on top drove slowly by.

'The road works have been going on for ages. But I've never seen those two in town before.'

Penny laughed. 'There must be a few hundred workers on highway jobs. No doubt they chew through staff more often than we change our underwear.'

It was true. The turnover in the civil and mining industry was well known. Workers followed the money and skipped from company and worksite accordingly. Still, she couldn't ignore their reaction to her uniform, or the evasive behaviour last night when she asked where they usually drank. She couldn't budge her suspicion it was all linked to the chemical spill.

She held the coffee tray while Penny closed her door, then passed it back. Reaching for her brekkie wrap, she slipped it from the baking paper and bit off a mouthful before placing it back on the coffee tray in Penny's lap.

'Last night, did Tim say where all the patients came from?

Penny sipped her coffee as she nodded. 'Sort of.'

Jenny backed out of the parking space and tried to drive quietly toward work.

'What does *sort of* mean?'

Penny swallowed a mouthful of wrap. 'Tim said it was weird. Two guys turned up at emergency, then he got the call out to pick up more patients.'

'Where?'

'Just out of town, but Tim said it wasn't the scene of a chemical spill.'

Jenny changed gears as she navigated the roundabout toward the station.

'How did he know?'

'There were three more victims. Tim thought they suffered smoke inhalation at first but then tests confirmed it was some sort of chemical poisoning. They are waiting on lab results, but Tim said Nev would likely know more today.'

'So what was the weird bit?'

Penny swallowed another mouthful and Jenny's stomach tightened in silent protest.

'Well, the SES arrived on location, ran some checks, found nothing. So the spill can't have been on the premises.'

'That explains why it wasn't reported through proper channels.'

'Exactly. Tim said once the paperwork lands, you'll likely get the call to investigate.'

'Or…'

Penny read where Jenny was going immediately. 'You could get a headstart on it.'

Jenny nodded. 'So where did Tim pick up the patients from?'

Penny grinned. 'A car wrecking yard out on Kempel Road.'

'No time to check it out now but if I'm out that way later, I'll call in.'

Penny nodded agreement, bit into her breakfast and giggled as melted cheese oozed over her chin. Jenny's stomach protested aloud this time.

They laughed as the station came into view. But the merriment disappeared as Jenny considered the case. It was

now obvious Tanya had a reason to be afraid. But who was
Katie and why would anyone want to kill her?

Chapter 10

The rising sun cleared the ochre and white ridgeline as Jenny parked outside the station. She was one foot out the door when a vehicle slid to a stop in the dirt carpark. A dust cloud lifted. She squinted and slammed her door before the car could fill with red dirt.

Jenny recognised the William Creek Station Troop Carrier, but knew Nick was driving his own ute this weekend.

Goosebumps erupted on her arms as Ben Stokes jumped from the vehicle and stormed toward her.

'Where's Katie?' His eyes scanned the front of the police station as though the woman were locked in the cells.

'Ben. Take a breath.' Jenny kept her tone calm. 'Did Nick call you?'

She barely spoke to her fiancé when she got in early this morning. He was awake before she left for work, but talking shop wasn't high on their agenda.

Ben nodded vigorously. His eyes were grief-stricken but her mistrust of Ben made her wary.

'Nick called last night.' Ben shoved his hands in his pockets, then pulled them out a second later. 'I would have been here straight away, but it was late when I got Nick's message. Sam is on uni break, but he's been MIA with Mick, so I waited until early this morning to brief Al and Ed.

'It was a good call,' Jenny reassured him, silently surprised he was being so responsible. 'Sam might be Nick's little brother, but he's not experienced running the property much over the years. Al and Ed know what they are doing.'

Jenny waved toward the station as Penny balanced the coffee tray.

'How about we talk inside?'

Ben hesitated as O'Connell's four-wheel-drive police Landcruiser pulled down the side driveway to park at the rear of the station.

'All I want to know is what happened to Katie? Can't you tell me out here?'

Jenny understood Ben's reservations. He was a convicted criminal, who, if you believed his sister, was set up. The police weren't his friend. The fact he trusted her was unexpected.

'Ben, Nick told you Katie has been found dead, right?'

He slipped his hands back into his moleskin pants pockets and nodded vigorously.

'We have questions, but you aren't a suspect.'

Senior Constable O'Connell arrived to open the front doors.

Penny lifted the coffee cups toward the station entrance. 'Come on inside Ben. The coffee is getting cold.' She tried to lighten the mood.

Ben's eyes jumped from Penny to O'Connell, before landing back on Jenny.

'Not a suspect? So it wasn't an accident?'

Jenny patted the back of his shoulder lightly, directing him toward the front door.

'No Ben, it wasn't. But I know you have an alibi.'

His shoulder shuddered, and for a moment, Jenny thought he might break down. Instead, he lifted his chin and straightened.

Jenny gave his bicep a gentle squeeze.

'But we could really use your help working out how Katie ended up like she did. Come in, have a coffee, not Niko's espresso though. Those are all taken so it's instant I'm afraid.' She tried to make light.

No one laughed, but the tension around Ben's eyes eased. O'Connell held the door. Ben entered. As Jenny followed, she reminded herself to keep an open mind. Nick trusted Ben, despite his link in the federal investigation into the mining company extortion.

She knew Ben's alibi checked out. Nick confirmed Ben left for a short time, but it was less than an hour. Coober Pedy was a four-hour round trip from Nick's. Still, her cop instincts weren't entirely satisfied Katie's death wasn't linked to Ben's past.

And then there was the Fergusson fire. The old man was sure it was deliberately lit and one hour was long enough for Ben to be involved. She reminded herself there was a murder to solve and the CFS were yet to finish their report.

She planned to follow up the fire with her boss again when she got the chance.

'Williams!'

Speak of the devil.

'What's up Sarge?'

She grinned at her relaxed reply. When she first came to town, the sound of her boss's voice yelling her name made her blood curdle or drain from her head, depending on her mood. Now, she realised the gruff manner was a barrier he chose to employ at work.

'You need to…' He halted as he stepped into the foyer and saw Ben standing by the counter. 'Never mind. See me when you're done.'

He brushed past Ben, lifted the counter, dropped it down heavily and strode to his office. Jenny silently quizzed O'Connell, who shrugged he wasn't aware of any issue.

Maybe it was lack of sleep? They'd all been running around in circles last night searching for Mikey's abductor.

Katie's death was unsettling for everyone, but maybe it reminded Sergeant Mackenzie of his own loss. His daughter Lily wasn't murdered, but she died young and losing her cost the sergeant a lot.

She ushered Ben into the main office area.

'If you don't mind, it might be quieter and more private if you join me in an interview room.'

'Or not.'

Jenny bit her bottom lip. 'Ben. The details of the case aren't pleasant...'

Ben's nostrils flared. A curt nod followed.

'I'll join you.' O'Connell lifted two coffees from the tray as Nellie and Phillips arrived. 'One of you two make our guest a coffee, then see Sarge. Lots to do today.'

Phillips hurried around the counter. 'I'll get one. How do you have it?'

Ben shook his head. 'Nothing for me. I'm wired enough.'

Nellie dragged her feet toward the front computer. Jenny knew she stayed at the hospital most of the night to make sure no one came back to bother Tanya or Mikey.

Ben turned to Jenny. 'Can we get this over with? I don't know how much help I'll be, but I'll try my best. Whoever hurt Katie better hope you find them before I do.'

Jenny's stomach knotted. What was he going to do once he saw the photos?

'I'm sorry for your loss Ben.' Jenny accepted her coffee from O'Connell and waved for Ben to follow the Senior Constable down the hallway. 'I hear you were engaged.'

'Just proposed last week.' Ben's voice hitched on the last word.

Jenny joined O'Connell on one side of the table. Ben dragged his chair a good distance away from the table and sat, not bothering to shuffle back in.

'Are you recording this?'

'No.' Jenny smiled. 'I'm not lying to you Ben.'

O'Connell slipped a manila file her way. Jenny turned it so she could view the photos and details.

'This is the best place for…'

'I don't want to see her dead.' Ben's voice quivered.

'Alright. You don't have to. She's been identified by Tanya Rothchild.'

'Tanya?'

'Yes. Do you know her?'

Ben shrugged a little too casually, then shuffled his chair closer to the table.

'Sort of. Katie babysits,' he shook his head, 'baby*sat* her kid sometimes, and I hung around a few times.'

'Mikey. Yes.' Jenny pressed on, trying not to let Ben get too lost in the past. 'We are also asking Tanya this, but do you have a photo of Katie we can use?'

'Why?'

Jenny licked her lips.

'A few reasons. One, Katie might have changed her name at some point because we can't find any birth certificate, or driver's licence to match her age and description. We need to formally identify her.'

Ben frowned.

Jenny wondered if he was genuinely confused.

'Still doesn't explain why you need a photo.'

Jenny suppressed a shiver. There was no easy way to explain why the morgue photo wasn't going to be useful.

'I'm sorry Ben, but Katie's face was…'

He threw his hands up in front of his face. 'I don't want to know. If I know details, I'll be too angry.' His entire body shook. 'They better hope I don't catch them.'

That was the second time he alluded to taking revenge into his own hands. She understood the rage. But it was a side of Ben she'd never seen.

'I understand Ben. Really, I do.'

Ben rummaged in his pocket, dragged out his phone and tapped the screen. The phone slid across the table, revealing a headshot with smiling brown eyes, light brunette hair and the top edges of a light, summer floral top or dress.

She slipped the phone to O'Connell, not missing the sadness in her colleague's eyes.

'Do you mind if we forward this to the station email?'

Ben shook his head. Jenny continued.

'Do you have any family contact details for Katie?'

She kept her questions general, not wanting to get Ben offside, but knowing her next line of questioning would aggravate him.

'No. Only child. Parents are dead.'

O'Connell handed the phone back. Ben studied the picture a moment before putting it back in his pocket.

'But I only know what she told me. It pisses me off I can't be more help.' He slammed his fist onto the table hard enough to make Jenny jump.

She watched as his fingers flexed open and closed. She understood the frustration, but something about his posture was off.

'Did she ever mention a name, even in passing? A name you didn't recognise? Someone you don't know?'

He picked at his fingernails, then gripped his hands together in his lap and shook his head.

'Where did you meet Katie?'

Ben's eyes jolted to hers. His lips pursed, then flattened.

'Why? What does it matter?'

Jenny wondered over his tone. It was a common question most couples were asked. She changed tack.

'Tanya was Katie's friend.' Ben frowned. Jenny continued. 'Do you know where they worked?'

Ben sat back in his chair and crossed his arms. Jenny glanced at O'Connell who seemed to have noticed the defensive behaviour.

'Nah. Sorry. You'll have to ask Tanya.'

'So you genuinely have no idea where Katie worked?'

Ben fixed his gaze on Jenny long enough to make her uncomfortable. Then shook his head.

'No. We never talked about work.'

Jenny bit her tongue to stop herself from challenging Ben's answer. Either he was lying, or Katie kept her occupation secret. Neither option was going to help them in this investigation.

'Okay. Now remember, you have an alibi for her time of death, so don't get all agro with me, but we need to know when you last saw Katie.'

Ben sucked in a deep breath through his nose, held it, then let it out slowly, puffing his cheeks as he did.

'Last Friday, on my day off.' He pointed to Jenny. 'You know Nick gets Wednesday night and Thursday off to come to town for you?'

The edges of Jenny's lip curled into a quick smile. She rolled her lips to hide it, but it wasn't missed.

'You two are good together.'

'Even for a cop?' Jenny joked.

'Even for a cop. And for once, I'm happy to know one.' Ben slid his chair back. 'Are we done?'

'Sure, but if you think of anything—like I said, a random name, even the name of a town, or place, mentioned in passing—let me know. Plus, if you find out where she was working, it might help us discover her tax file number or a prior address.'

Jenny rose. Ben extended his hand, and they shook.

He didn't let go.

'Find the bastard Jenny.'

'I'll do everything I can.'

She watched him round the desk and head for the door. 'Actually Ben...'

He turned to face her, a crease knitting his brow. 'Yeah?'

'Where did you stay when you were in town?'

Ben hesitated, then answered 'the Opal Miner's Motel.'

'So you don't know where Katie lived?'

'No, sorry.' He stepped through the doorway and disappeared.

Jenny's stomach tightened. Why was he lying to her about Katie's address?

Chapter 11

Jenny leant on the front counter and watched Ben leave the station before turning to O'Connell.

'He's devastated about Katie's death, but he knows more than he's letting on. I don't believe he didn't know where Katie was living.'

'He has an alibi for her murder.' O'Connell reminded her. 'We need to ask Marj if he stayed at the motel, and I think you're right about him holding information back.'

Sarge strode from his office.

'Did he give you a photo?' Jenny nodded. 'Good. Get it out to customs, run through all the missing persons files and see if anything jumps out.'

'I think I heard my cue.'

Heads turned to find the slim, curvy woman with immaculate makeup and six-inch heels, tottering into the station.

'What do you want, Gwen?'

Sarge's tone reflected everyone's opinion of the newspaper editor. But Jenny knew, for her boss, it was a case of protesting too much. Gwen was Senior Constable O'Connell's ex-wife, but Sergeant Mackenzie dated her on and off. There weren't a lot of available ladies in Coober Pedy and Gwen was an attractive woman.

'Don't be like that Mac. I might be here to help.'

O'Connell met Gwen at the counter.

'I doubt it.'

'Now now, Jon. Play nice. How is Gary anyway?'

It seemed O'Connell's ex still wasn't pleased about being replaced by a man.

'You know, I'd answer your question if I thought you were being even the slightest bit sincere. Like the sergeant said, what *are* you after?'

Gwen turned to Jenny with a cunning grin.

'A little birdy told me you found a dead body in a car boot yesterday. The public want more information.'

Sarge joined O'Connell.

'The public, you reckon.' He shook his head. 'We'll give an official statement once the postmortem is complete. At this stage, we are still making general enquiries.'

'You mean enquiries like, who she is. Sounds like you are struggling to confirm her ID. Maybe I can print an article to help you find out more about her?'

No one spoke. The last thing they needed was for the local paper to print anything yet.

'I'm off to Ted's.' Penny tossed her empty coffee cup into the bin beside O'Connell's desk. 'Who's giving me a lift, or whose car can I flog?'

Phillips pulled his keys from his pocket and hurried toward the exit.

'I'll drop you off.'

'Excellent. Let's go.' Penny leant into Jenny as she passed. 'You missed your cue. You snooze—you lose.' Her eyebrows wiggled.

Jenny stifled a grin.

Gwen slipped her faux Gucci handbag onto the counter, pulled a pen and pad out and flipped it open dramatically.

'I'm sure the local community can help you discover the victim's ID.'

Sarge crossed his arms.

'No need Gwen. We have two people who knew the woman and have given us her name.'

Gwen grinned knowingly.

'Yes, but it's not her real name, is it, or you wouldn't be searching the Missing Persons database.' She tapped her pen on her cheek and waited.

'We have work to do Gwen.' O'Connell rounded the counter. 'I think it's time for you to leave.'

'This is a public service building. You can't make me leave.'

Nellie jostled the mouse at the counter computer.

'She's right guys.'

Sergeant Mackenzie scowled, then opened his mouth to speak, but Nellie interrupted.

'We can't make *her* leave, but we can retreat to Sarge's office.'

Sarge stifled a snigger.

'Righto. Let's go team. In my office, now! Nellie, clean the whiteboard. Williams, bring the file with you.'

'Hang on!' Gwen tottered along the counter as they made their way into Sergeant Mackenzie's office.

'O'Connell, how are the CFS going with their fire report?' Sarge spoke as he stepped into his office, O'Connell two steps behind him.

Under normal circumstances, Sarge's office door was left open so the team could keep an eye on the front desk, but this time, everyone held their breath as Sarge's door closed.

For a moment Jenny thought Gwen might scream. A few seconds passed before her high heels stomped from the foyer.

'Good one Nellie. Nice work.' O'Connell patted her on the back. 'Make sure the coast is clear, then open the door and keep watch on the counter.'

Nellie mock-saluted with a wide grin.

'You got it Senior.'

Sarge rounded his desk and dropped into his chair. The air escaped from the vinyl in a rush.

'Williams, give us an update on your interview with Ben.'

Jenny relaxed in the chair opposite the sergeant.

'Ben appears genuinely devastated and Nick has alibied him, so he didn't kill Katie. He said he isn't aware of any family, or any prior names, but what was strange is he claimed not to know where Katie worked.'

'Or didn't want to say,' O'Connell offered.

'Exactly. He also said he didn't know where she lived. He claims he stayed with her at the motel, and he was extremely evasive when I asked where they met.'

'Confirm what he did tell you. But until we find out who this woman was, we don't have much to go on.'

Sergeant Mackenzie rose, picked up the file Jenny left on his desk and began writing information on the whiteboard.

'Estimated time of death is between Monday afternoon and Tuesday 2pm.' He drew a timeline and put the details at the far-left end. On the right, he added the date and time Jenny discovered the body.

The phone rang. Nellie stepped from the office as O'Connell lowered himself to the edge of Sarge's desk.

'We still need to trace the drop-sheet the victim was wrapped in. There are only two shops in town selling them.'

Sarge lifted the victim's crime scene photo from the file and placed it at the top, centre of the whiteboard.

'Print out the photo from Ben and get it up here. I'd rather not endure this one any longer.' He turned to Jenny. 'You need to interview Tanya again. Find out who grabbed Mikey and if it's connected to our case. Ask her where Katie lived while you're at it.' He turned to O'Connell. 'Get Phillips to chase down CCTV footage from the accident and last night's abduction as soon as he gets back from dropping McGregor off at Ted's.'

Jenny rose. 'I'll get started.'

Nellie tapped the doorframe. 'That was the hospital.'

'Go on,' O'Connell coaxed.

'Tanya is checking out soon, but apparently there is some sort of commotion going on in her ward.'

Phillips drew up behind Nellie. 'What's up?'

'Williams, sounds like you better take Phillips with you. Get Tanya's statement. Pry as much info out of her as you can. Then go to the hardware stores. Their systems are all digital these days. Find out what time anyone bought a drop-sheet, then view their security footage and see if we can find ourselves a suspect.'

'Will do.' Phillips turned on his heel.

Jenny hurried to her locker and grabbed her utility-vest, then signed out her service weapon. A few minutes later they strolled into the hospital entry to find Nurse Pat busier than usual.

'Hey!' He half smiled over the counter. 'She's in room 4.'

'Thanks Pat.'

Jenny wondered how Pat knew who she was looking for but a high-pitch voice filtering down the hall answered her question.

Phillips lifted an eyebrow as they checked their Tasers and weapons and hurried down the shiny white corridor.

A woman in pumps and lightweight pants backed from the room as they arrived. Her hair was in a bun, and she carried a large patchwork bag over one shoulder.

'You can't take him.' Tanya grabbed at the child in the woman's hands.

Jenny's heart ached as Mikey held out his arms to his mother. Tears ran down his chubby cheeks.

'Excuse me. Can we help?'

The woman let out an exaggerated sigh. 'Thank goodness you've arrived.'

'She's taking Mikey,' Tanya screamed. Mikey howled.

'Hang on a second.' Jenny held her hand up in front of the woman. 'What's going on?'

'I'm from Children's Services. Unfortunately, there's been a complaint, and we are under an obligation to act on it.'

'*One* complaint?' Jenny, like all police officers did her mandated child protection training. One complaint wasn't enough to have a child removed from their mother.

'It's a reliable source. A judge has signed off on an Immediate Removal Order.'

Jenny shook her head as Phillips physically restrained Tanya with his hands on her shoulders.

'You can't take him!' Tanya shoved Phillips aside.

'Stop!' Jenny spoke louder than intended. 'Everyone,' she held her palms out either side facing between Tanya and the case worker, 'just stop right now.'

Tanya stepped back from Phillips who puffed out a breath.

'I have the paperwork.' The children's services officer shoved a sheet of paper in Jenny's face so hard she was forced to step back.

'Let's see.'

Jenny held out her hand. The woman slapped the order into it. Jenny read through, knowing the complainant wouldn't appear, but wanting to understand the reasons.

Immediate Risk of Serious Harm, was cited as the reason. She knew the police hadn't made this complaint. Did someone know about the attempted kidnapping? Tanya wasn't responsible, at least not directly.

'Look, Mikey has been through enough over the past day. We have reason to believe he is a target after last night's abduction. I'm not sure removing him from his mother's care right now is the right thing. Can we get this investigated further?'

'I'm sorry. I don't make the rules.'

'Mum. Mum. Mum,' Mikey cried, followed by baby googly talk Jenny couldn't understand. His pudgy little hands reached for his mother.

'Mikey is in good health. A minor car crash isn't grounds for this, and last night's incident was outside anyone's control.' Jenny's heart was racing, and she knew she was growing frustrated.

'A thorough investigation goes into those orders.'

The case worker pointed to the paperwork still in Jenny's hand.

'I fail to see how that's possible given Tanya's accident was less than a day ago.'

'Not my concern.' The woman stepped around Jenny and started down the hallway.

Phillips intercepted Tanya as she lunged forward.

'Don't let them take him!' Tanya's voice broke. 'Please!'

Mikey's cries carried down the hallway. Jenny turned to Tanya who frantically tried to step around Phillips.

'I'll make a few calls. But you need to come clean with us. Children's Services must know something more. Something you're not telling us.'

Tanya turned from Phillips, crossed to the bed, snatched up her mobile phone and stormed past Jenny.

She resisted the urge to grab her by the arm.

'Tanya. What's going on?' She followed, Phillips two steps behind.

'Nothing!' Her hand waved behind her head as she stormed down the hallway, past Pat on the desk and out the front doors.

Jenny was running out of options. 'Tanya, stop or I'll have to arrest you.'

The woman turned so fast her long blonde hair whipped her cheek. 'What the hell for?'

Jenny scanned the parking area. Finding it empty, she said what needed to be said.

'We found a dead woman in your car, Tanya. You've been uncooperative with our police investigation, avoiding our questions about the victim. We need to talk to you about who would take Mikey and why. Then there is a list of other charges we are yet to formally lay. Don't make me lay those charges.'

Tanya's shoulders slumped. Jenny drew closer.

'Your son was abducted. If I wasn't right around the corner, you might be dead and Mikey would be gone. Why won't you help us find who did it? Why won't you say where you and Katie were working? We can protect you.'

Tanya threw her head back and laughed loudly. A man carrying a bunch of flowers scurried to the opposite side of the carpark and rushed toward the hospital entrance.

'You can't protect me. No one can.' Tanya stormed toward the taxi rank.

Jenny slipped her cuffs from her belt and jingled them intentionally.

'Tanya Rothchild, I'm detaining you for further questioning in relation to the suspicious death of Katie…'

'Okay. Okay!' Tanya rounded on Jenny, eyes blazing, lip raised in a near snarl. 'I'll come to the station willingly, but I won't answer any of your questions until I get my son back.'

Jenny replaced her handcuffs and nodded. 'I'll make some calls. Find out who filed a report with Children's Services.'

'Oh, I can save you the trouble.'

'You know who did this?'

Tanya grimaced. 'Like the lady said. Someone powerful.'

'Who Tanya? I need a name.'

'His father, Terrence Sullivan.'

Jenny swallowed hard.

'As in the union boss?'

'The very same.'

Chapter 12

Phillips parked the police Landcruiser up outside the hardware store.

'Terry Sullivan is so connected. No wonder Children's Services acted so quickly to take Mikey.' Phillips yanked the keys from the ignition and stepped out.

Jenny adjusted her utility belt as she slammed the passenger door.

'So, one of his minions threatened Tanya and tried to snatch Mikey last night? Seems like a stupid thing to do when he can call in the officials and take him through the court.'

'Maybe it was supposed to be a threat last night. But you interrupted the thug, and he improvised.'

'Possible. He might have panicked. He did leave Mikey behind in the end.'

Phillips pressed *lock* on the key fob and frowned.

'If the attack was only a threat, why would Sullivan get Mikey officially removed now?'

'Maybe Sullivan doesn't want Tanya talking to us. If Katie's death has anything to do with the union boss or his bikie connections, removing Mikey sends a clear message.'

'O'Connell is digging into the Child Protection Order. Hopefully we get confirmation Sullivan made the complaint.'

Jenny rolled her shoulders as tension rose in her neck.

'No wonder Tanya is a drunken mess. The union boss must have a judge on speed-dial to act this fast and if he did, we have to believe there's a connection between Tanya, Sullivan and our victim.'

Phillips led the way across the parking lot. 'If there is, this case might land with the AFP.'

They entered through the automatic glass doors into the high roof shed. Tepid air enveloped them as the airconditioner struggled to keep such a large area cool.

'The union has three divisions. Depends on which one Terry is linked to,' Jenny offered.

'Queensland and Northern Territory, as far as I know.'

Jenny lifted her eyebrows at her partner.

'Impressive. Either way, I doubt the AFP will jump in over a child custody dispute. It might be an issue if we link the union or Sullivan to murder.'

'True.' Phillips approached the counter.

'Officers.' The cheery woman, with purple-dyed Princess Leia buns and earrings all the way to the top of her ear, adjusted her apron and fluttered her false eyelashes at Phillips.

'What can I do for you?' Her tone flattened as her eyes fell on the white band where Phillips usually wore his wedding ring.

Jenny found the woman's name tag.

'Denise. Sorry to bother you. Can we please speak with your manager?'

The woman rolled her eyes. 'Good luck with that.'

'Sorry?'

'He's probably out to lunch, or in the loo, or doing a delivery.' She used air quotes for the last part.

'We do need to speak with him, or an assistant manager.'

'You're looking at her.' She tapped her ample bust.

'Okay. We need a list of purchases of one item in the store. If there are multiple brands, we need all of them.'

The woman frowned. 'Do you need a warrant?'

'Why would we?'

Denise's cheeks flushed as her eyes flicked from Jenny to Phillips.

'It's only a paint drop-sheet,' Phillips offered jokingly.

'Oh,' she frowned. 'I guess that can't incriminate anyone.' She laughed. 'From what day?'

Phillips put his hand on the counter and leant forward.

'Well, I'm sorry but we don't have a specific date. We need all the transactions on all the models of the product for the past month.'

'A month!'

'Yes, is that an issue?'

Jenny tried not to gawk as Phillips laid on the charm. He was usually a straight up, matter of fact kind of guy. This side of him was new.

Denise glanced back at the hand Phillips left on the counter. Jenny could see the cogs turning and read the assistant manager's thoughts. Was the wedding band line because he recently split up with a partner?

'A month of sales will take a little while to go through.'

'We can wait,' Phillips grinned. 'We'll need to get someone to collate security footage from the date and time of each purchase too.'

Denise frowned, curiosity rising. 'Is this about that dead girl, in the boot?'

Phillips shook his head and tutted.

'Can't comment on an ongoing investigation I'm afraid.'

'So it is?'

Phillips stepped back, suddenly less confident.

'No,' Jenny interrupted. 'What my partner here just said is we, can't confirm or deny anything and we can't comment on this particular investigation.'

Denise frowned again.

'So if it isn't about the dead woman, why are you willing to wait for it? If it was a shoplifter or something trivial, you wouldn't wait around. That footage could take a day, by the way.' She waved her hand around the almost deserted shop. 'We don't exactly have a lot of staff on.'

Jenny bit her cheek to calm her tone before speaking.

'You don't exactly have a lot of customers either.'

Twenty minutes later, Jenny rolled a chair out from under a desk as her stomach growled. The stench of body odour suppressed her hunger as the security officer brought up the first video file.

'We want footage of anyone who doesn't look like they should be buying a drop-sheet.'

The security officer nodded vigorously.

'This is so exciting. Nothing interesting ever happens around here. Shoplifters galore, but nothing linked to a murder.'

'As we've already explained, no one said this was about a murder and we can't comment on an ongoing investigation.'

'Yeah. Yeah. Sure. Sure.' His long thin neck poked forward as he began cueing up the video.

'Let's start with the most recent purchases.' Jenny sat on the wheeled chair and positioned it in front of the monitor.

'You got it.' He sat too close to the screen, eyes squinting as the first video file played. 'That's Clem, he's a local painter.'

Jenny rolled her lips.

'Please skip past the tradesmen for now.'

The screen blurred, another file opened and began to play. Ten videos were started and stopped, according to time stamps, cross referenced with sales receipts from the past few days.

Nothing unusual came into view. Jenny scanned the list of sales.

'How many people buy a bloody drop-sheet?'

'Thousands. Painters use them of course, but my mum always puts one over her bed in the caravan when they travel. The red dust is like baby powder and gets into everything.'

Jenny bit her lip. Denise was right. This was going to take ages, but Jenny's gut told her the purchase must have been in the past few days. Likely picked up after Katie was murdered.

But why dump her in Tanya's car? It seemed deliberate. And how did they get access to the car? She hoped Tanya was answering that question down the station now but doubted it.

A thought popped into her head.

'What if they didn't purchase it?' Jenny turned to Phillips who hovered over her chair. 'I've got an idea.'

'Anything to stop this torture,' Phillips moaned.

Jenny swivelled her chair to face the tech as he cued up another video.

'Download all the footage from this aisle from Sunday 12pm to Wednesday 2pm.'

'You got it. But it'll take a while.'

Jenny pulled a card from her utility-vest.

'Pop it up on a storage file and email the link here when you're done.'

'No worries.' He saluted.

Jenny shook her head, rose and joined Phillips as they exited the smelly little room.

'There is another possibility.'

Jenny nodded, knowing what Phillips was about to say.

'They used one they had lying around already.'

'Exactly. And if they did, they could have purchased it years ago.'

'Let's hope the lab can narrow it down more.'

As the words left Jenny's lips, she knew it was unlikely. Lab tests could be done in hours, but there was a backlog, and priority went to cases due to go to court, high profile deaths and investigations linked to anything political. Who was going to care about a woman who was not even using her real name, bashed to death in the middle of nowhere?

She was.

Chapter 13

Cool air pumped full speed from the car vents. Jenny adjusted the stream to blow on her face. Beads of sweat dried as more raced to replace them. She reached for the insulated water bottle in her door, drank deeply, then sighed when her stomach growled loudly.

Phillips laughed. 'Lunch time, by the sounds of it.'

'Yeah. I was going to meet Nick, but it's too hectic.'

Phillips glanced at Jenny, then returned his gaze to the road. 'Never too hectic to spend time doing the important things.'

Jenny realised the significance of those words. Having nearly lost her cousin and aunt because no one listened, paid attention or cared enough to see what was going on, right in front of them, should have been enough.

Watching her partner struggle with his son's illness was an eye opener. Danny was shocked and like most dads, wanted to fix his son's cancer. But he adjusted quickly and was there for Dianna and Tommy. He was present during the treatment and supportive once his wife and child were home.

She needed to be present with Nick. 'Can you drop me off at the motel?'

'Sure.'

Jenny texted a message to Nick. The reply came as Phillips turned down Hutchison Street and stopped outside the Opal Miner's Motel reception.

Jenny hopped out but leant back inside before closing the door.

'I hate leaving you with all the video footage.'

'I doubt it's in yet. Plus, I need to chase up CCTV footage from last night and the accident scene. I'm sure I can save the hardware videos for you to watch.'

'Thanks for that.' She heard his chuckle as she slammed the door. She waited for the police Landcruiser to pull away, then jogged across the road. Regretting it almost immediately as sweat soaked into her armpits.

She entered Marj's office to find Nick leaning on the counter, while Marj perched on her stool. She opened her mouth to speak but stopped when Nick put a finger in the air, his eyes never leaving the television screen hanging on the wall.

She scanned the show and grinned at the over-filtered, perfect hair and makeup staring back at her and waited for the scene to end.

'Another cliffhanger.' Marj slapped her forehead dramatically. 'Why do I watch these things?'

Nick grinned past Marj to Jenny.

'Because we all know how much you love drama,' Jenny announced as she reached Nick and wrapped her arms around his neck. His warm hands circled her waist.

'Get a room you two.'

They laughed.

'We already have one.'

Marj slipped off her stool.

'In that case, give an old lady a hug and get to it.'

'Marj!' Jenny gaped as Marj slipped from her stool and shimmied into the hug.

'Group hug.' She squeezed, then let go. 'Now get out of here.' She waved her hand toward the door on the restaurant side. 'The *Bold and the Beautiful* starts in a minute.'

Jenny laughed as Nick dragged her from the office. The mood grew heavy as they entered the motel restaurant.

'Is Ben under arrest?' Nick's voice was barely a whisper.

'No. You gave him an alibi for the murder.' She didn't tell him Ben was lying about something. She didn't ask Marj to check her records while Nick was there either. It didn't seem right holding the information back from him, but he was keeping the AFP investigation about the extortion close to his chest.

'That's good.' Nick's tone was wary.

Jenny thought about asking him to clarify his alibi again, but Stan interrupted them.

'Hey you two. What can I get you?' The barman's slim face never appeared jovial, but the tight lines and the twinkle in his eyes always conveyed warmth.

'I'm still on duty, so a non-alcoholic ginger beer for me thanks Stan.'

'I'll grab a cola.' Nick slid a menu to Jenny, then laughed. 'And a bowl of chicken pesto for Jenny.'

'You're not eating?'

Nick grinned. 'Do you know what time it is?'

Jenny scanned her watch, but Nick continued.

'It's after 2pm Jenny. I ate a few hours ago.'

'I'm sorry.'

'Don't be. You've got work to do. I'll head home soon. Ben's not in a great place. Can we catch up at William Creek Saturday?'

Jenny wanted to say yes, but she knew the chances were slim. Not unless the investigation was handed over to Adelaide detectives. Deep down, she hoped it wouldn't be. She hated not seeing cases through.

'I'll try. I need to get out to Fergusson's to interview him, but Sarge isn't making it a priority. Maybe I can convince him to let me do it Saturday.'

'Fingers crossed.' Nick lifted the drinks from the bar. 'Thanks Stan.'

Stan nodded politely, but his face darkened. Jenny turned to follow his gaze and found the two men who briefly shared their table the night before, strolling in.

'You know those two?' Jenny asked, as the lean guy with the neck tattoos eyed Jenny's uniform.

'*Know*, is an ambiguous word.'

'So, you recognise them, but don't know their names?' Jenny kept her eye on the tattooed guy as she spoke.

The man slipped his hands into his pants pockets and glanced at everything in the restaurant except her.

'One on the right is Leigh Mundy. Don't know the other fella's name.'

Jenny recalled Leigh calling him Dave last night.

'How do you know Leigh?' Jenny's gaze followed the men as they entered the beer garden.

Stan pursed his lips.

'I don't. They rocked up with last night's crowd, new in town, or so I thought.'

'And.'

'And it's not my story to tell. Ask Marj.'

Jenny's curiosity piqued. 'Trouble?'

'Nothing Marj and I can't handle.'

Stan was tall, and lean, but Jenny knew he could take care of himself. He'd been Marj's barman since before Jason, Marj's partner died. He would look out for Marj, but why did he need to?

'I know that look Jenny. I'm not saying anything. Ask Marj.'

Jenny lifted her chin, then nodded.

'Let's get some food into you first.' Nick coaxed her to a table. 'Because I know that look too, and you can't fight everyone's fight Jen.'

'Why not?' she half teased.

'Because one day, you'll pick a fight you can't win.' Nick's tone made her stomach lurch.

'Nick, is everything okay? Is this about the Fergusson fire and Ben's alibi? Is he threatening you?'

'Ben isn't threatening anyone.' Nick rubbed the back of his neck.

'Is this about the AFP investigation? I thought it was wrapping up with a lack of evidence, but now the Fergusson hayshed fire...'

'I can't comment on an ongoing investigation.'

Nick placed the glasses on the table and pulled a chair out for Jenny.

She didn't sit down.

'That's my line.'

'Feels like crap, doesn't it?'

Chapter 14

Condensation dripped onto the cardboard coaster. Jenny reached for her drink, sipped, then lowered it back in silence. She should have given herself time to digest Nick's words. Not only his words, but everything about the statement.

But she didn't.

'Have the AFP progressed with their investigation? Has something happened to you or the farm, I should know about?'

Nick spun his coaster around. 'Let's talk about something else?'

'Like what? Ben just lost his fiancé. The Fergusson's hayshed was burned to the ground. Is my murder case connected to the AFP investigation?'

'You know I can't say.' The coaster made another rotation. Nick kept his eyes on it as he lifted his drink to his lips.

'Am I going to get this murder case ripped out from under me?'

Nick shook his head, then dropped his drink onto the moist coaster heavily.

'Jenny. Katie's death isn't *your* case. There is more than one police officer in town.' He leant in closer. 'And what the AFP are up to is outside my brief.'

'The fire at Fergusson's is the first sign of anything happening on the local properties in nearly a year. Are the Feds getting *anywhere*?'

'Ask your superiors.' Nick's tone was sharp.

Jenny sighed. She'd gone too far again. Swallowing hard, she reached for Nick's hand. He drew it into his lap before she touched him.

'I'm sorry Nick. I'm such an idiot.'

Nick glanced her way but didn't give up the hand in his lap.

'You came for lunch Jen. I thought you'd put a few minutes aside for us?'

'I did. At least I meant to. But then those guys came in the door and Stan's reaction and then you going all weird when I talked about…' She shook her head as she recalled something her mum often says. *You can't control anyone or anything Jenny, only yourself.*

'Did you ask Sam when his mid-year or Spring uni break is next year?'

She hoped changing the subject would help alleviate the tension. A slow grin curved Nick's lips and she relaxed.

'He gets two weeks in late July, and another week mid-semester in late September.'

Jenny pictured the landscape during both those dates. After nearly two years, she knew September was a wild-flower month.

'Where are we having the wedding? Location is going to affect the best time of year.'

'I'd like to hold it on the property, but it's a long way from accommodation. How many people do you think we'll have?'

Jenny considered her extended family. Her brothers loved camping. Her parents bought a caravan last year. They were due to arrive in it this weekend.

'I think we can make that work. Camp, caravans, get Mrs B. to cater from the William Creek Pub.'

Stan arrived with Jenny's meal.

'Not sure Marj will like that.'

'Stan's right.' Nick rubbed his chin. 'Maybe Marj can help Mrs B. with the catering.'

A thought struck Jenny. 'But the crew from work will be on standby. They can't be all the way out at the farm in case something goes wrong.'

Stan cleared Nick's empty glass from the table.

'Have you considered eloping?'

'Considered and binned. Marj and my mother would kill me.'

Stan grinned.

'I'll leave you love birds to sort out the mess then.'

Jenny watched Stan, then noticed the two men from the beer garden reappear. Leigh stopped in front of Stan, who brushed past without a word.

'Making sure your work mates can attend is important, so we know we can't have it on your parents farm in Myponga.'

Jenny snapped her attention back to Nick.

'True. July or September could work, but I love September, with all the wildflowers.'

'September it is then.'

Jenny squeezed Nick's hand and leant in for a kiss. The sound of breaking glass made her spin in time to witness the two men shoving one another.

She jumped to her feet and rushed across the dining area instinctively.

'What the hell is going on?'

Leigh sneered at her as his eyes roamed over her uniform.

'The cops are pretty hot in this drop-kick town, hey Dave?'

'Come on Leigh, let's get going.'

The stocky man glanced past Jenny as Nick arrived at her back.

'Sounds like your mate has the right idea, *Leigh*.' Jenny repositioned her Taser for emphasis.

Leigh shook his arm free of his mate and barged past Stan toward the door, but not before leaning in and staring at Jenny eye to eye.

'You have no idea who you're dealing with little lady.'

Nick reached out toward Leigh. Jenny grabbed his hand as Stan dropped to his haunches to pick up broken glass.

'Oh I think I do.' She sniffed the air, catching Stan's eye. 'Can you smell that?' She eased Nick's arm behind her back, willing him to take the hint.

Stan rose, the bottom of the broken glass in hand.

'Can't mistake dog shit when you smell it.'

Jenny nodded.

'The kind of smell you can't get out of your nasal hairs.'

Nick stepped around Jenny to help Stan. Jenny noticed he kept his eye on Leigh, but as Dave nudged his friend to the door, Nick let his guard down.

Jenny held her breath until they left the restaurant, then rounded on Stan.

'Now, will you tell me what's going on?'

Chapter 15

Jenny wandered along the covered veranda and stopped outside the motel reception. A fly crawled over her sweaty face. She waved it away from her nose as she counted to ten, plastered a smile on her lips and entered Marj's office.

'Hey Marj.'

'Jenny. I thought you were having lunch.'

Her food was being transferred into a takeaway container and Nick agreed to bring it to the station. After watching the altercation with Stan, he wasn't sulking about her lunch being cut short.

'All sorted. I needed to speak to you without Nick,' She glanced out the reception door, 'so managed to sneak away for a sec.'

It wasn't entirely a lie.

The motel owner placed her open book, pages down, on the counter and waited without her usual curiosity. Jenny's stomach knotted. Why wasn't Marj assuming this was a wedding chat, or a catch up on town gossip?

'What do you need?'

What made Marj go from buzzing, to flat so quickly?

'It's about Ben.'

Marj appeared to relax. Jenny wrestled with the guilt. She was going to get to Leigh and Dave next, but the last thing she wanted to do was upset the motel owner.

Marj was her mum away from home. Even more reason there shouldn't be secrets between them.

The vague thought her mother kept secrets about her cousin for years slipped away with Marj's words.

'He's a good one you know.'

The statement caught Jenny off guard. Marj didn't know everything Jenny knew about Ben. She was aware Nick's fall wasn't an accident. She said so herself. Nick Johnston was born riding. But Marj was unaware Ben was in the frame for the sabotage.

Jenny didn't know what to say to Marj's comment. So she asked the question she needed to.

'Can I confirm Ben has been staying here Friday nights?'

Marj frowned. 'Why?'

Jenny smiled, trying to make light of the question. 'I'm just ticking boxes Marj.'

Marj slid from her stool and rounded the counter. Leaning in close she whispered.

'Is this about his fiancé's murder?'

Marj was back in gossip mode.

'You know I can't discuss details. Has he been staying here?

Jenny's heart broke. She knew, any second now, she was going to wipe away the woman's mischievous grin.

'Well, I can't confirm he sleeps in the room, but yes, he's been booked in every Friday night for over a month now.'

She wondered again where Ben met Katie. A month was a very short time to be seeing someone before proposing. Maybe Ben knew his fiancé before she came to Coober Pedy? She buried the thought for later.

'And you've never seen Katie with him?'

'No.' Marj placed her finger over her lips and tapped. 'It's strange, isn't it? Why would he sneak her into his room and not eat at the restaurant?'

It was a good question. Jenny was sure Ben knew more about Katie's background than he told them, but why not eat in the restaurant? Jenny reminded herself that Ben did five years in prison. Even if he wasn't guilty and did the jail sentence in exchange for money or some other coercion, he was an ex-con. Being cautious came with his past.

Jenny focussed back on the real reason she was in Marj's office and not eating lunch with Nick.

'Thanks Marj. I've got one more question.'

Jenny thought about beating around the bush with Marj by asking if she heard anything about other bars in town yet. But decided Marj was a friend. She needed to be straight with her.

'What is it Luv?'

Marj must have read her hesitation. She swallowed, then pressed on.

'I needed to know about Ben, but I came straight in here now because I witnessed an altercation between Stan, and someone called Leigh in the bar, only moments ago. It got rough Marj. Stan refused to explain what it was about. He said I needed to ask you, and you need to tell me what's going on before things get nasty.'

Marj put her hands on her hips. 'That's not a question.'

Why was she being evasive? Jenny reminded herself she needed to hit this issue head on.

'What does Leigh want?'

Marj licked her lips. Jenny knew the woman's hesitation meant she was only going to get half the story.

'He wants a venue for an event, and I said I couldn't accommodate him.' She waved absently and returned to her stool behind the counter.

'A venue?'

'Yes.'

Marj lifted her book from the top of the counter as though the conversation should be over.

Jenny studied the motel owner as she pretended to read her book.

'So this event isn't legal?'

Marj didn't look up immediately. When she did, Jenny found her expression difficult to read.

'I didn't say that.'

Why wasn't she coming out and saying what was on her mind?

Jenny leant over the high countertop, resisting the urge to rip Marj's book from her hands.

'Why does he need your bar now?'

Marj peered over her book. 'I don't know.'

'And he approached you when?'

'Last night. Told me he could guarantee last night's crowd every week if I host this major event.'

'So why did you refuse if it isn't illegal?'

Marj snapped her book closed and dropped it on the counter.

'Because I don't like him, that's why.'

'Well, it seems he isn't taking no for an answer.'

Chapter 16

Jenny paced back and forth in front of Sergeant Mackenzie's desk as she explained the incident in the motel bar. Her hands wouldn't stay still as her mind went back over Marj's weak response.

'I can't believe she lied to me.'

'Sit down Williams.' Sarge's tone was calm as he waved to the seat and her full takeaway container abandoned on his desk.

Jenny continued to pace. 'I know she was holding something back.'

Sergeant Mackenzie nodded with unusual patience.

'Like Stan said, they said no thanks and probably thought the problem would go away.' He pointed to the seat once more.

Jenny shook her head.

'But they didn't. Marj claims she said no because she didn't like Leigh, but I believe she said no because whatever Leigh Mundy wants to do at this event is illegal.'

Jenny noticed Phillips scanning through missing persons reports in the main office. Nellie tended to the front counter with one ear open to what was going on in the boss's office. Jenny eased the door until it sat ajar.

'This has to be connected to our victim's murder.' She plonked down in Sarge's spare chair.

O'Connell sat on the corner of Sergeant Mackenzie's desk with a frown.

'Quite a leap.'

'It's only a hunch, but Tim attended patients out at the wreckers on Kempel Road last night. The same direction Tanya was coming from when she crashed Wednesday afternoon.'

Sarge leant back in his chair, clasped his hands together, steepled his fingers and tapped his top lip.

'Not seeing the connection.'

'Leigh Mundy and Dave, whatever the face's name is, were at Marj's bar last night. When I started asking if they usually drank somewhere else, maybe where the chemical spill was, they hurried away.'

'And you think the chemical spill is connected to Leigh and Dave hassling Marj?'

'They told Marj, every week could be like last night if she agreed to host an event.'

'I read Marj's statement.'

'But where have all those guys been drinking up until last night?'

'I see where you're going, but they probably usually drink at the worksite bar. Companies working with FIFOs like to keep tabs on how much alcohol their staff consume.'

'Then why suddenly turn up at Marj's the same night Tim is called out to handle five patients from some unknown chemical spill? And if it was a legal bar, why haven't we been called to investigate the spill?'

'This is all speculation Williams. We need proof.'

'Exactly. I need to run background on Leigh, but Tanya already told me Mikey's father is union connected.'

'Not all union roads lead to corruption and illegal activities Williams.' Sarge rose and lifted the marker from the shelf on the whiteboard as he spoke. 'But let's nut this out.'

'All roads do when we're talking about the CWU.' Jenny snatched the pen from her boss's fingers and began scribbling.

The only reason Jenny knew Terrence Sullivan's name was because he was head of the CWU and the union was under investigation over claims of corruption. The CWU were all over the news.

'Terrence Sullivan, the union kingpin, snaps his fingers, and Tanya loses custody of Mikey.' Jenny wrote Terry S. next to the photo of Tanya on the board.

'Nellie is still digging for the paper trail on that one. We all know Children's Services are overworked, but the paperwork went down a rabbit hole too quickly,' O'Connell offered.

'With Tanya's relationship to Terry Sullivan, she must know more than she is telling us, but she's refused to say more until we get Mikey back. I tried threatening to arrest her. She still didn't talk. Maybe if I say the right things in front of her, we might be able to gauge her reaction. I think the chemical spill, and whatever nightlife kept all those FIFO workers busy until last night is connected.'

'Another infamous gut feeling is it?' O'Connell grinned.

'It is, but it makes sense.'

Sergeant Mackenzie fell back into his chair. The vinyl groaned.

'Okay Williams. We'll play along. McGregor has finished up with the VW. Take her to the wreckers with you and see what you can find.'

Jenny tossed the whiteboard marker onto his desk.

'But Williams, we have no grounds for a warrant. I read the CFS report. They ran tests and found no evidence of a chemical spill. If the wrecking yard refuses any further tests, there's nothing we can do. You need to tread carefully.'

'You got it Sarge.'

Jenny bumped into Nellie on the way out.

'Got the file on Leigh Mundy and known associates.'

'Priors?' Jenny followed Nellie back into the office.

'No prison time.'

'What you got Nellie?' Sarge half rose.

Jenny wondered why her boss used Nellie's first name, then put it down to the fact she was a civilian staffer before she became a cop.

'Mundy has a few arrests, but charges were never laid. He's thirty-seven, unmarried, has worked for various construction companies, and…' Nellie's white teeth shone.

Jenny filled the hung silence.

'He's connected to the CWU.'

'Give the girl a jelly baby.' Nellie tapped her nose. 'He's a fully paid-up member of the CWU and is on the committee with Terrence Sullivan.'

'Of course he is.' Jenny turned to leave.

'Wait up.' Phillips waved a piece of paper in his hand.

'What?'

'I got a hit on missing persons.'

Phillips rushed into the stuffy office.

'I think I've found our victim?' He crossed to the whiteboard, taped a picture on the board and stepped back.

Everyone studied the photo from Ben's phone and the missing person's picture.

'I think you might be right.' Sarge broke the silence. 'Let's have her details.'

'Maryam Suleiman, aged twenty-five. Born in Syria. Parents are refugees from the conflict.'

'And now we have to tell them their daughter is dead.' Jenny swallowed the acrid taste in her mouth.

'Local detectives will handle the death notice,' Sarge sighed. 'You get McGregor and check out the wreckers. Good work, Phillips.'

'Thanks Sarge, but there's one more thing.'

'Spit it out.'

'Maryam has applied for a restraining order on her ex.'

'Was she here to hide?' Jenny wondered if her theorising about a link between their victim's work, the chemical spill and the CWU might be superfluous now.

'Possibly.' O'Connell waved for everyone to leave. 'Phillips, see where the victim's deadshit ex is now. Williams, carry on with McGregor. Even though the CFS didn't find a chemical spill, we know five people required medical attention. We need to follow up regardless.'

'Will do.' Jenny nodded as Phillips strolled by. 'Good catch.'

'It's a start.' He seemed tense.

'Is Tommy doing alright?'

Phillips nodded. 'Yeah, he's all good, I just can't imagine what it would be like to flee a war-torn country, only to see your daughter beaten by her ex-husband and then brutally murdered.'

'Husband? She was married?'

'She was Syrian,' Phillips offered in explanation.

Jenny considered the information. Maybe she was promised before leaving Syria.

'How old was the ex?'

'I'm still getting details in.'

'The MO seems to match. Katie, or Maryam, was viciously beaten to death. Sounds like something an abusive ex could do.'

O'Connell slipped between Jenny and Philips.

'Yes, but was the facial injury to cast suspicion on the ex?'

Jenny laughed as she collected the police Landcruiser keys from the peg next to O'Connell's desk.

'You're beginning to sound like me.'

O'Connell touched his brow with the back of his hand and flopped into his chair.

'Oh, heavens no.'

'You got that right. One of you is more than enough.' Sergeant Mackenzie called from his office door. 'Get going Williams.'

Chapter 17

Jenny stepped from the airconditioned station into a clear blue sky, red dirt and a visible heat haze shimmering over the horizon.

She reached O'Connell's vehicle parked under the carport at the rear of the building and relished the shade a moment. Opening the car, she turned the key and leant in to crank up the airconditioning before getting in.

Five minutes later, she drove into Ted's Garage carpark to find Penny standing outside.

'What are you doing in the sun?' She slipped from the vehicle and opened the rear doors.

Penny stowed her bags. 'Believe it or not, it's cooler out here than in there.' She pointed to the shed where the roller doors were still down.

'Why didn't Jed open the doors?'

'He's not here and they are locked. Stuffed if I could figure out how to open them.'

She returned to the shed for more of her gear. Jenny joined her, lifting the evidence box.

'Did you find anything else of use? A mobile phone would be good.' She asked as she placed the box in the back of the vehicle and closed the doors.

'No phone. Nothing else of note. I'll get everything off to the lab.' Penny grinned over the bonnet. 'Let's check out this wrecker. Tim said the lab results on the patients are back too.'

'Great. I'll call Nev on the way.'

Penny sighed as she aligned all the vents onto her face.

'It's hot enough to bake a cake out here.'

Jenny giggled. 'Cook an egg maybe, but a cake might be pushing it.'

'You should feel inside my disposable overalls. I've sweated ten litres of water.'

'At least you didn't need to use Jed's loo then.'

'Oh, I used it. Disgusting.'

'I've seen you pull putrid fingers from drainpipes and pick bits of flesh from a truck grill. So *disgusting* is a big call.'

'Exactly.'

Jenny dialled Nev's number on her phone. The handsfree in O'Connell's vehicle picked up the call.

'Jen, what's up?'

'Hey Nev. Sorry to bother you. I know you're pretty busy there still.'

'Yeah, flu has a few staff off, and the heat has sent a few packing their bags for the city.'

'I hear you. Can you give me the short version of the lab report from the chemical spill patients?'

'Not a chemical spill.'

'Really?' Jenny glanced at Penny.

The forensic tech leant forward toward the car mic.

'Tim said they presented with poisoning.'

'They were poisoned, but not by any chemical spill. It was gas.'

'Like LPG?' Jenny asked.

'Yes. Weird, I know.'

'Did they all stick their heads in a barbie or something?'

Nev chuckled. 'I'd say you're looking for a location where a large volume gas storage has leaked out into a confined space.'

'LPG stinks to high heaven,' Penny stated.

'Yes, but it's possible they were using the LPG to power a burner inside without adequate ventilation.'

'It's too hot to run a heater and commercial cooktops have huge vent hoods.' Jenny turned the vehicle down Kempel Street and slowed as they approached the wrecking yard.

'I'll leave it with you two, but there's always the possibility it's been caused by burners in a drug lab.'

'Oh no. I can hear Sergeant Mackenzie now.' Penny pursed her lips and put on her best impersonation of Sarge. '*You bloody kids, it's always drugs with you lot.* It's always the baby-boomer fallback position.'

Nev laughed.

Jenny parked outside the yard.

'Nev, I'd usually agree with you, but wouldn't there have been drug residue if the patients weren't wearing PPE.?'

'Good point.' An alarm sounded in the background. 'Gotta go.'

'Thanks Nev.'

Jenny disconnected the call and turned to Penny, the motor still running. Cool air continued to pump from the air vents.

'Any other reason why someone would be using a large LPG tank and not notice the smell of a leak?'

Penny adjusted the air vent, scrunched her face into the airflow and sighed. Jenny wasn't sure if it was a response to the refreshing cool or an attempt to psych herself up before heading into the heat again.

'I'll think about it. Nothing counteracts the smell of LPG. It's deliberately made to stink like rotten eggs so people can't die of inhalation. But I might be missing something.'

Jenny turned the car off and laughed as Penny pouted.

'Come on. It's not getting any cooler out there for at least four more hours.'

Penny collected two pairs of gloves and shoved them into her pocket along with a few paper bags.

'I don't know how you live out here.'

'You get used to it.'

'Keep telling yourself that.' Penny waved for Jenny to lead the way.

Jenny approached the tall chain-link fence, complete with razor wire.

'Bit of overkill,' Penny offered.

Jenny said nothing. The locals didn't understand ownership in the same way as European culture did. Nev tried to explain it to her once. Thousands of years ago, whatever was found on the barren land was theirs to use. It used to be berries, plants, kangaroos including their leather, stones to grind grass seeds into flour and any other naturally occurring resource.

Nowadays, it was full of cars, fuel, alcohol, food and other possessions modern society owned and didn't want to share.

The friction point was obvious. How to overcome the cultural void wasn't.

The wrecker was surrounded by expansive red dirt stretching to the horizon. Sparse patches of grass dotted the landscape, while two scraggly mallee trees struggled for life either side of the gate.

They entered between the open gates and were met with harsh barking. They flinched at two German Shepherds, baring their teeth and yanking against heavy chains tied to a rusted old Jeep.

'Sorry ladies. They get a little protective.'

A lean guy with a long beard, worn tank-top and shorts that threatened to expose more than Jenny wanted to see, stepped out of a transportable office. A window airconditioner rattled noisily as he pulled the door closed and descended the two concrete steps.

'What can I do for you?'

Jenny approached the office building. Penny waited near a shed, far enough away the still barking dogs couldn't reach her.

'I'm Constable Williams, this is our forensic tech, Penny McGregor.'

The dogs continued to bark, each taking turns. The man studied Penny a moment, then shouted at the dogs.

'Be quiet you two!'

One dog sat back on his haunches, ears back, eyes alert. The other burrowed under the Jeep out of the sun.

'Sorry to bother you. We're here about the three men who were taken to hospital yesterday. Were you here when the ambulance arrived?

The man rubbed an open hand over his chin, and down the greying beard until he created a peak at the tip.

'I was. Called the ambulance myself.' His eyes followed Penny as she strolled between the dogs and the corrugated-iron shed. 'What's she doing?'

'Hospital tests confirm the patients were overcome with fumes. We are here to make sure the Country Fire Service didn't miss anything.'

'Fumes?' He shook his head. 'All we have here are old cars Luv.'

'I understand, I still need to get a statement. Can you talk me through the incident?' Jenny continued.

'Not much to tell. Dogs started barking. I came out, found one passed out here.' He pointed to his feet, while his eyes followed Penny picking her way past the dogs toward an outbuilding. 'The other two were puking up on the dirt over there.'

He pointed past the shed Penny circled, to a transportable donga. Jenny wondered what a wrecking yard needed an accommodation building for but focussed back on her questions. She needed to give Penny space to find anything of interest.

'Where did they come from?'

He crossed his hands over his chest and scoffed. 'How the hell should I know?' He waved his hand beyond the stacked, crumpled wrecks and various outbuildings. 'I'm just a wrecker Luv.'

Something clanged to the ground out of sight. Jenny peered between the office and a single bay shed.

'Is someone else here?' The man remained silent. 'Maybe they can help. Were they here yesterday?'

A dark face with brown hair, streaked with blond appeared from the work bay. The Aboriginal boy studied Jenny, then Penny before scampering out of sight.

The wrecker waved his hand dismissively.

'He's just a kid. Helps me pull the parts from the cars and trucks. I'm teaching him mechanics.'

'He's only about ten.'

The beard jostled.

'I'm just keeping him busy and out of trouble Luv.' He grinned, opening a previously split lip, which began to weep. He reached into his pocket and produced a stained rag, then dabbed at the spot.

Jenny cringed. 'Can we speak with the boy?'

'He's shy.'

Jenny nodded, then turned to scan the yard as Penny wandered toward the donga beyond the shed.

'Been doing this long?'

He shifted his weight from one foot to the other impatiently.

'Most of my life.'

'We'll finish taking a look around then,' Jenny smiled. 'We'll be out of your hair soon.'

He chewed his bottom lip but stopped when a tooth connected with the cut.

'Maybe I can save you some trouble if you tell me what you're searching for.'

'It's routine. We need to confirm there's nothing here responsible for making those people sick.' Jenny kept her tone casual.

'Like I said, dogs started barking. I came out, found them spilled out on the ground. Nothing here but oil and grease.'

'And you didn't hear a car?'

He tightened his arms over his chest again. 'Nope.'

The dogs were now hunkered down in the dirt, under the Jeep, panting to stay cool. Penny stopped at the side of the donga. Jenny noted there was no airconditioning and wondered again what the building was there for.

She turned back to the owner.

'There's nothing for miles out here. Where do you think they came from?'

His chin jutted out.

'No idea Luv. I'll leave that for you to figure out.'

Jenny watched as Penny slipped her phone from her pocket.

'You sure I can't chat with the kid?' Jenny stepped closer to the office. 'He might have seen something.'

'He's a minor. His parents aren't present. I don't think it's a good idea.'

'Can I look around the office?'

He lifted his chin again.

'Not without a warrant.'

Jenny nodded.

'We'll leave you to it then.' Jenny pulled a card from her pocket. 'If you think of anything that might help, please…'

'I know where the cop shop is Luv.' He waved his hand dismissively at her card.

'Fair enough.' Jenny turned to see Penny start toward the car. 'Thanks for your help,' she waved.

'All good Luv.'

She joined Penny at the police vehicle.

'How'd you go?' She opened the driver's side door as Penny got in the passenger's side.

'I think I know how they were poisoned.'

'And.'

'And start the bloody car, it's stinking hot in here.'

Jenny did as instructed.

'*And,*' she repeated.

'And out the back of one of the dongas is a large LPG tank on a stand. It outdates my grandad.'

Jenny frowned as she steered the car into a U-turn.

'I don't get the connection.'

'I'll need to check, but the first few batches of LPG released in Australia didn't contain ethyl mercaptan.'

Jenny shook her head.

'Still not getting it.'

Penny laughed.

'Ethyl mercaptan is what stinks in gas. Without it, natural gas and LPG are odourless.'

'So the patients *were* poisoned at the wrecking yard. How come the CFS didn't find the leak?'

'I'd guess they were looking for the obvious signs. Smoke, vapour, liquid spills. I doubt they were carrying an LPG detector with them and even if they were, they may not have gained access inside the building to take readings.'

'So we need a warrant.'

'Your department.'

'I know. But I don't think we have probable cause with Nev's report alone.'

'You sure?' Penny opened her phone to reveal various pictures of the gas tank.'

'Will it be enough?'

'Only one way to find out.'

Chapter 18

Jenny hit *send* on the warrant request and crossed her fingers. After compiling the patient test results, enhancing the photos Penny collected and doing her best to date the LPG tank to around 1937, she was hopeful.

'Good spot McGregor.' Sarge leant against his office door frame. 'You done here then?'

'I am. I've sent the evidence boxes from the VW ahead and I'm on a flight first thing in the morning back to Adelaide.'

'Always good to have your assistance.' Sarge waved, stepped into his office and pushed the door so it sat ajar.

Penny scanned the time on the station wall clock.

'I'll see you for drinks tonight.'

'I'll be there. Nick's back at the property. Hopefully he can get Ben to say where he met our victim. I'm sure he knows more than he's telling us.'

Penny shook her head.

'I've done my bit. The rest is up to you lot.' She lifted the counter and headed for the door. 'I'm catching up with Tim at the pool.'

Jenny crossed to the counter. 'Lucky you.'

'That's for sure.' Nellie added with a sigh.

Phillips grunted as Penny disappeared out the door. Jenny shimmied up alongside as he scanned the CCTV footage from the hardware store.

'Find anything?'

'Not yet.'

'Williams,' O'Connell called from his desk.

'Yep.'

'I've organised for a unit to inform the victim's parents. They have taken a cultural liaison with them. Keep an eye out for their report.'

'Roger that.'

'Follow up the restraining order. See when it was lodged. If it's been granted. Get details of the request and find out where this guy is. If he's in town, he could be our killer.'

'On it.'

Jenny crossed to her desk, wiggled the mouse to life and typed in Maryam's details. Maryam's date of birth was included, but the document didn't reveal the husband's details.

Typing, she added his name and last known address to the registration database and waited.

'Got you.' She hit *print* on the file, knowing O'Connell and the sergeant liked paper copies. 'Omar Suleiman is fifteen years older than Maryam.'

'Any kids?' O'Connell joined her to view the computer screen.

'I've only got registration and licence details here. He drives a navy blue Hi-Lux ute. I'll add the registration details to the board.'

'After you're done, check and see if they have any kids. We could be looking for a missing child.'

Jenny's stomach flipped at the thought.

'I hope not.'

She joined Phillips, reached under the counter for the still warm sheet of paper, then turned, ready to bother the sergeant and add the details to the whiteboard.

'Hey. Check this out.'

Jenny fixed her eyes on the screen as Phillips hit *play*.

'I think this kid flogs a drop-sheet.'

Jenny frowned at the screen, then tapped Phillips' hand away from the mouse, hit *rewind*, then used the arrow keys to advance the video frame by frame.

'It's a pretty weird spot for a kid to linger if he didn't.' She slowed the footage. 'I think he shoves something down those shiny red trackpants. Who wears a tracksuit in this heat?'

Nellie joined them as Phillips replayed the footage.

'He looks familiar,' Jenny frowned

'Apparently, we all look alike.' Nellie's tone was mocking, but the pinch at the corner of her eyes told Jenny there was more to the comment than Nellie's usual fun-loving nature.

'Don't be silly,' she offered. 'I think this is the kid I saw at the wreckers today. Same tracksuit. Same age and height.'

'That's Flynn.' Nellie pointed to the screen. 'If you think he flogged something, he most definitely did. The kid has Velcro fingers.'

'You know him?'

Nellie suppressed a grin.

'He's a local boy. Contrary to popular opinion, we aren't a plague out here. There's only about 400 of us, spread out around the region.'

Jenny focussed on the screen.

'We know this little guy couldn't possibly have picked up our victim and dumped her in Rothchild's boot. But maybe he sold the drop-sheet on to someone.'

'So did Flynn steal the drop-sheet for the wrecker?' Phillips printed the screenshot.

O'Connell joined the small gathering around the counter.

'Have we run the owner yet?'

'It was next on my list.' Nellie pointed to the computer. 'When Phillips finished.'

'We need another computer.' O'Connell pointed to his workstation. 'Use my desk.'

Nellie scurried away.

'We need to find this kid.' Jenny lifted both sheets of paper from the printer.

'Good luck with that.' O'Connell grabbed the paperwork from Jenny's hand. 'I'll update the boss. You follow up and see if the victim has a child.'

'I've lodged a formal request. Maybe I should ring Mack at Births Deaths and Marriages?'

The clerk was a friend of Penny's and was known to slip a little early information Jenny's way if she lodged a formal request and the matter was urgent. A possible missing child would qualify.

'Hey.'

All eyes fell on Nellie.

'I think I've got something?'

O'Connell joined Nellie.

'Go on.'

'The owner of the wrecking yard isn't too interesting. No priors, no obvious gang affiliation, but...'

Nellie clicked a few more keys.

'But what?' Jenny's stomach knotted as she wondered if she might have missed vital information.

'I need to double check something.'

Everyone waited silently.

'The property, not the business, but the land is owned by a shelf company. I did an ABN search and found this.'

The laser printer whirred into action. Phillips reached under the counter to retrieve the printout. O'Connell snatched it from his fingers.

A whistle escaped the senior constable's lips.

'The CWU.' He scanned faces, landing on Jenny last. 'I'll be...'

'I missed it.' Jenny's tone was forced.

'Easily done. The warrant would have asked for the occupant's details, not the owner's.'

Jenny shook her head.

'Still. I should have found it.'

'Let's see if the warrant is in yet. And take Nellie. If Flynn is there, find out what you can.'

'You got it.' Nellie's smile lit the room.

Chapter 19

Two police Landcruisers drove in convoy. The setting sun radiated enough heat to still be considered uncomfortable. Jenny adjusted the vents and willed herself to relax as Phillips and she rode in tense silence.

Carrying out a search warrant came with inherent dangers. The earlier visit didn't raise too many red flags. Two dogs, not overly vicious but protective, plus the owner, in his late sixties and not particularly fit or strong.

Still, the location was now linked to five poison victims, and possible illegal activities involving the CWU. Tanya Rothchild was the link between their victim and the CWU, making her their best chance of getting answers. But until they got Mikey back with his mother, there was no way she was telling them anything.

Then there was Omar Suleiman. Details of the restraining order were still pending, but why would anyone take one out unless they were genuinely afraid. So far, there was no obvious link between Omar and the CWU. Two lines of enquiry. Both going nowhere.

'How do you want to play this?' Phillips dragged Jenny out of her own head as the high fence and wrecked cars came into view.

'If he's still on his own, I'm not expecting much resistance. Phillip Zeigler doesn't have a record, and we are only talking about a gas leak at this stage.'

'If he's involved with the CWU, he could be armed.'

'Let's hope not. Keep your Taser ready. If the dogs are off lead, they might be an issue.'

'And what if he's not alone?'

'Let's not get ahead of ourselves.' Jenny nodded at the open gate. 'I can't see a mob of cars.'

Phillips lifted his chin, scanned the area and drove the police Landcruiser slowly inside the gate. Nellie parked in the gateway, blocking the entrance.

Jenny adjusted her utility belt as she stepped from the vehicle to a chorus of barking. Finding the animals restrained, she relaxed and approached the office.

'Mr Zeigler,' Jenny called at the closed office door.

The aged airconditioner rattled as it laboured to keep the small office cool. Condensation dripped from the unit, hitting the parched red sand and rapidly evaporating in the heat.

Jenny lifted her utility-vest, hoping to pump some air between it and her sweaty shirt and sports bra as Nellie slammed her vehicle door and strode up to join them.

The office door flung opened with a thud.

'What are you back here for?'

'Mr Zeigler, we have a warrant to search the premises.'

'What the…'

'Here.' Jenny held out a printed copy. 'You are welcome to read it, but I can explain the terms if you prefer.'

Mr Ziegler leapt from the top step deftly. Jenny glanced at Phillips whose lifted eyebrow mirrored her thoughts.

Had she misjudged the man?

Snatching the paper, he scanned it between squinted eyes.

'Why do they have to print this stuff so bloody small.'

'I can read it,' she offered.

He massaged his beard, scrunched his face, then shook his head vigorously.

'I'll get my glasses. You do what you need to do.'

He waved her away casually. She wondered if they were wasting their time. Was the place already cleared? Were they going to come up empty? She hoped not.

'We'll start over here.' Jenny waved Phillips past the dogs who now sat on their haunches, quietly awaiting instructions.

'This is where Penny found the gas tank,' she whispered as Phillips joined her.

'Do we need to get the dogs removed?'

'No, it's up at the donga.' She pointed ahead.

'What are you doing?'

Jenny turned to see Mr Ziegler, arms clamped across his chest, staring Nellie down.

'This warrant doesn't include the office building or any of the contents.'

He waved the four-page document in one hand.

Not so blind, after all, Jenny thought.

'I'm here for Flynn.' Nellie explained with a smile in her voice.

'He's not here and you don't have a warrant for *that*.'

'I don't need a warrant to collect a minor and return him to his mob.'

Jenny suppressed a grin. Playing the Indigenous card was clever. The line between First Nations law and colonial law was thin, and often frustrating for Police. On this occasion, it was to their advantage.

'I told you he's not here.'

A flash of colour sped between a rusty Bedford truck and a Dodge ute in worse shape than Jenny's.

'Flynn! Auntie Dot wants to see you.'

The boy stopped at the sound of Nellie's voice. His dark face split with a huge white tooth grin, then he darted through the wrecks and out of sight.

'You gotta go home eventually,' she called after him and waited.

Silence greeted her. Nellie huffed, then turned to Jenny.

'Where do you want me?'

'Do you want to go after him?'

'Nope. Kid's got lightning bolts on his feet. Way too fast for me to catch.'

'Check behind the office,' Jenny pointed. 'You know what we're looking for.'

Nellie nodded.

'You got it.'

The warrant was specific to the LPG poisoning, but they were taking the opportunity to search every square metre of the exterior in case they could find a link to the murder victim or any CWU illegal activity.

Mr Ziegler plonked down on the concrete step outside the office, put his elbows on his knees and guarded his domain.

Jenny couldn't help wondering what they might find if they could get inside the office but pushed the thought aside for now. No point focussing on something she couldn't change. The warrant was clear. Outside, in the wrecking yard, in the vehicles and external shedding and unlocked buildings only.

When the judge found out the CWU owned the land, he restricted the search to protect any confidential paperwork not pertaining to the poisoning case. Frustrating, but not exactly unexpected.

They reached a large, oblong cylinder, mounted on a platform at the rear of the first donga. A padlock hung on the door.

'Can you open this?' Jenny called to Mr Ziegler.

'It's not on the warrant.'

Jenny chewed the inside of her lip. He was right. Plain sight, vehicles and unlocked outbuildings.

She circled the building for another unlocked door. Nothing. Dropping to her haunches, she peered under the raised transportable flooring to find pipes, plumbed into the sewage system.

Why would the donga be plumbed if it was there as a derelict or to be resold? She pressed up to her tiptoes to see into the building through a high window. Only to find it covered in newspaper.

Maybe Nev was right about a drug lab. But the CFS found no meth or other chemical residue in the area.

Circling the building once more, she noticed another high window with a horizontal slide panel sitting ajar. Searching around, she found a tin bucket, upturned it and carefully balanced on it to reach the window.

Sliding it back, she sighed when it jammed after a few centimetres.

'What you got?' Phillips peered up at her.

'I can't see in. Can you give me a hoist up?'

'Sure.'

Jenny hopped down. Phillips lifted one leg to the bucket, braced his shoulder against the building and held out his hand.

Jenny gripped his hand, climbed to the edge of the bucket, then stepped up onto his thigh. Using her free hand, she held the edge of the window and peered inside.

'See anything?' Her partner's voice wasn't strained by Jenny's weight.

She scanned the interior to find a long kitchen bench and gas cooktop. There was no rangehood, and little ventilation. It was possibly the reason five people succumbed to the tasteless, odorless gas?

Two shower and toilet cubicles lined the other end of the donga.

'A kitchenette, toilets and showers and they are plumbed in, so must be in use.'

'Weird.'

Jenny was about to jump down when she spotted a piece of fabric hanging from the cupboard below the sink.

'Bingo!'

'What is it?'

'Bad news for Penny.'

'Why?'

Jenny jumped down.

'Because I'm about to ruin her afternoon plans with Tim.'

Chapter 20

Strobing red and blue lights reflected around the mangled and rusty wrecks. Penny crossed the yard, a bag of gear in each hand.

'Set up the tripod light there.' She lifted one heavily laden arm and pointed. 'Did either of you go in?'

'No. Saw the floral fabric and knew we needed to leave it to you.' Jenny realigned the light as she spoke.

Phillips trotted up behind Penny, carrying two more cases.

'Where do you want these?'

'By the door thanks. I'll do a perimeter check first.'

'Roger.' Phillips lowered the bags to the dirt as Penny flashed her torch around the exterior.

'You guys traipsed all over everything.'

'We were looking for a gas leak.' Jenny kept her tone even.

It was late. They were all hungry and Penny was torn from the only quiet time she'd managed to snatch with Tim during her quick visit.

Her own relationship with Nick was difficult enough with him living two hours away. She couldn't imagine how hard it was for Penny and Tim. She silently hoped he got his transfer soon, even if it meant losing one of her roommates.

Penny flicked the beam of her torch to a purple UV light and continued to scan. As the light reached the door, she stopped, turned and retrieved something from her kit.

Jenny watched with fascination as Penny swabbed the handprint for DNA, bagged and tagged it, then dusted it with powder and skilfully pressed the tape into the metal door.

Gently, she lifted the tape and pressed it onto a large piece of white card, placed it in an evidence bag and lowered it into a box before carrying on inside the stifling hot building.

Jenny slipped on shoe covers and ensured her disposable overalls were zipped up fully, before following the forensic tech.

'This fabric is the exact same pattern our victim was wearing in the photo Ben gave us.' Jenny pointed as Penny retrieved the peasant top, opened it out in the air, revealing grease stains.

'Appears someone chucked it in the rag bag.'

Penny bagged the top, then retrieved an electronic gas sensor. The apparatus reminded Jenny of a personal alcohol meter. The tech used it under the sink and near the gas cooktop. No alarm sounded and the gauge remained steady.

'Either the gas cylinder is empty, or someone managed to contain the leak.'

Sergeant Mackenzie stuck his head into the shed.

'All going alright in here?'

Penny gave a gloved thumbs up and carried on.

'Good.' He turned to Jenny. 'Where's Zeigler?'

'Nellie has him cuffed in the shed by the office.'

Sergeant Mackenzie stuck his head back outside.

'Phillips, caution him and get him to the station. O'Connell is getting our warrant upgraded. Then we can search this entire lot from top to bottom, inside and out.'

'You got it.' Phillips turned to leave.

'And Phillips, find all the victims from yesterday's gas incident. They might know more about our victim.'

'Yes Sarge.' Phillips disappeared.

Penny lifted a garbage bag from under the sink.

'I'll finish up in here while you get the warrant sorted.'

'Thanks McGregor. Sorry to make you stick around town.' Sergeant Mackenzie's tone was sympathetic.

'You might have ruined my afternoon swim, but I've got at least another day's work processing this place as a possible murder scene. Not pleasant, but the extra day will give me a few more nights to catch up with Tim.'

'Always look on the bright side, hey McGregor.' Sarge turned to Jenny. 'Get ready for another late night.'

He waved for her to follow him.

Jenny should have been exhausted, but finding Maryam's clothing meant they might have finally discovered their primary murder scene. At the very least, the link between the gas leak, the poison victims, the sudden influx of bar patrons at Marj's and the CWU was a positive step in the investigation.

Nellie met them as they stepped out.

'O'Connell has confirmed the warrant has been extended to everything.'

'You two with me.' Sarge strode toward the office. 'Let's start in here. I want employment records, anything to connect this place to any of the patients from the hospital yesterday, the CWU or our victim.'

Jenny followed Sergeant Mackenzie inside. The odour of sweat and grease made her cringe. Nellie stepped over the dirty vinyl floor and opened a four-drawer metal filing cabinet. Jenny rounded the desk, mounted high with open books on various vehicle mechanics and strewn with loose papers.

A red FINAL NOTICE caught her eye.

'He's got an unpaid council parking ticket here.' She waved the paper in the air, then scanned the location.

'That's weird.'

'What?' Sarge drew up alongside.

'It's from the parking lot behind the disused shops and accommodation where Mikey was found.'

'It could be a coincidence.' Sarge chewed his lip. 'But worth checking out. There's no reason to park there since the sale fell through. No one will be doing any renos anytime soon.'

It was a shame, because Tash's clothing store was closed for the renovation. If they never happened, she wondered if Tash would reopen somewhere else.

Placing the parking fine in an evidence bag, she returned her focus to the dark grey metal desk drawers.

Nellie slammed the last filing cabinet drawer closed with a clang.

'Nothing in here. Only old tax records.'

Jenny tugged the top desk drawer twice.

'This one is stuck.'

Nellie rounded the desk, dragged the ancient swivel chair aside and bent over to study the drawer.

'Locked?'

'No. Just stuck.' Jenny braced one gloved hand on the top of the desk and tugged with more effort. The drawer came free without warning, spilling her to the floor.

Pens, notepads with greasy fingerprints and thumb tacks were strewn everywhere.

Nellie chuckled.

'Do you need a hand up?'

Jenny rolled her eyes at the new constable's extended hand.

'No,' she huffed, then studied the drawer to figure out why it was stuck in the first place. 'That's strange.'

She cocked her head and peered inside the hole the drawer left. The underside of the desk surface was oddly shaped. Rolling on to all fours, she reached inside, touched an envelope, felt the tape holding it in place, then pulled her arm free.

'What is it?' Nellie leant over, hands on her knees as Jenny retrieved her mobile phone.

'What you got Williams?' Her boss peered over from his search of the tea and coffee facilities.

'I don't know yet. Thought I should grab a few pics first.'

Sergeant Mackenzie abandoned his search and joined Nellie to wait as Jenny tried to retrieve an A4, yellow envelope taped to the underside of the desk.

With gloved hands, her fingernails were no help lifting the edges of the tape away from the metal surface. Jenny patted her utility belt, unclipped her knife and used it to cut the tape free, section by section.

The envelope eventually came away.

'It's thick. No wonder it jammed the drawer.' Gently, she lifted the flap to peer inside.

'What's in there?' Sergeant Mackenzie leant around her to see inside.

'A reason to charge Mr Phillip Ziegler.'

Her gloved hand dove in and retrieved a wad of passports. Placing the envelope down, she opened the first to find a middle-aged man of Indian or Asian descent. As she opened the next, a knot gripped her stomach and words caught in her throat.

'What?' Sergeant Mackenzie used a loose glove to snatch the passport from her hand. 'Shit.' He showed the owner's photo to Nellie.

'Another solid link between the gas leak, this yard and our murder victim.'

Nellie handed an evidence bag to Jenny, who scanned each passport as she placed them back in the envelope.

'And an operation employing international workers and judging by the passport stamps, ones who have overstayed their visas and are here illegally.'

'Ziegler is going down.' Nellie fist-pumped the air.

'Yes, but our victim wasn't an illegal. Where does she fit in to all this and why have her passport? I don't think Ziegler will be brimming with information anytime soon.'

Sergeant Mackenzie slapped her on the back.

'Take the wins where you can, Williams.'

Jenny nodded understanding, but her earlier excitement was waning. The leads were piling up, but like any case connected to this level of organised illegal activity, finding someone to talk wasn't going to be easy.

Chapter 21

The evening was balmy and under any other circumstances, it might have been pleasant. Jenny watched for a shooting star, hoping it would ease her tension, but gave up after a few seconds.

She tried unsuccessfully to quell her frustration as she trudged along the crushed rock pathway toward the dugout she shared with Nev and Tim. Finding the victim's top was a win. And the passports gave them a new line of enquiry. But what they found in the second building left a foul taste in her mouth.

She slipped her key in the door, then jumped as it flung open. Nev handed her a beer and offered a weak smile. If it were Nick at the door, she would have collapsed into his arms.

'Tim got home about an hour ago. Heard about your shit night.'

Jenny swigged her beer before answering.

'My faith in humanity is definitely diminished.'

She brushed past as Nev pulled her keys from the lock and tossed them onto the kitchen bench. Jenny placed her backpack alongside them.

'Have you eaten?'

Jenny's stomach growled.

Nev grinned.

'I left you some chicken curry.'

Jenny's stomach tightened.

'I don't think I can eat right now Nev. Thanks for the offer.'

'Maybe later.' Nev crossed the small living area and flopped onto the sofa. 'I did some digging though. Might help.'

Jenny remained in the small U-shaped kitchen and drained her beer, knowing it would go straight to her head.

'Digging?'

She opened the fridge, lifted out a beer and held one up for Nev who nodded.

'The patients Tim brought in, plus the two who arrived in ED before he was called out, were all using fake Medicare numbers.'

'Damn.'

'Yeah. Didn't flag in the system straight away, but Pat, you know Pat?' Jenny nodded. 'He found two numbers were from recently deceased patients. One was from an international on a temporary residential visa. They left the country a few months ago.'

Jenny knew accessing dubious Medicare numbers required insider connections. Connections the CWU would have.

She passed Nev his beer and flopped onto the sofa alongside him.

'We were hoping to interview the patients, but I guessed something like this would happen. Thanks for trying though.'

The bathroom door opened. Tim exited, wrapped in a towel from the waist down. A second later, Penny appeared, dressed in cargo shorts and a tank top.

'Hey.' She joined Jenny on the sofa. 'Got any wine?'

Nev shook his head.

'Nah. Sorry. Scotch, gin or beer.'

'Gin will have to do. I don't think I'll be sleeping easy tonight, no matter what.'

Jenny was surprised. Penny rarely showed any signs of discomfort with her work. In fact, her morbid sense of humour usually broke the tension for everyone else.

She put her beer on the coffee table and rose to get Penny's drink.

'Do you want tonic with it?'

'Yes thanks.'

Jenny lifted a glass from the open shelf over the sink as she recalled unlocking the second building, ready for Penny.

Four bunk beds, crammed into a 6 metre, unventilated, unairconditioned transportable building created a stomach-churning stench.

'Did you find more evidence amongst the workers' personal effects?'

Jenny passed the drink to Penny.

'Nothing in particular. They didn't have much.'

Tim joined the sofa.

'I wish I'd seen what was going on when I picked up those guys Wednesday.'

Penny squeezed his arm.

'It's not your fault arseholes treat people worse than dogs.'

'Doesn't make it any easier.'

Jenny lifted her beer from the table and sipped it absently.

'I need to give Nick a call.' She glanced at her watch.

'Hang on. We've got news.' Penny snuggled up against Tim.

'Good news then?'

Tim's freckles bounced on his nose as he grinned.

'I've finally been granted a transfer to Adelaide. Based close enough to Penny's place to finally move in.'

Jenny dropped her beer on the table and flopped back onto the sofa next to Penny.

'I hope that doesn't mean we'll never see either of you again.'

Penny dragged Jenny into a hug.

'We'll be back for your wedding, and I can't speak for Tim, but I'm sure this case won't be the last one to drag me back out here.'

Jenny was flooded with mixed emotions. She loved having Penny around. Even sharing her with Tim this past year wasn't all bad but wanting to see her friend and only getting the chance over a dead body, was wearing thin.

'I wish we could catch up for something other than a case.'

'I told you already. Come to Adelaide for your hen's night. Mack would love to see you.'

Jenny laughed at the thought of dragging a trans guy out with her on a hen's night.

'He's wicked fun. Believe me,' Penny assured her.

Jenny's phone pinged in her pocket. She glanced at the screen. Text messages rarely made it through the thick stone walls of the dugout, but she was glad it did.

'I have no doubt.' She rose, phone in hand. 'It's Nick. I need to call him.'

'Tell him, he should be here.' Nev lifted his beer as he spoke.

Jenny chuckled, picked up her own drink and headed outside. This time, she embraced the warm air, dark sky and twinkling stars.

As she dialled Nick's number, she wondered if Tim would miss this when he got to Adelaide.

'Hey Jen. I got your message earlier. Everything alright?'

Hot tears sprang to her eyes with his gentle tone. In the near dark, she found the large sandstone rock she often sat on when speaking to Nick when he was on the property.

'It was a tough day. But we'll start digging for answers again tomorrow.'

Nick cleared his throat.

'I asked Ben about Katie, you know, you wanted to know where he met her.'

'And he told you?' She failed to keep the surprise from her words.

'Not exactly. I think he was being careful not to let anything slip, but wherever he met her, I don't think it was legal.'

'That was the impression I got when I spoke with him.'

With a clear connection between the CWU, illegal workers and their victim, getting Ben to share what he knew was more important than ever. But why was he staying quiet?

'I think he's worried the AFP might link him to all this.' Nick answered her question.

'You told him he was under investigation?'

'I didn't have to. You and Penny grilled him after my accident. He knows I kept him on, even though you two thought he tried to kill me. We've been talking.'

Jenny struggled to remain calm. Sharing the AFP investigation with Ben was reckless. Or was she annoyed he was talking to Ben, and not her? At least he was being more forthcoming now.

'Do the AFP know Ben knows?'

Nick scoffed.

'The AFP are the ones who told me to get close to him. Everything cooled down after the real estate agent was murdered and Sid's car blew up. When the guy responsible was shanked in prison, I guess the mining company decided to play it cool for a while.'

'And the feds thought you could pump Ben for info?'

'Something like that.'

'Why are you telling me now, Nick?' Her tone was sharper than she intended, but Nick was keeping dangerous secrets.

'I'm not supposed to, but Ben's behaviour makes me think the cases could be connected, despite him not wanting the AFP to join the dots.'

'You think Ben's fiancé could have been killed by the mining company?'

'No, at least I don't think so. You know Ben has a past. He's told me a little about it over beers. But Jen, I've never seen him this jumpy. He knows more than he's telling us.'

'Lots of people know more than they are telling me.' She didn't try to hide her frustration. 'But I'll talk to Sergeant Mackenzie and see if I can get out to investigate the Fergusson fire tomorrow. Maybe I can call in and catch up with Ben while I'm there. Hopefully he's ready to talk.'

'As much as I'd love to see you, there's no point.'

'Why?'

'I gave him tomorrow off. He took off about an hour ago.'

Jenny scanned her watch. It was after midnight.

'Where's he going?'

'I don't know but take it easy on him Jen. He's lost the love of his life. I know what I'd be doing if someone hurt you.'

Jenny swallowed hard.

'And I'd do the same if anything happened to you.'

Silence hung a moment before a thought popped into her head.

'Did he mention anything about where I was today or the investigation?'

'I don't think so, but it's a small town. News travels fast. My guess is the whole town probably already knows.'

Nick was right. The wrecking yard was lit up like a side show until only a few hours ago. But Ben didn't need to guess where to start his search. She was sure he knew exactly where their victim worked.

'I need to find him Nick. Maybe Trudy knows where he's gone.'

'If anyone does, his sister should,' Nick agreed.

'It's going to be another busy day tomorrow.'

'I wish I could be there with you.'

'Me too.'

Chapter 22

Jenny's body ached and her head was weighed down with fog as she filed into Sergeant Mackenzie's office. Sleep didn't come easy last night and what little she got, was interrupted by an early alarm this morning.

Nellie was on the coffee run, so Phillips hovered by the door to keep an eye on the counter. O'Connell was poised with marker in hand, ready to update the whiteboard.

Sergeant Mackenzie listened to her explain what Nev said about the Medicare numbers and then shared Nick's information on Ben.

'Did you get a hold of Trudy then?'

'No. But I'll call again shortly.'

'Phillips, you run all the passports. See if you can track down any relatives in Australia or overseas. Hopefully someone has kept in contact with their loved one and we can get some questions answered.'

'Got it.' Phillips wrote details on his notepad.

'Who's interviewing Zeigler?' Jenny asked.

Her boss grinned.

'Maybe we should give the new girl a go?' His eyes met Nellie's as she appeared in the doorway.

'Yes!' Nellie fist-pumped the air, then steadied the coffees with an embarrassed grin.

'You go with her Williams. I get the impression Zeigler might have looser lips with you two.'

Jenny recalled the appalling conditions Zeigler kept the workers in. Even now, the stench coated her nostrils. Urine, faeces, dirty clothing and stained bedding. She shook the memory away.

'I wouldn't count on it,' she offered.

Her boss carried on undeterred.

'O'Connell, chase up who made the 000 call. Zeigler told Williams it was him, but I don't see the guy who locked eight people into a hot box having enough compassion to call for help. Plus, the ambulance drew unwanted attention.'

All heads nodded as Nellie passed out coffees. Sergeant Mackenzie sipped his, then fixed his gaze on O'Connell.

'Where are we at with the victim's ex?'

'I've circulated Omar's vehicle details. No hits yet. Might need to call around the accommodation places in town because local uniforms have done numerous call outs to his home and he's not been there. So far, no success contacting him on his mobile phone either.'

'Not a good sign.' Sergeant Mackenzie frowned at the whiteboard. 'Did they check with his employer?'

'He's a self-employed concreter. But like I said, not answering his phone and we have no idea where he's currently contracting.'

'Get on to his relatives. See if we can locate him. I'd like to eliminate him from our enquiries, but with the restraining order, and him being uncontactable, he's got to be a prime suspect.'

O'Connell nodded, then returned his attention to updating the whiteboard.

'Surely finding Maryam's passport at the wrecking yard can't be a coincidence?' Jenny asked.

'I'm not discounting anything Williams. But why would they kill her? She could easily have been the one recruiting the illegal workers.'

Her boss was right. They couldn't discount anything or anyone.

'Maybe she threatened to expose them?' She tossed out the idea.

Sergeant Mackenzie pursed his lips.

'It's one of many possibilities. Prostitution, maybe a client killed her. Her ex still needs to be eliminated.'

Jenny nodded, but in the back of her mind she doubted Ben would be engaged to a prostitute. Even with his background. Sergeant Mackenzie turned to Nellie.

'When you're done with Zeigler, find that kid.'

'Flynn?' Nellie shoved her hands in her pockets. The gesture seemed odd. 'Not sure he'll be any help.'

Sergeant Mackenzie dropped into his office chair.

'He's been working at the wrecking yard, and we know he stole the drop-sheet from the hardware store. We need to know who he gave it to.'

'I called Dot last night, but he hasn't turned up yet.'

Sergeant Mackenzie pointed a finger at Nellie.

'I said find him. So keep looking.'

'Will do Sarge.' Nellie shifted her attention to Jenny. 'When do we get started with the perp?'

Jenny stifled a grin.

'I'll call Trudy while you get Zeigler out of holding. Meet you there in a few minutes.'

Jenny turned to O'Connell and Sergeant Mackenzie as Nellie left the office.

'I can't see why Zeigler needed so many illegal workers on his property. So where were they being utilized?'

'I might be able to help with that.'

Jenny turned as Penny entered the office.

'I just got off the phone with Doc. He's finished the postmortem on our victim and trace has come back on her clothing.'

Penny strode past Jenny and plonked into the free chair in front of Sergeant Mackenzie's desk. For a moment, Jenny thought the forensic scientist might pop her feet up on the desk, but instead of relaxing back, she fixed her gaze on the sergeant.

'As suspected, victim died of blunt force trauma to the back of the head.'

O'Connell lifted the marker pen and returned to the whiteboard.

'What's with the facial injuries then?'

'Tissue analysis leads us to believe they were postmortem. Maybe to cover up her identity. Maybe the killer couldn't stop hitting after she was already dead. It could also be her killer wanted her disfigured. Some kind of message.'

Penny's words sent a shiver down Jenny's spine.

'Not being able to stop hitting, might indicate a personal relationship to the victim.' Jenny leant on the edge of her boss's desk. 'Making her unrecognisable doesn't fit with dumping her in Tanya Rothchild's car to be found later though.'

Sergeant Mackenzie nodded.

'So personal could mean the ex-husband.'

'But sending a message makes more sense,' Jenny countered. 'Was the message for Tanya? Her car? Her friend?'

Sergeant Mackenzie slammed his palm on the table.

'We need to get Tanya talking! She must know who had access to her car and when. And if the message was for her, she'll know who sent it and why.'

'I'll chase Children's Services as soon as I finish with Zeigler, because Tanya isn't talking until we get Mikey back.' Jenny tried to keep the agitation from her voice.

'She might not have a choice. I've got the Chief breathing down my neck, asking me why we haven't laid charges against Tanya Rothchild.'

O'Connell tapped the whiteboard.

'There's not enough evidence to convict her, even if we did arrest her. Why would the Chief be pushing so hard to close the case?'

'Maybe the CWU connection is putting pressure on him.' Jenny voiced her concerns without thinking about it first.

Sergeant Mackenzie shook his head vigorously.

'Bite your tongue, Williams. That sort of talk, even in jest, could cost you your job.'

Penny cleared her throat. All eyes fell on her.

'Can I finish?'

Sergeant Mackenzie lifted an eyebrow. O'Connell coughed behind the whiteboard marker and Jenny licked her lips.

When no one answered, Penny continued.

'Tissue damage to the victim's ring finger indicates the engagement ring was torn from her finger in a hurry.'

'That could be important. It supports the personal angle,' Jenny offered.

'It's not the best part,' Penny grinned. 'I might be able to help you work out what the workers were doing.'

In Penny's usual manner, she let the thought sink in.

'Out with it McGregor.'

Penny grinned again.

'Trace on the victim's clothing indicates she was in contact with alcohol before her death.'

'What, like a spill on her dress?' Sergeant Mackenzie slumped back in his chair. 'Hardly a smoking gun.'

'No Sarge. We are talking a lot of alcohol, and various varieties. Scotch, rum, beer, wine, and when I read this, I got thinking.'

'I bet that hurt.' O'Connell physically ducked. Luckily Penny only threw daggers with her eyes. 'Sorry. Go on.'

Jenny suppressed a surge of adrenalin as Penny opened a manila folder.

'I found this in the victim's pocket but thought nothing of it. Who doesn't have a set of these at home?'

She turned the photo so everyone could see. Jenny focussed on an evidence marker, then the item circled in the photo.

'A poker chip.' Jenny lifted the photo from Penny's fingers and passed it to O'Connell. 'Add it to various drinks, and you get…'

'Drinking and gambling!' Penny sat back in her seat. 'And last time I checked, you don't have a licensed casino in Coober Pedy.'

Sergeant Mackenzie placed his palms on the desk and pressed to his feet.

'Pokies, yes. Poker and blackjack tables, definitely not.' He pointed to Jenny. 'After Zeigler, get Tanya Rothchild in here. I want answers or we'll start tossing out charges.'

Jenny knew Tanya was holding back, but so was Ben.

'I think the illegal gambling is how Ben met her. It explains why he wouldn't tell us where she worked.'

'Agreed. Find Ben. If we tell him what we know, maybe he'll help.'

Jenny wasn't holding out hope. Not with the AFP investigation and his prior record. Any connection to the CWU, corruption or organised gambling could put him back on their radar. She kept the thought to herself.

'Could there be a disused mine near the wreckers? The CWU own the property,' Jenny suggested.

Sarge nodded, then pointed to O'Connell.

'Check the title out.'

Something niggled at Jenny.

'If Maryam's body was left in the boot as a message to Tanya, how did they think she'd dispose of it later? I doubt Tanya could have lifted the body on her own.'

O'Connell jotted details on the whiteboard. Sarge frowned. It was Penny who spoke.

'Not my department, but they obviously didn't expect her to crash on the way home.'

A thought popped into Jenny's head.

'Maybe it wasn't a warning. Maybe it was about covering Maryam's ID after all. They kill her, plan to use Tanya's vehicle to dump the body in a mine somewhere. That way, if we search later, the evidence in Tanya's car implicates her. But Tanya grabs the car and leaves work early for some reason.'

'Tanya was pickled.' O'Connell pointed to the alcohol reading which was barely below .05 hours after the accident. 'I doubt she was working anywhere.'

'I don't care,' Sergeant Mackenzie huffed. 'Get her back in here this afternoon, with or without Children's Services cooperation.'

Nellie stuck her head in the door.

'Ready when you are.'

'Ask Zeigler about the casino. Let's see if he flinches.' Her boss rounded his desk and headed for the door.

'Where are you off to Sarge?' She knew the question was the wrong one the moment it left her lips.

'Last time I checked Williams, I don't report to you.'

Chapter 23

The temperature in the cramped interview room gave a whole new meaning to sweating a suspect. Jenny quizzed Nellie with her eyes as she dragged a chair out.

The new constable revealed white teeth in a cheshire cat grin, confirming Jenny's suspicion. Jenny adjusted the temperature before sitting opposite Zeigler.

'Mr Zeigler. I'm Constable Jenny Williams and this is Constable Nellie Miller.' Nellie checked the recording equipment as Jenny continued. 'Can you confirm you've been cautioned?'

'No comment.'

Jenny reiterated the caution for the recording, then tried again.

'Phil. You don't mind if I call you Phil.'

'No comment.'

Jenny smiled sweetly.

'Phil. You'll be charged today. There's no doubt about that. Holding on to the passports of workers, even those on a working visa is illegal.' Phil glanced up from his hands for a split second. 'The big question is if we *add* charges relating to the obvious imprisonment and forced labour of said workers.'

Phil sat back in his seat, crossed his arms over his chest and sucked air in loudly through his nose. For a moment Jenny thought he was going to hack up a snot-ball.

'No comment.'

'I think we might have more charges to come,' Nellie reminded Jenny.

'Oh, yeah.' Jenny slapped her forehead with an open palm and played along as planned. 'Nellie is right. I almost forgot.'

She rummaged through a folder and with a flurry, dragged out the photo Penny provided. Instead of revealing it, she placed it face down on the desk, retrieved a photo of Maryam's passport and turned the image around so Zeigler could see.

'We've linked your little illegal activities with a recent murder, and I have to say, it's not looking good for you Phil.'

She slid the photo closer.

Phil's arms slipped from his chest as he recognised the picture. His lips parted, then pressed back together.

Jenny continued.

'You see this woman was found murdered a few days ago.' Jenny tapped the photo. 'It's strange you should have her passport. How does that happen Phil?'

He opened his mouth. Jenny stopped him, knowing what he was about to say.

'We also found a piece of her clothing in one of the dongas on your property. Got to say, murder is a big wrap to take for someone else.'

She thumbed the corner of the upside-down photo. Phil's eyes focussed on it.

'But you don't have a record Phil. I've checked.' His eyes met hers. 'You're a good bloke. Been struggling away to make a living from the wrecking yard for a while. Maybe you started out mining?'

Phil's left eye twitched, indicating she might be on the right track. Would they find a disused mine below the wrecking yard? A place to run an illegal gambling house?

'We know about the illegal casino.'

Phil's hands clasped together in his lap tight enough to make his knuckles whiten. He remained silent as he squinted at the photo under Jenny's hand. She watched the cogs turn. He was weighing up his options.

'You see, we've connected you to our victim with her confiscated passport, and her clothing was found in the utility donga at your yard. But we've also connected our victim to an illegal gambling operation.' Jenny turned the photo over, revealing the poker chip. 'If you point us in the right direction, it will go a long way to helping you avoid a very long prison sentence.'

Phil sat back once more, crossed his arms and sucked in a deep, audible breath.

'No comment.'

Whoever Phil was working for, he was willing to do time for them.

'I understand.' She slipped the photos back into a folder and rose. 'We'll be digging through your life Mr Zeigler. Whatever you're hiding, we'll find it.'

She leant over the desk.

'And I'll be sure to let everyone know how helpful you've been with our inquiries.'

'You can't.' Phil surged to his feet.

Jenny pointed at his chest.

'Sit down Mr Zeigler. You don't want to add assaulting a police officer to your already long list of charges.'

He slid back into the chair.

'You'll be formally charged and remanded in custody until the judge decides what to do with you. If you'd like to give us a statement and help us find this illegal casino operation, then I'll be sure to tell the world how *uncooperative* you were.'

Jenny turned to Nellie and nodded toward the recording equipment.

'Interview…'

'Wait!'

She suppressed a smile.

'I didn't kill anyone, and I don't know where they run the gambling.' His hands shook until he clamped them together in his lap. 'It moves around all the time.'

'Who are *they?*'

He shook his head.

'I don't know.' He was lying, but she let it slide for now. 'I just supply the workers, but after the gas leak, everyone was too sick to work. A few split from the hospital before I could pick them up. They could be anywhere.'

Jenny hoped they were on their way home as she returned to the seat opposite Zeigler.

'Where are the workers you *did* pick up?'

'After the leak, I got…' He touched his cut lip. 'I'm out of the loop.'

'The workers weren't given any freedom, so someone drove them to each venue. Where did you last take them?'

A long silence greeted her before Zeigler shook his head and crossed his arms over his chest. 'That's all I'm saying. I'm done talking. I want a lawyer.'

Jenny considered pushing him, but she knew it was a waste of time. The man was far more afraid of his boss than her.

Hopefully forensic evidence found with the workers' personal effects would lead them to a venue or some other break.

'Interview ended.' She checked the time on the wall as she turned to Nellie. '10.45am.' She rose as the red light blinked out. 'Get him back to holding and contact his lawyer, thanks Nellie.'

O'Connell met her in the hallway.

'Nice work Williams.'

'We didn't get the location.'

'No, but we confirmed it isn't likely to be out at the wreckers.'

'How so?'

'The check on the land came back during your interview. There's never been a mine out there. No other places where they could be running an illegal bar and casino nearby.'

'Damn.' Jenny entered the office area. 'I could really use…'

'A coffee?' Phillips passed her a cup. 'Caramel latte for the lady.'

'You're a keeper Phillips. Dianna and Tommy are lucky to have you.'

Phillips blushed.

Jenny was about to rub it in, when Sarge stormed into the foyer. The vein at the side of his temple visibly pulsing. 'Report!'

Jenny didn't know how to react to his mood. Wherever he went earlier, it wasn't a happy place. O'Connell met Sergeant Mackenzie at the counter passthrough.

'The 000 recording has come through. I'll update you on the interview while Williams and Nellie have a listen.'

Sergeant Mackenzie strode toward his office.

'Fine.'

O'Connell turned to Jenny.

'I've got this.' He tilted his head toward her boss. 'The recording is up on my computer.' He pointed as Nellie arrived in the office. 'You two have a listen, but I'm fairly sure I know who it is.'

'I'm guessing it's not Zeigler then.'

'You'd be guessing right.'

Chapter 24

Jenny waved Nellie to O'Connell's desk as the senior constable joined Sergeant Mackenzie in his office.

She wanted to listen in on the conversation and find out what was upsetting her boss, but right now, finding out who called 000 might help them find their next lead.

'What's up?' Nellie joined her.

'O'Connell said we might recognise the 000 caller.' Jenny dropped into the senior's chair and scanned the file open on his desktop computer.

'Give it a whirl then,' Nellie said.

Jenny cued up the call and hit *play*. They leant into the computer screen to hear the call.

"The white fellas are sick as, falling all over the place."

The voice was young, but unusually calm.

"Tell me where you are calling from?"

The emergency services call-centre, operator's voice was calm and reassuring.

"Out at the wrecking yard on Kempel Road."

"Can you give me the full address?"

The caller was young enough to not realise the call connected with a major call centre, not a local one.

"They're real sick. You betta come quick."

'That's Flynn,' Nellie declared.

It made sense. The boy spent plenty of time in the yard. He stole the drop-sheet from the hardware store. Jenny couldn't help wondering what he knew about their murder victim.

O'Connell appeared from Sergeant Mackenzie's office.

'Phillips. Have you gotten anywhere with the relatives of our passport holders?'

'Nothing yet Senior.'

'Okay, Boss wants you and Nellie door-knocking. Let's see if we can find where the visa overstayers went after they left the hospital.'

Phillips crossed to the lockers. Nellie joined him as Jenny nodded towards the now closed office door.

'What's that all about?'

'Gwen.'

The one-word answer told a story they all knew well.

'Nellie says the caller was Flynn. I don't know the kid, but it makes sense. But we can't find him anywhere.' Jenny changed the subject.

'Nellie. Get the word out. Make sure Flynn knows he isn't in trouble, but we need to find him.'

'Will do,' Nellie waved as she left with Phillips.

Jenny reached her workstation.

'I still need to bring Tanya in for an interview, so I need to chase up Children's Services again. And I can't get an answer from Trudy about Ben's whereabouts.'

O'Connell tapped keys on his computer.

'You do that. I'll run a search for disused buildings that might work as a makeshift casino.'

'Zeigler gave the impression the illegal gambling racket was likely moving on, but then Marj was approached to host some sort of event for Leigh Mundy. Maybe the other staff know something?'

O'Connell glanced up from his computer screen.

'Might be worth quizzing Cheryl or Kelly.'

'I was thinking the same thing. I'll do it after I've contacted Children's Services.'

O'Connell waved his hand dismissively.

'Get on with it then.'

Jenny chuckled as she searched for the details, lifted the handset and made the call.

The last thing she wanted to do was to argue with a case worker. Their job wasn't easy. So many of the cases they worked on were tragic. But sometimes they got it wrong. And despite Tanya's drinking problem there was no doubt in Jenny's mind the woman loved her son.

It was also obvious Terrence Sullivan was behind the order to remove Mikey from his mother's care.

The call connected.

'Morning. This is Constable Williams from Coober Pedy Police. I'd like to speak with the case worker dealing with Tanya and Mikey Rothchild.'

'Speaking.'

'Oh. Great. We met at the hospital.'

'I recall.'

Jenny frowned at the woman's tone.

'We are in the middle of a murder investigation and Ms Rothchild's cooperation is paramount to our case. I'm trying to work out a way we can reunite mother and son and get Ms Rothchild on side.'

'I'd like to help you Constable.'

Nothing in the woman's tone conveyed her words.

'But Mikey's father has been awarded temporary custody.'

'He what!'

O'Connell glanced up with a frown.

'It's out of my hands. You'll need to take it up with the Family Court.'

'Hang on.' Jenny could sense the woman was about to end the call. 'Terry Sullivan is known to police. He's a thug, a dangerous one.'

'I'm sorry Constable. As I said to you in the hospital, a judge signed the order to remove the child.' Jenny noticed her lack of personal connection by avoiding the use of Mikey's name. 'A private hearing was called this morning and the judge ruled in favour of Mr Sullivan.'

'Which judge?'

'I don't have the case file in front of me, but I'm sure Ms Rothchild can answer your question. She was at the hearing.'

Jenny was stunned into silence.

'Thanks for your call Constable.' The case worker hung up.

Jenny frowned at the handset in front of her face, then slowly lowered it to the cradle and turned to O'Connell. Her stomach knotted as she contemplated their next move.

'We might need to officially charge Tanya and bring her in. The situation has gotten messier and she's not going to cooperate willingly now.'

O'Connell's reply was interrupted as the foyer erupted with noise.

'There she is!' The deep voice hit her in the chest. 'Hey baby sis. Long time no see.'

'Leave her alone Nat.' Her brother Ben's fine features were the exact opposite of Nathaniel's broad forehead and wide nose.

'God you two, can you not be quiet anywhere? This is a police station.' Her father wrapped an arm around her brothers. 'Hey bub. Where can we park the van? Your mum's nicked to the loo.'

'Er.' Jenny stammered.

Sergeant Mackenzie's office door flew open.

'What the hell!'

Jenny stepped in front of him.

'I'm so sorry Sarge. You've met my dad. These two idiots are my brothers.' A thought popped into Jenny's head. Turning back, she frowned at Nat.

'Where's Kimberly and the kids?'

The grin on her brother's lips flattened. She changed the subject. Turning to Sergeant Mackenzie instead.

'Can I take a minute? I'll get them settled at Marj's.'

'You can grab lunch and ask around the bar while you are there,' O'Connell interjected, exchanging a nod with Sarge to reassure him she was on police business.

'Will do.' Jenny rounded the counter. 'Come on you lot. Bloody bulls in a china shop. Don't you know how to make a quiet entrance?'

Her brother Ben wrapped an arm around her shoulder. His slim frame and height matched Jenny's.

'Missed you too Jen.'

Chapter 25

Cool air, the smell of food and beer and a whiff of her mother's perfume greeted Jenny as she crossed to the bar.

'Hi Mum.' Jenny wrapped her arm around her mother's slim shoulder, then turned to Marj with a smile. 'Who's watching reception?'

Seeing Marj and her mum huddled in conversation gave her butterflies. Marj was her mum away from home, and if it weren't for the motel owner, Jenny would have cried herself to sleep for her entire first month in town.

'Cheryl said she'd take a stint. It's not super busy today.'

Jenny scanned the worn carpet, glossy timber bar-top running along one wall and the many empty tables.

'Where is everyone?'

Marj shivered, the way people did when an unpleasant thought filled their mind.

'No idea Luv. Feast or famine this time of year.'

Jenny caught Stan's eye as he placed a sparkling water in front of her mother, and a tumbler in front of Marj. His eyes told her nothing, but the brandy in Marj's glass spoke volumes.

Marj rarely drank during the day. The last time Jenny recalled her sipping brandy was when she broke her leg from a car ramming into her office.

She needed to find someone willing to tell her what was going on, before something terrible happened to Marj.

'Can you take care of this mob for me Marj? I've got to run to the loo.'

'Sure thing Luv.' Marj slipped from the barstool with renewed energy. 'Follow me you lot. Let's get you a table and organise some lunch. You're a day early, but I think I've got a spare room for the lads. You brought your van, right?'

Jenny didn't hear her father's reply as she wandered toward the toilets.

Stan wasn't going to talk. He was loyal to Marj and their story about refusing Leigh Mundy's offer for CWU patronage was feasible. But thugs like Mundy rarely backed down. Marj's lunch brandy told Jenny they hadn't this time either.

She glanced at Kelly, who was dusting plastic plants on the other side of the room. The barmaid grew up in a commune. Marj helped her get out, which made the motel owner Kelly's new family.

After Jenny closed the cult down when it was linked to a recent murder case, Kelly began coming out of her shell. But keeping secrets was part of her DNA. She wouldn't betray Marj's trust.

Jenny washed her hands and studied her image in the mirror. Strands of auburn hair hung loose from her ponytail. With damp hands, she released the band, retied her hair and made the obvious choice.

She brushed past the round table, full of smiling faces and chatter as she made for the door.

'Order me a chicken parmie. I'll be back in a sec,' she called as she whizzed by.

Heat engulfed her as she pushed the glass door open and jogged down the covered veranda to reception.

Cheryl glanced up from behind the counter with a bored expression, then a grin split her lips.

'Hey. Saw your brothers. Hot as! Can I get an introduction later?'

Jenny considered telling Cheryl that Nat was married but decided it wasn't her job to screen prospective dates.

'Sure. If you can do me a favour first.'

'Anything you need.'

'Don't be so hasty. You don't know what I want yet.'

Cheryl's expression darkened.

'It's important you tell me the truth though.'

'A…bou..t?'

'What do you know about Leigh Mundy and the issue Stan and Marj were having with him and his big bruiser mate?'

'Oh damn. I was hoping it was something to do with your wedding, or Nick or…'

She interrupted Cheryl.

'What do you know about him?'

'Nick?'

Jenny rolled her eyes. 'No, Leigh.'

'You sure? I have wedding ammo for Nick if you know who his best man is yet?'

Cheryl's teenage history as a working girl in town was well known. The death of her friend Tiffany was Jenny's first case and the investigation confirmed Nick never slept with Tiffany. But did Cheryl sleep with him? Did it matter?

She shook the thought away.

'Leigh, Cheryl. Leigh Mundy. What do you know about him?'

Cheryl's bored expression returned.

'Not much. He offered to pay me cash to work after hours, but I told him to piss off, I don't do tricks anymore.'

'Was that what he wanted?'

Cheryl shrugged. 'Who knows? Who cares?'

Jenny considered if Cheryl was the right choice after all. Kelly was quiet, but observant. She persevered though.

'Stan and Marj claim they were being pressured to host some sort of event for the CWU. In exchange, the union would make this their regular watering hole. Know anything about that?'

Cheryl didn't flinch.

'I see nothing. I know nothing.'

'Cheryl. This could be connected to a woman's murder.'

'I heard about that. Nasty.' She bit her lip. 'I did hear a few guys talking the other night, you know, when the big crowd rolled in?' Cheryl glanced around conspiratorially. 'One said something. It kind of makes sense now I think about the work offer, but I only heard bits of the conversation.'

'Anything might help,' Jenny coaxed.

'One guy said something about staff shortages. He could have been talking about the highway roadworks for all I know.'

'Anything else?'

'He mentioned finding a new place, with staff already on tap. Then the other guy made a show of looking around the bar and said he heard Leigh was doing a deal.'

Jenny's stomach knotted. Was this why Marj was so tense? Did she make a deal with Mundy?

'Thanks Cheryl.'

She hurried from the office.

'Don't forget that intro.'

Jenny waved over her shoulder as she strode down the veranda, back to eat lunch. But before the food arrived, she was going to have a serious talk with Marj.

The former miner, come motel owner was a gossip queen. If she was holding back about the relocation of an illegal gambling house to her own establishment, what else was she hiding?

Chapter 26

Jenny arrived at the table as her food was placed in front of her. Her stomach grumbled over the hot chips and delicious smelling chicken parmigiana.

'You need some meat on those bones girl.' Her dad slapped her on the back harder than she liked.

'Leave her alone Allan.' Her mum's tone was firm. 'Nat, pass me the pepper thanks.'

Jenny leant around her mother's back to catch Marj's eye.

'Are you joining us?'

'No Luv. I've got work to do.'

Jenny scanned the still empty restaurant.

'I'll come find you when I'm done.'

'Sure.' Marj turned to address the table. 'Lovely to meet you boys.'

Her brothers grunted a reply with full mouths.

Jenny picked up a chip and popped it into her mouth, letting the family conversation wrap around her like a comforting blanket.

Last Christmas, an emergency on the farm prevented them getting together. She stayed in Coober Pedy and missed the family celebrations. She was glad they were able to come to her this year.

Warmth spread through her body, reaching her stomach which growled once more. Her brothers' laughter peeled out as Jenny caught sight of a vehicle through the front windows. She absently shoved another chip in her mouth as the vehicle parked in front of a room.

The registration number wasn't visible, but the make and model were a fit. As the driver stepped out, Jenny's heartrate quickened.

She reached for her lapel mic, then recalled her utility-vest was still in her locker.

'Excuse me guys. I'll be right back.' She almost stumbled as she shoved her chair back. Lifting her phone, she strode to the restaurant entrance dialling the police station.

'Coober Pedy Police…'

'O'Connell. I've found Omar.'

As the man's name left her lips, his head turned her way. There was no way he heard her words, but her uniform was obvious. A split second passed. Jenny was vaguely aware of O'Connell speaking, but she didn't hear a word as Omar dropped his bag and ran.

'He's running!' She shoved her phone back in her pocket and followed, aware she was unarmed and on her own.

'Stop Omar! I only want to talk,' she called as he disappeared around the back of the motel, running full speed toward the camping area.

She sucked air into her lungs as her legs pumped. Skidding on the loose red dirt, she rounded the corner of the last motel room and searched between the mix of caravans and tents strewn sparsely around the yard.

There were no trees, a few outbuildings and large gaping unfilled sites, leaving little cover, but Omar was nowhere in sight.

'Need a hand?' Nat's voice made her jump.

They must have seen her take off across the car park.

'You're not a cop.'

'Looks like you need a hand.' Ben drew up on her other side and nodded to Nat.

Jenny licked her lips. Omar was her boss's prime suspect, but even if he didn't kill his wife, they needed to question him. Still, if he was a killer, he could be dangerous. He could be armed.

'What I need, is for you two to wait for my backup to arrive and send them my way.' She pointed toward the rear of the caravan park. 'The fence will keep him in, but he might sneak back this way.'

'We'll cover your butt.' Nat saluted.

Jenny stifled a chuckle. Always the clown. She turned to Ben.

'Make sure he stays here.'

'You got it.' His words didn't fill her with confidence.

She stalked past a Millard caravan older than her father. Stopping at the edge, she peered beyond, aware of one small section of the fence line where someone could scale it.

Omar wasn't local. He wouldn't know about the commercial bins, but he could find them any second. She watched, and waited, hoping if Omar did double back, Phillips would be there to catch him.

The vein at her neck pulsed as her heartrate slowed from the sprint. A click from behind her made her spin.

'Whatcha doin'?'

She snapped her finger to her lips and tapped.

'Shoosh!'

Flynn smiled widely, reminding Jenny of the children she met at the Umoona community with Nev.

She was about to berate him over how hard he was to find but stopped herself. She needed to keep him around to answer questions, not spook him.

She bent down to meet him at eye level and wiggled her finger for him to come closer. Flynn glanced around suspiciously, then scooted toward her.

She squatted to her haunches.

'Can you help me out?' she whispered.

He nodded.

'Can you stand here, and if you see a tall, broad man with an almost black bushy beard come this way, call out to me really loud?'

Flynn frowned, then nodded. Jenny circled around to the other side of the caravan but stopped when voices carried from behind her.

'Damn!' She swore as she recognised Nat's voice. Sprinting, she entered the carpark to find her brothers draped over a struggling figure. Phillips was sprinting from the opposite direction.

'Get off me.'

Jenny reached the seething mass of limbs before Phillips.

'You heard the man,' she growled.

'He was sneaking out.' Nat sounded defensive.

'He was.' Ben backed him up as he got to his feet and attempted to brush the red dirt from his navy boardshorts.

Phillips reached Omar, pulled his arm behind his back and closed a cuff around his wrist.

'What do you want?' Omar struggled as Phillips clamped the other cuff closed. 'Why are you arresting me?'

'You got him?' Jenny asked.

Phillips nodded and dragged the man to his feet.

'Let's go Mr Suleiman. I'll explain everything once we get you to the station.'

'I'll go get Flynn.'

'Flynn?' Phillips glanced over his shoulder with a frown.

'Yeah, he's here somewhere.'

Phillips lifted his chin in the air. Jenny turned to follow where he was indicating. Flynn's head poked around the corner of the motel building.

She watched in slow motion as the Aboriginal boy
caught her gaze with a wide smile, then darted back behind the
building.

'Flynn!' she yelled as she followed.

'Don't waste your time Williams,' Phillips called.

Jenny ignored him, rounding the corner in time to see
black feet with white soles disappear over the wall. Nellie was
right. He was damn quick.

Chapter 27

Phillips grinned as Jenny lifted her shirt and pumped it to cool her body. This summer was hot enough to seriously consider a desk-mounted fan.

'I told you not to run after him. Sprinting is in their genes.'

'Hey!' Nellie protested. 'That's racist.'

'No. It's a generalisation,' O'Connell corrected. 'It's like saying all gays are camp.'

Nellie frowned.

'Sorry Nell.' Phillips blushed. 'I only meant your mob are super quick. Great footy players, runners…'

'I get it,' Nellie sighed. 'And I know you don't have a racist bone in your body mate. It's just…'

'We get it Nellie.' Jenny smoothed her shirt and tucked it back into her pants. 'But the little bugger was fast.'

Nellie grinned.

'Told you he was. He could have a future in the Aussie footy league if he didn't have such nimble fingers.' Her expression darkened once more.

'It's not a problem we're solving today.' Sarge appeared from his office. 'O'Connell and Williams will take Omar's interview.'

Nellie fixed her gaze on Sarge.

'Did I do something wrong?'

Sergeant Mackenzie shook his head.

'Nope. But this guy is a wife beater, at least that's what the restraining order indicates and culturally, he's not going to respond to a woman.'

'Another stereotype.' O'Connell pointed his pen at Nellie, who chuckled.

Sarge puffed out his broad chest and crossed his arms over his ever-increasing belly.

'They are called stereotypes for a reason O'Connell.'

'Not for a *good* reason.' Nellie mirrored the sergeant's stance. 'Stereotypes are almost always fiction. A broad brush, swept across a race, gender, religion or culture. They don't take into account the individuals within a culture…'

'Are you channelling McGregor or something?' Sergeant Mackenzie's tone relaxed.

'Let's go Senior.' Jenny lifted her chin toward O'Connell. 'I'm keen to find out what Omar knows about where Maryam was working. Nick's manager is still missing.'

'Speaking of which.' Her boss pointed. 'Phillips. Get back out doorknocking for those visa overstayers and keep your eyes open for Ben Stokes. I want him interviewed ASAP.'

He fixed his gaze back on Nellie.

'I'll hold the fort here while you use your association with Tanya Rothchild and her kid and get her in here for a formal interview. Williams has been informed by Children's Services Tanya lost custody this morning. Try every bar in town.'

It wasn't a pleasant thought, but Sergeant Mackenzie was right. Tanya would be depressed over Mikey, and with her drinking problem she could be in a bar, but there was another possibility.

'Or she could be at home with a bottle of scotch, drowning her sorrows.'

'Good idea Williams.' He turned to Nellie. 'Get going and keep an eye out for Flynn. He's playing hide-and-seek and I'm getting a bit sick of it.'

'Yes Sarge.' Nellie didn't seem overjoyed with the assignment.

Jenny collected a pen from her desk, along with a lined notepad, then turned back.

'Is there anything we can do to get Tanya's son back?'

'It's not our job Williams.'

'I know Sarge, but what legit judge gives a guy like Sullivan custody? He's still under investigation for corruption with the CWU.'

'He's not been convicted, and not everyone sees the man as a thug Williams. If we can link him to this murder, Tanya will get Mikey back by default.'

'Let's hope so.' Jenny joined O'Connell in the hallway. 'Let's see what Mr Suleiman has to say.'

O'Connell opened the door to a wave of body odour. Jenny's nose twitched. She rubbed it, then reached for the airconditioning controls and cranked up the cool and fan speed.

As she opened her mouth to introduce them, the taste of sweat tainted her taste buds. Swallowing, she forced the bile down and reached for a sealed bottle of water. Cracking the lid, she gulped down half the bottle while O'Connell passed one to Omar.

Replacing the lid, Jenny nodded she was ready. As usual, O'Connell managed the recording equipment. Jenny would take lead. The pattern worked well for them. O'Connell would hold back in case a rougher, more masculine approach was needed.

Jenny only ever saw O'Connell lose his cool once. She didn't want to ever be on the receiving end of his anger.

Reaching across the table, she unlocked the handcuffs as she ran through the formalities.

'Mr Suleiman. I'm sure we simply got off on the wrong foot. We only needed to ask you a few questions.'

'I'm not speaking without a lawyer.'

'But you're not under arrest.'

Jenny waited. He remained silent.

'I'm sorry for your loss.'

'What?'

Jenny glanced at O'Connell whose expression mirrored her thoughts.

'I know you were estranged, but your wife…'

'What about my wife? Where is she?'

Jenny exchanged another confused glance with O'Connell.

'I'm sorry to inform you, Maryam has been killed.'

Omar surged to his feet. O'Connell with him. The senior constable was tall, lean, but very strong. Omar scanned O'Connell's square-set shoulders, even stopping to take in the shield on his shirt sleeves, then lowered himself back into his chair.

'How?' The word was barely audible.

'We are still investigating the circumstances, but maybe you can help us with our inquiries?'

Jenny readjusted her earlier game plan. Omar's reaction wasn't fake. He genuinely wasn't aware Maryam was dead.

'How did she die?'

Jenny rolled her shoulders and steadied her breathing.

'We aren't able to release the details yet Mr Suleiman, but her death has been ruled as homicide.'

Omar reached for the water bottle, sipped sparingly and swallowed hard. Sorrow filled his eyes as they met Jenny's.

'What do you want from me?'

'We are trying to piece together her life, which means working through her past.'

Jenny waited for Omar to understand what would come next. He nodded for her to go on.

'Maryam took out a restraining order against you and as we understand it, you were divorced.'

Omar shook his head vigorously.

'Divorce is frowned upon in our religion. I had not signed the papers. I wanted to stay married until the day we…' he wiped his thick beard with the palm of his left hand.

'When was the last time you saw Maryam?'

Omar reached into his pocket and produced a pale blue chequered handkerchief.

'Nearly two years ago.'

Jenny noted the dates on a yellow lined pad.

'Did you hit your wife?'

'I did not.'

Jenny studied Omar's features—his body language. Nothing indicated he was lying.

'Then why the restraining order?'

Omar fell back in his chair. His stiff back returned with hunched shoulders.

'Maryam wanted to leave the faith.' He swallowed. 'She said Australia offered a new life. A new way of thinking. She is, was young. Easily led.'

'By whom?'

Omar shook his head.

'I don't know. She ran away. I found her in a women's shelter. She told them I hit her, and they believed her.'

'You're saying you never hit her?' Jenny repeated the question, trying to make sure she was reading the man correctly.

'I never laid a hand on my wife. She was a gift from Allah.'

Jenny swallowed hard.

'How long were you married?'

Omar's features softened.

'Seven years.'

Jenny did a quick calculation.

'She was eighteen, and you were?'

'Thirty-two.'

Jenny forced herself to keep her personal opinions to herself. Every culture was different. And a woman's expectation of marriage also differed.

She recalled a Greek family who used to shoot for rabbits on the home farm. The wife would chat with Jenny's mother and her when she got older, about life and love and marriage. Maria's words stuck in Jenny's memory like super-glue.

You marry an older man and he'll be yours forever. Men want sex until their old age. Women grow bored of it, or go through the change and find it hard, but if they are twenty years younger, the man's eye will never stray.

Maria's view of men assumed true love didn't exist and being faithful through every stage of life was a pipe dream. Jenny hoped Maria was wrong. She hoped Nick and she would be different.

'Okay, Mr Suleiman, if you haven't seen Maryam for nearly two years, why are you here now?'

'I got a call from someone called Ben. He told me I needed to sign the paperwork and let Maryam go, but I burned my copy.'

'So, he told you to come here?'

Omar nodded.

'He said they had a new copy. I should stay at the motel, and he would contact me.'

'Why did you run?

'I saw your uniform. I've been wrongfully arrested twice for brutalising my wife.'

'But you were never charged?'

His hands waved frantically in front of his face.

'I told you. I never hit my wife!'

A search revealed no hospital records or police report photos to support Maryam's claims. Every word out of Omar's mouth appeared to be the truth. But abusers could be cunning, manipulative and very charismatic.

'We'll need to confirm where you were from last Friday to this Monday, when your wife's body was found.'

Omar buried his face in his hands a moment, then used the chequered handkerchief to wipe his eyes.

'I was home when I got the call from this, Ben.' He spat the name. 'That was Saturday morning. Then I was at the soccer match.' A weak smile crossed his lips. 'My nephew plays and I coach under-nine's. I was with family on Sunday, then worked up until Thursday, then I packed and came here today.'

'We'll need the names and contact details of everyone you mentioned, but I think we have what we need for now.'

Jenny turned over a page on her notepad, then spun it toward Omar with a pen. His eyes never left hers.

'Did this Ben, kill her?'

'We can't discuss details, but Ben isn't a suspect at this time. Like you, he has an alibi.'

'Then who and why?'

'Mr Suleiman, please leave those questions to us to figure out. We'll inform you of our findings as we get updates.'

Jenny's phone buzzed in her pocket. She scanned the caller ID and lifted a finger to O'Connell.

'It's Penny.'

O'Connell nodded.

'Mr Suleiman. I'll stay here while you finish your list of names.'

Jenny heard O'Connell speaking as she opened the interview door and answered.

'Hey Penny. What you got?'

The sound of keys tapping, greeted her before Penny spoke.

'The top you found at the wrecking yard is a match to the one in the photo. We are running DNA, but it will take a while.'

'Okay?' Jenny wondered why this confirming information warranted a call. 'What else did you find?'

'That's it. We checked all the evidence we bagged. All the personal effects from the donga with the bunk beds. Nothing in there was a match to your victim. There wasn't one outfit in her size. No photos, brush with her hair colour, make up bag to match her DNA.'

A slow ache crept up the back of Jenny's neck and into her scalp.

'So our victim never lived with the other workers.'

'Only an assumption, but I think it's a good one.'

'If she didn't live with Tanya, and Ben is telling the truth, we still have no idea where Maryam has been living and what role she played in any of this.'

Chapter 28

Sergeant Mackenzie glanced up from the front counter as Jenny returned to the main office. The sight of her boss looming over the desktop computer, hunting for keys made her stifle a giggle.

'How'd you go?'

'He's given us a long list of alibis. We'll need to check them out, but I don't think he's our guy.'

Sarge pursed his lips, nodded and returned his gaze to the computer screen.

'I'm inclined to think you might be right.'

Jenny crossed to the counter.

'You don't sound so surprised.'

'I'm not. Your instincts are good but never overlook an obvious suspect.'

'Of course.' Jenny watched as a file popped up on the screen. 'What's this?'

'The Family Court transcript.' He pointed at the screen. 'Check this out.'

Jenny studied the name his finger lingered on.

'Judge Temperance Povich.' Her stomach tensed. 'That can't be a coincidence.'

'I agree.'

'If Temperance is related to Ms Jamie Povich, we have a link to the mining company extortion and the CWU king pin Sullivan.'

'Tenuous at best Williams, but I agree, it needs investigation.'

Jenny grinned.

'And we need to keep it out of the AFP's line of sight.'

Sarge tapped his nose.

'Exactly. So not a word to Nick.'

Jenny's heart sank. Nick finally filled her in on the AFP investigation and now she was going to have to keep her own secrets.

'This comes back to Ben Stokes, but we know he didn't kill Maryam. Nick said he got the impression Ben's relationship with Maryam was somehow linked to his past.'

Sarge hit *print* on the file and bent, hand held out over the printer as it whirred into action.

'Povich could be the link between Sullivan and Ben, but we have no proof and if we get it, we'll need to pass it on to the AFP team investigating the Foresight Mining extortion from last year. Let's focus on our victim for now.'

'I agree. With Omar and Ben in the clear for the murder, we are left with everyone connected to the illegal workers and gambling.'

Nellie entered the foyer.

'And Tanya.'

'Did you find her?' Sarge lifted the paperwork from the printer and crossed to O'Connell's desk.

'I tried every bar in town. Nothing. Then I called over to her place. The door was open, so I knocked, then entered to do a welfare check.'

'Good thinking. Any sign of a struggle?'

Nellie shook her head.

'No obvious signs of an intruder, but I did find this.' Nellie lifted a bottle of nail polish inside a Ziploc bag.

'That's…'

'A match for the victim's.' Nellie nodded excitedly. 'But I don't think Tanya would have killed her friend.'

'Maybe Maryam was living with Tanya? Penny didn't find any sign she was living with the visa overstayers at the wrecking yard.'

'It's possible, but I didn't find a toothbrush or deodorant in the whole place.'

Sergeant Mackenzie plonked on the edge of O'Connell's desk.

'So Tanya is on the run? Where would she be going?'

Jenny crossed to her locker and flung it open.

'I can't believe she killed her friend, but even if she did, she isn't going anywhere without her son.'

'Where do you think you're going Williams?'

Jenny slipped her utility-vest on and turned to answer her boss.

'To Sullivan's place. This is the perfect chance to get inside his place and check things out. I can offer our support.'

Sergeant Mackenzie shook his head as he rose.

'I like the idea Williams, but no. Sullivan has his own personal security team. No one is breaking into his place and taking Mikey anywhere.'

Jenny opened her mouth to protest but stopped herself. Sergeant Mackenzie was right. Leigh Mundy and his burly offsider were never far from Sullivan. Mikey was not going anywhere while Sullivan was nearby.

Sergeant Mackenzie nodded at the wall clock.

'It's stinking hot and it's beer o'clock. Something is going on over the road tonight and I think we need to make an appearance.'

Jenny slipped off her vest.

'What do you mean?'

'Two trucks rocked up about an hour ago, now the carpark is filling up.'

'Marj said she told Mundy to get lost, but I saw her throwing down a brandy today. I was going to ask her about it, but Omar decided to go for a run.'

'Get changed and get over there. Keep your ears and eyes open. Cheryl's info might prove helpful. See if you can get Marj talking.'

'I'll join you.' Nellie crossed to her locker. 'I could use a drink.'

O'Connell appeared from the interview rooms, guiding Omar to the front counter. Jenny busied herself at the lockers with Nellie, while O'Connell opened the passthrough and led Omar out.

O'Connell returned as Jenny lifted her backpack out of her locker and closed it. Sergeant Mackenzie filled him in, then turned to Jenny.

'Follow up his alibi tomorrow. I'll get a BOLO out on Rothchild.'

'She's not going anywhere without Mikey.'

'Maybe not, but the nail polish at her place needs explaining and it's about time she gave us a straight answer about her relationship with the victim, and her past with Sullivan. Zeigler lawyered up, by the way. But we might get another run at him because I couldn't find a local judge to process his bail today.'

'Oh, what a shame.' Jenny didn't hide the sarcasm.

O'Connell switched off his computer and rounded his desk.

'They picked Ziegler for a reason.'

'Yeah. No record. Runs a cash business. Easy to shift money around. And smart enough to keep his mouth shut,' Sarge agreed.

Jenny slung her backpack over one shoulder.

'We still need to find Flynn. He dialled Emergency Services. He's keeping his distance but seems to turn up in all the wrong places like today when I spotted Omar.'

'He'll do anything for money,' Nellie offered.

Jenny thought about Omar's statement. Ben was going to contact him at the motel.

'Could Flynn have been there to give Omar a message from Ben?'

Sarge pointed to her.

'First thing tomorrow, you and Nellie need to find Flynn. He's right smack bang in the middle of all of this.'

'It's nearly Christmas.' Nellie's whining tone surprised Jenny.

'It's just a day on the calendar. We've got another week yet. Otherwise, we'll have to delay our family celebrations.'

Jenny's heart sank.

'My parents have travelled hours to be here. My brothers…'

'We'll do our best Williams, but we have a murder to investigate.'

Jenny nodded understanding. It didn't ease the pain in her chest.

'Now I really need that drink.'

She trudged through the foyer, Nellie at her side.

'You better get changed first.' Nellie pointed to her uniform. 'Come back to mine for a few minutes and we'll freshen up.'

Jenny stepped outside into a wave of heat. The thought of a cool shower sounded perfect.

'Thanks for the offer, but I'll drop in to Marj's. I need to talk to her anyway and my family are staying there.'

Nellie crossed the carpark to her bright red Vespa, lifted a shiny black helmet from the seat lock-box and shoved it on her head.

'See you in twenty.'

Jenny waved as the moped pinged and buzzed out of the carpark, then braced herself for a tough conversation she didn't want to have. Marj was her friend. Her mentor. Jenny knew she'd never do anything illegal, at least not willingly.

She reminded herself to take it easy, recalling how hard she pushed when Marj was linked to the death of her defacto's sister. It was Nick who pulled her back. But Nick wasn't here to temper her vigour. Not today.

She adjusted her backpack and crossed the road. As she rounded the corner, her mouth dropped open involuntarily. Her boss was right. The carpark was full. The road was lined with white utes with strobing yellow lights on the roof and high-vis stripes down the side.

It seemed every miner, roadside worker and truck driver was at Marj's bar tonight. Jenny's instincts told her it wasn't the food, or the renowned Karaoke dragging them in the door.

Chapter 29

Jenny prepared herself mentally for how best to approach Marj as she wove between the cars toward reception. Her pulse quickened and her palms grew sweaty as she plastered a smile on her lips and stepped inside the office.

The TV screen was blank. The room, eerily silent. Marj sat slumped behind the counter, her hand devoid of the usual romance or crime novel.

'Hey Marj. Can I use your room to do a quick change?'

Marj's eyes regarded her blankly. The ever-present red lipstick smile was nowhere to be seen.

'Go for your life.'

Jenny dropped her backpack at the front of the counter and rounded it. The act was foreign. Marj always joined Jenny on the other side for a hug or vibrant chat.

'What's going on Marj? The place is jam-packed and you're in here, all alone and…' Jenny searched for the right word but found nothing.

'I'm alright Luv. You get changed and go have fun.' She pointed to the door leading to Marj's apartment.

Jenny licked her lips, then swallowed hard.

'Does this have anything to do with Leigh Mundy? I see you've got every construction worker known to man in the bar tonight.'

Marj patted Jenny's hand on the countertop and smiled weakly.

'Let it be, Jenny.'

Jenny clasped Marj's hand and waited for the woman to make eye contact.

'Let what be, Marj?'

She eased her hand free of Jenny's and shook her head.

'I was thinking of retiring. Now might be a good time.'

Jenny's stomach tightened.

'Marj, tell me what's going on. I can help.'

'Marjorie. Thanks for the venue tonight.'

Jenny spun at the deep, husky voice and tried unsuccessfully to keep the surprise from her face.

Terrence Sullivan's eyes scanned her uniform. A forced smile curved his lips. Jenny glanced from him to the woman on his arm and fought to keep her lips sealed.

He nodded toward Jenny.

'Constable.'

'What's so special about tonight?' She managed to keep her tone even.

'We are hosting a benefit event. The CWU run them regularly. Come and join us Constable. We'll be running a casino for the night.'

His expression was challenging.

'That's illegal,' Jenny replied flatly.

Sullivan's laughter peeled out, the woman on his arm giggled. Jenny physically bit her tongue as her eyes locked with Gwen's.

'It's only illegal if you keep the proceeds.' The newspaper editor's voice dripped with contempt. 'All the proceeds are going to the CWU Family Fund which supports families who've lost a loved one on the job. It's such a good cause. I'll be covering it tonight for the paper.'

Jenny ignored Gwen and turned to Sullivan.

'Where's Mikey, if you're out here galivanting around with…' She nodded toward Gwen clearly not wanting to give the woman a name or title.

Gwen's reputation for hanging on the arm of powerful men was well known. Even so, she was surprised to see the ambitious reporter stoop this low.

Sullivan's eyebrows lifted for a microsecond.

'He's with the nanny and having a great time.' His attention shifted to Marj who continued to stare blankly at the wall.

'I'll see you inside later Marjorie. Don't forget our arrangement.'

Jenny sneered as Sullivan and Gwen strolled past the office window toward the restaurant.

Jenny counted in her head, willing herself to remain calm before turning back to Marj.

'What arrangement?'

Marj dismissed her with the wave of a hand.

'There are some fights you can't win Jenny. Let it go.'

'You know I can't.'

'The world is full of powerful people.'

'Only if we let them get away with it.'

Marj forced a smile to her lips.

'Oh Jenny. If only it were that easy.'

'Sullivan is running an illegal gambling ring. We know it, we just need to prove it. You can help Marj.'

Marj's back straightened. Her eyes refocussed. Jenny held her breath.

'I have no proof Jenny. He's no pushover. The man's been doing this a very long time. He keeps it squeaky clean on the outside and lets people like me take the fall. He'll be moving back to where he came from soon enough. Let it go.'

'What do you mean moving back?'

Marj bit the inside of her cheek.

'I don't know all the details, but he's been operating elsewhere. This charity event is a farce. A way to continue his activities and not raise suspicion. I hate to think how much of the money he makes tonight will be syphoned into his personal coffer.'

Marj glanced around nervously.

'Our arrangement is temporary and hardly voluntary.'

Jenny reached out and wrapped her arm around Marj. Finding her shaking, she squeezed.

'How did he manage to keep you quiet until now?' Jenny watched the reception doorway, aware Sullivan was gone, but one of his minions might be within hearing.

She lowered her voice. 'He knows you know the local cops.'

'He made threats when I said no. Eventually, we agreed this was a one-off event. He needed my staff to take care of the drinks and meals, while his team runs the casino. Apparently, he was down a few workers due to illness.'

'The gas leak.' Jenny slapped her hand over her mouth. 'You didn't hear that from me.'

Marj's lips turned up at the corner as a familiar twinkle lit her eyes.

'I heard about the leak and something about passports.'

'Don't go there Marj. Let me call the sergeant and loop him in while I get changed. Stay in here. Nellie will be here any minute. Let her know I'll be out soon and don't worry, we'll get this sorted.'

Marj's bright smile melted Jenny's heart, but as she reached for her backpack and headed to freshen up, all she could think about was how she was going to sort this mess out. Proving Sullivan was running an illegal gambling syndicate, and using illegal workers wasn't going to be easy.

Zeigler wasn't talking. Tanya would only help them if they could get Mikey back. Ben was in the wind and even if he knew more, his past would keep him quiet.

If this event was illegal, they'd need to raid it, and they simply didn't have the manpower to do so effectively. Even if they exposed the illegal gambling ring, they were no closer to finding a motive for Maryam's murder.

Chapter 30

Nellie ran her fingers through her thick wavy hair as Jenny slipped the straps of her floral top up, and wrapped her long, straight loose auburn hair over one shoulder.

'Here goes.' She opened the door. 'Just another Friday after-work drink.'

Nellie licked her lips and entered as Jenny held the door. The usual cool air was replaced by dense, stale air fuelled by too many warm bodies. A faint waft of various aftershaves mixed with body odour made Jenny swallow.

A sea of colour jammed the room. Gwen's flowing after-five cocktail dress, jarred against a burly construction worker still in his Hard Yakka Stubby shorts and long-sleeved high-vis shirt. The scene was a cacophony of activity.

A cheer erupted from a table set up at the rear of the main dining area, right near the stage where Marj performed her annual Liza Minnelli impersonation.

The group was gathered around a roulette wheel, tossing chips down and sculling beer in equal measure.

In front of the bar, a deep line of patrons waited for service. Cheryl, Kelly and Stan rushed to pass out drinks and keep patrons appeased. Jenny turned to Nellie.

'Sarge and O'Connell will join us shortly. I briefed them on what Marj said and hopefully we can ask the croupiers a few questions.'

'What about Danny?'

Nellie would never get used to calling Phillips by his last name. They'd known one another all their lives.

'He's got commitments with Tommy.'

Nellie merely nodded.

Although Tommy was all clear from leukemia now, he was still prone to illness with a compromised immune system.

'We should probably get a drink, but it looks like a long wait.'

Nellie pointed to a ginger mop of hair alongside a dark brown head as they reached Stan at the bar.

'That's Nev and Tim.' She whipped out her phone and punched out a text with rapid fingers.

A ping came back immediately. Jenny saw Nev wave as Stan spoke with Tim.

'I told them we would meet them in the beer garden. Maybe we'll be able to breathe in there.'

Nellie shimmied past a milling group of men in tight-fitting tee-shirts and bright shorts, but it was more familiar faces that caught her eye.

Jenny tapped Nellie on the shoulder.

'I almost forgot they were staying tonight. I better say hello.'

Nellie followed Jenny's line of sight.

'Nice!'

Jenny chuckled as the curvy woman smoothed her gumleaf-green maxi dress and pulled back her shoulders to accentuate her full bust.

The preening was a common scene around her brothers. Ben was lean, with thick hair and an easy smile. While Nat was the complete opposite. Broad, strong, ripped to the max and he knew it. She wondered again about Nat's family but as she wound her way through the milling crowd, she realised now wasn't a good time to ask.

As they passed two blackjack tables, a poker game and a chocolate wheel, Jenny noticed the poker chips matched the one they found on their victim. It was hardly conclusive evidence. The multi coloured chips were much like the ones found in the silver box of cards and poker chips in nearly every home in Australia.

Once O'Connell and Sarge arrived, she planned on playing a few rounds and collecting one for evidence. Maybe Penny could find a fancy way of matching the batch of material used. At this point, she was willing to try anything.

'Hey guys.' She hugged Nat, then Ben. 'Where are mum and dad?'

'This was a bit intense for the oldies. They are up the road at some café mum keeps raving about.'

'Nikolic's.' Nellie and Jenny answered in unison.

Nellie thrust her hand forward.

'I'm Nellie, you must be Ben and Nat.'

Nellie fluttered her eyelashes. Jenny wasn't sure if her brothers noticed, but as Ben reached out, his expression assured her he did.

'I'm Ben.'

'That's going to get confusing.' Nellie addressed Jenny but kept her eyes on Ben.

'Yeah. I wondered about that. Nick has a Ben on the property. Would it be alright if…'

'You call me Benji?' He laughed, then shrugged. 'It's been a while, but yeah, why not?'

Nat slapped him on the shoulder.

'Always thought your hair looked a bit like the Hollywood mongrel.'

Benji swiped Nat's arm away playfully.

'Watch it mate, or I'll start calling you *Nathaniel*.'

Nat cringed.

'Point taken.' He returned his attention to the pile of chips in his hand.

Nellie chuckled, then hoicked her thumb over her head.

'We're having drinks out in the beer garden if you guys want to join.'

'I'm on a roll.' Nat pointed to the chocolate wheel.

Jenny noticed his missing wedding ring.

'Sounds good.' Benji turned to Nat. 'You all good here?'

Nat waved over his shoulder as he placed a bet on number 21.

'Lead the way,' Benji waved.

Jenny glanced at the croupiers, recognising three from the passports found at Zeigler's wrecking yard. The crowd was too thick and the staff too busy to answer any questions right now.

She turned to follow Nellie but stopped as the back of Ben Stokes' head disappeared around the corner near the toilets.

'Look.' Jenny whispered over Nellie's shoulder.

Nellie spun in time to see Ben disappear. Nev and Tim pushed free of the ever-increasing waiting line seconds later.

'Things could turn nasty,' Nellie whispered.

'They could. But we need to question him. Now might be our only chance.'

Tim and Nev joined them. She eyed her brothers, then tapped Nellie on the shoulder.

'I'll be back in a second.'

She didn't wait for a response. Out the corner of her eye, she spotted Sergeant Mackenzie and O'Connell arriving. Gary, O'Connell's partner wore a tight-fitting, round neck tee leaving nothing to the imagination.

O'Connell caught sight of her. She pointed to Nellie, then disappeared around the corner to wait outside the toilets for Ben.

Ben reappeared moments later and stopped dead when he saw her.

'Hey Ben. Got a minute?'

'No!' He tried to brush past her.

She reached out and grabbed his arm.

'You lied to me Ben.'

He yanked his arm free and stormed away. Jenny followed.

'Don't make me arrest you.'

He rounded on her with a smile that made her skin crawl.

'In that outfit.' He made a show of peering around her body. 'I don't see a Taser or gun.'

He turned away. Jenny hurried after him.

'Ben. You said you didn't know where Katie worked. But you knew she was married. You knew Maryam's real identity all along.'

Ben turned so fast, Jenny nearly bumped into him.

'How do you…' He shook his head. 'It doesn't matter now, does it?'

'You said you wanted me to catch Katie's killer before you got to them, but you didn't really mean it, did you?' Ben turned to leave. Jenny followed once more. 'We know her husband is here. We've got his statement.'

Ben spun back around. His expression darkened.

'Omar has no idea why anyone would kill his wife. We can't find a motive. Do you know why she was targeted? Is this all about you? Has your past come back to haunt you Ben?'

Ben's face contorted and his eyes blazed with anger. Jenny wondered if she might have pushed him too far. Stepping back, she swallowed rising bile.

Ben closed the gap and spoke inches from her face.

'You have no idea what you are involved in. This isn't about Katie. This is…' Ben stopped as something over Jenny's shoulder caught his eye.

Jenny spun around to see Terry Sullivan smirking at Ben. The men exchanged a glare. Jenny shivered.

'I can help you Ben,' Jenny whispered.

'No one can help me.' His words were forced out between firm lips and a clenched jaw. 'This issue runs deep, and I was a fool to think the cops could fix it.'

Ben's eyes were still on Sullivan. Jenny glanced back to see him run his finger across his neck. When he noticed Jenny, the pointed finger transformed into a cutesy wave. Jenny fought the nausea clenching her stomach.

Turning back to Ben, she found him shoving his way through the crowd which closed in around him. She struggled to keep up, finally reaching him as he shoved the glass entrance doors open and stepped into the stifling evening.

'Ben!' He raced away. She rushed to keep up. 'Please let me help you.'

He turned to face her once more. His lips turned up in a snarl.

'I tried that route already. No one gives a crap about me, just the information I can give them. It's time I stopped being everyone else's stooge. I'm taking control of my own life.'

He stormed across the artificial turf toward the roadside parking.

'Ben! Don't do anything stupid.'

'Too late,' Ben yelled back as he reached Nick's old Toyota Troopy, jumped in and slammed the door. Jenny watched dust lift and heard gravel crunch as the vehicle disappeared.

O'Connell stepped up behind her.

'That sounded ominous.'

O'Connell's words dug deep into her chest. Ben was going to do something stupid and all she could hope for was that no one would die tonight.

The crash of breaking glass and raised voices made her heartbeat spike. O'Connell shoved the restaurant door open ahead of Jenny. She entered two steps behind him to find Omar waving a broken bottle and screaming in Terry Sullivan's face.

Chapter 31

Jenny chased after O'Connell as he powered through the crowd. People hovered, stunned, while others jostled and scurried for a better position to see what was going on.

'You killed my Maryam!'

Sullivan raised his hand in front of the waving beer bottle, his eyes never drifting from the sharp, jagged edge.

'Hey, mate. I have no idea who…'

'Don't call me *mate*!' Omar stepped in close, hand slashing back and forth toward Sullivan's neck. The CWU boss's eyes widened as he stumbled back into Gwen, who fell from her six-inch heels to her backside with a squeal.

Two men cautiously helped her to her feet as the crowd around the fighting men thinned.

Jenny scanned the bar to find Sergeant Mackenzie steering people away. His words were impossible to hear over the panic rolling through the room.

Nellie appeared at the beer garden doorway. Benji, Nev and Tim hovered right behind her. Jenny instinctively sought out Nat, finding him with his arms crossed over his chest, calmly studying the scene intently.

She continued to follow O'Connell between a burly man with tree trunks for legs and a woman with dreadlocks and a nose ring. Comments rippled around her, some goading, some frightened. Patrons began arguing and taking sides in a fight they knew nothing about. The incident was on the edge of escalating out of control.

'Omar!' She heard the panic in her voice. 'You don't need to do this.'

The whites of Sullivan's eyes were visible as he fixed his gaze on Jenny and O'Connell.

'I don't know what he's…'

'Shut up Sullivan.' Sergeant Mackenzie's gruff voice boomed over the hubbub of the mob as he closed in from the opposite direction.

'You've done nothing.' Omar waved his makeshift weapon from Sullivan to Sergeant Mackenzie and back. 'He's walking free, and Maryam is gone.'

'We haven't given up on your wife's case Omar.' Her boss glared at Sullivan. 'We are closing in on possible suspects.'

'Justice works differently where I come from.' The bottle stabbed at Sullivan.

The man lifted his arms high, curved his back and drew his stomach away from the offending weapon. Sarge reached Sullivan and stepped between Omar and his intended victim.

Her boss cried out and lifted his hand to reveal a dripping wound. Omar stumbled back into Jenny.

She wrapped her left arm around his neck and gripped Omar's right wrist with her free hand. The bottle smashed to the floor as Jenny struggled to drag Omar's arm up behind his back.

Leigh Mundy and his mate Dave surged forward, forming a protective wall in front of Sullivan.

O'Connell reached sergeant Mackenzie, gripped his wound and glanced around for assistance.

'Here!' Stan tossed a towel from behind the bar. O'Connell snatched it from the air and wrapped it tightly around the wound.

'Nev!' He called, but the doctor and his paramedic roommate Tim were right behind him as Jenny continued to grapple with Omar.

The man was Jenny's height, but stronger and enraged enough to block out the pain she inflicted in every joint in his restrained arm and shoulder. With a groan, he bent forward and tossed her over his shoulders to the ground. She landed heavily. Glancing up, she saw O'Connell hand his patient over to Nev.

She struggled to her feet as Nat and Benji stormed inside the circle of jeering onlookers. From the corner of her vision, Jenny watched Sullivan edge back toward the bar. Leigh kept watch on the crowd and Omar, as Dave used his bulk to create a path through the crowd and steer Sullivan toward the kitchen.

'Don't you go anywhere Sullivan,' she shouted.

An eerie hush fell over the crowd. Nat shoulder-charged Omar to the ground. The wind left their lungs as O'Connell dug into his pocket for handcuffs. He joined the tangled bodies, found Omar's wrist and snapped the cuff shut.

O'Connell struggled to pull Omar to his feet as Nellie forced her way through the crowd to join Jenny.

'Sullivan is on the move.' She pointed to three retreating backs, heading through the staff kitchen entrance.

'Sullivan. I said wait!' She turned to Nellie. 'Get out the back and head them off.'

She worried over their lack of weapons, but Sullivan wasn't under arrest. There was no need for him to resort to violence.

Nat was at her side as the group disappeared into the kitchen.

'More fun than chasing rabbits.'

She didn't need to see his face to know he was grinning.

'Just keep back Nat.'

'That's gratitude for you.' He was still smiling as she pushed the swinging kitchen door open.

They were met with the backs of all three men bunched together, hands raised, stepping backward, toward her and the kitchen door.

'You go nowhere.' Mateo, the chef, held a foot-long knife. The man's dark eyes regarded the group with pure malice.

'What the hell!' Sullivan turned to seek another escape but found Jenny and Nat blocking the exit.

'*I'm* the victim! I want to press charges.'

'Of course you do and I'm more than willing to take your statement.' She forced a smile to her lips. 'Down the station.'

Leigh Mundy crossed his arms over his chest with a sneer. Sullivan clenched his jaw, then drew his mobile phone from his pocket.

'I'll organise my lawyer and meet you there in the morning.'

'I think it's best you sign a report tonight, Mr Sullivan,' She tapped her temple. 'While it's all fresh in your mind.'

Nellie entered through the rear kitchen door, Benji right behind her. Mateo lowered his weapon, nodded to Jenny, then crossed to a stainless-steel workbench and continued cutting vegetables.

The CWU boss pursed his lips ready to argue.

Nat drew up alongside Jenny.

'All good Sis?'

'All good, thanks for the help, but I'm a bit busy right now.' She failed to keep the tension from her voice.

'I can see that.' Nat nodded toward Leigh, whose legs were spread wide, arms still crossed. His eyes begged Nat to take him on.

Sullivan gave Leigh an instructive wave. The henchman let his arms drop to his side with obvious regret.

Jenny relaxed.

'Mr Sullivan and Mr Mundy were just organising to come to the station and make a report.'

'Sarge is injured. O'Connell has Omar. I think you might need to finish up here.' Nellie continued to block the exit from the kitchen. 'I can escort them.'

Creases appeared at the corner of Sullivan's eyes.

'There's no need. I've decided to let the whole matter go. He's obviously got me mixed up with someone else.'

Jenny remained silent.

'I don't even know the man, or the person he was referring to.'

Jenny waved Nellie forward.

'Thanks Nellie. O'Connell will have the station open by now, so if you can show these gentlemen into interview rooms, I'll be over as soon as I mop up here.'

'I really think…'

'We'll be pressing charges Mr Sullivan.' Jenny cut him off.

A muscle twitched at the edge of Sullivan's jaw. Leigh stepped between the CWU boss and Jenny. Nat stood shoulder to shoulder with her and met the henchman's threat with one of his own. Benji stepped up beside Nellie, further barricading the rear exit.

Jenny noticed Dave ease back from the conflict.

'Pressing charges means you are a victim of an attempted assault, and we will subpoena you to give a statement if necessary. You might as well comply now.'

Chapter 32

She watched Nellie escort Sullivan from the kitchen. A sense of urgency made her shiver. She needed to catch the croupiers before they disappeared again. At least three faces matched the withheld passports found at the wrecking yard.

Nat slapped her on the shoulder.

'Best fun I've had in ages.'

'Thanks for the back-up Nat, but I've still got work to do.'

She turned toward the exit but stopped when the chef cleared his throat.

'I speak with you?'

'Of course Mateo.' Jenny turned to Nat. 'See you a bit later. It's going to be a busy night.'

Nat patted her shoulder.

'You always were a crusader Jen. This job suits you.'

She allowed herself a slight grin, then nodded for him to leave. As the kitchen door swung closed, she turned back to Mateo. Dinner service was over. Gleaming stainless-steel benches were almost empty, and the quiet hum of the dishwasher was all she could hear.

'What's up Mateo?'

'I speak with one of the extra staff.' His South American accent was still strong, even after years of living in Australia and working for Marj.

She nodded for him to go on.

'She says she's a backpacker, trying to get her extra year visa, you know?'

'I understand the 417 Visa.' Jenny left a question in her voice. What did this have to do with her.

'She said they stay in shit hole. That this man, he put his hands on her.'

'You mean Sullivan.'

He nodded.

'I understand the knife then.'

Mateo grinned. His hazel eyes twinkled.

'Where I come from, men like him, we cut off their…'

Jenny lifted her hand in the air.

'Yep. Get the picture.' She retrieved her phone. 'If I show you some pictures, can you point out the girl you spoke to?'

'Si.'

'Great.' Jenny slowly slid her finger over the screen, shifting from one passport photo to the next.

'This is her.'

Jenny slipped her phone into her pocket.

'Thanks, Mateo. This could be very helpful.' She patted his shoulder. 'Did you hear anything else? Something about an illegal bar or gambling place?'

'I hear about the girl's friends getting sick and now they are here to use *my* staff and *my* restaurant.'

Jenny patted his shoulder once more, being careful not to point out it was Marj's restaurant.

'Thanks again, Mateo. If you hear anything else, let me know.'

The chef waved his knife and returned to his food preparation. Jenny rushed through the swinging kitchen door in search of the woman Mateo identified.

Sergeant Mackenzie controlled the crowd as they filed out the front door. His skin was pale as he fidgeted with the sling holding his arm across his chest.

Nev hovered nearby. His face worried. Jenny watched her boss stop two women with white shirts, silky black waistcoats and black skirts. Both fidgeted anxiously as

Sergeant Mackenzie indicated for them to take a seat. Jenny watched them scan the room anxiously as they found chairs.

Neither was the woman Mateo indicated moments before.

Sergeant Mackenzie returned his attention to vetting the exiting crowd.

'Steve, next time someone pulls out a broken beer bottle, I better not hear you egg 'em on. You got me?'

Tree stump leg man cleared his throat and grumbled incoherently as Jenny approached.

'Williams, there are two more casino staff unaccounted for. Take a look around and see if you can find them.'

'You got it Sarge.'

Jenny cast her eye around the room to find two nervous faces, framed by Akubra hats and close-cropped beards yet to thicken up. One watched Tree Stump bow his head, drop his shoulders and scamper from the bar. The other scanned over his shoulder, seeking an escape.

As his eyes fell back on Jenny, she stifled more than one emotion and crossed the room to meet him.

'What the hell are you doing here Sam?'

Nick's little brother was over eighteen. It wasn't unreasonable to find him in the bar, drinking, but something about his mannerisms sent a tingle down her spine.

'Hey Jen. It was just a fundraiser.'

His best mate Mick swallowed nervously.

'Then why do you look like you pulled off a jewellery robbery?'

A flash of black caught her eye near the stage.

'Don't go anywhere. I need to talk to you, but I need to find someone first.'

'It was only a charity bash,' Sam called after her.

'You better be here when I get back.' She didn't bother to turn back and make sure he was. Her words were loud enough her boss would have heard. He'd make sure Sam and Mick didn't go anywhere.

They might know nothing. But the expression on Sam's face said he knew something wasn't kosher with the whole evening's events.

The red curtain at the side of the small stage was still moving when Jenny reached it. She was unfamiliar with the backstage area, despite Marj's encouragement to take over her Liza Minnelli gig. The idea of donning a sequinned outfit and parading around singing scared Jenny more than staring down the barrel of a gun.

The velvet fabric made her senses tingle. Something about the texture reminded her of chalk on a blackboard. She stifled a shudder as she gently eased the curtain aside.

A hallway with doors on either side ran toward the rear of the building.

'Damn!' She rushed to the exit door, gave it a shove.

Relief washed over her when she found it locked. Glancing up, she spotted the Fire Exit sign and tutted to herself. Fire exits should never be locked, but in this instance, she was glad it was.

'Hey. I'm not going to hurt you,' she called as she picked her way back down the hall, trying each door on the way. All were locked. Lifting her mobile from her pocket, she dialled Marj's number in the hope of getting keys.

As the call began to ring, *Hey Big Spender* played on repeat behind door number two. Jenny chuckled as the phone continued to ring unanswered.

'Marj! It's Jenny. Open up.' Silence greeted her. 'I know you are in there and I know you have at least one of the croupiers with you.'

More silence.

Jenny slammed her fist on the door.

'I *will* break it down if I have to.'

The tap of heels on vinyl echoed around the room. When the door didn't open, Jenny placed her ear against it to hear what was going on. A door clicked closed, leaving Jenny wondering if there was a rear exit, but the sound of feet drawing closer reassured her.

Pulling back, she resisted the urge to put her hands on her hips as the door flew open.

'Oh Jenny. Sorry I missed your call Luv. I was…'

'Hiding in your dressing room.'

Jenny brushed past Marj into the room to find a dressing-table mirror lined with incandescent light bulbs she didn't know were still sold. An oriental screen, suited more to a Japanese bathhouse wrapped along the left wall. To the right hung an array of brightly coloured costumes.

'I came in here to get away from the crowd.'

'Was that before or after we arrested Omar and escorted Sullivan to the station?'

A twinkle in Marj's eye answered her question.

'I'm not with immigration Marj. I don't care what visa status the women have, but we are missing two croupiers and one of them might be able to help us solve a woman's murder.'

Marj pursed her lips.

'Can I trust you?'

'Of course you can Marj.'

She wasn't lying, but she also couldn't guarantee these women could stay in the country. If they were overstaying their visas, they could be deported. Immigration wasn't her department.

'Marie, Carmen, it's safe. Jenny is one of the good guys. You can come out now.'

Jenny followed Marj's gaze to the wall of clothing. A black ball gown began jostling as though possessed with an unfriendly ghost. Jenny held her breath as a crack appeared in the wall and a face peeked out from behind it.

A hidden room. She made a mental note.

Marj crossed to the hidden doorway with her hands outstretched.

'It's all right girls. Come on out.' A hand reached out and gripped Marj's hand with shaking fingers.

'Jenny is only going to ask you a few questions about your nasty boss. Then she's going to put him in jail for a very long time.'

Marj lifted an eyebrow in Jenny's direction. The expression obvious. Jenny swallowed, forced a smile to her lips and hoped with all her heart she could keep Marj's promise.

Chapter 33

Jenny passed a bottle of water across the scratched and battered table, dragged out her chair and sat opposite the curvy woman. The only sound was the second-hand ticking on the clock above the table. Jenny noted the time with a silent sigh.

It was after 1am and they were yet to interview Sullivan. O'Connell and Nellie were interviewing the other women, but Carmen would only speak to Jenny.

The woman wrung her hands together as Jenny reached for a yellow lined pad.

'Carmen, we found your passport amongst others at the wrecking yard outside town. Can you explain how it got there?'

Carmen's eyelids slowly lifted to reveal intense brown eyes, framed by luscious black lashes and dark eyeliner. A glistening of moisture made Jenny reach for the carton of tissues. As she slid the box across the table, she scolded herself for beginning the interview so abruptly.

If Marj and Mateo were correct, Carmen was a victim of workplace harassment. While criminal charges in such cases were rare, Jenny was willing to push hard if Sullivan was involved.

'Sorry Carmen. Take your time.'

She needed to build trust with this woman. Not launch straight into Maryam's death or the details surrounding the illegal gambling.

'How long have you been in Australia?'

It was a moot question. Immigration records confirmed Carmen Perez overstayed her visa years ago, but it was the only conversation Jenny could think of to help the woman relax.

Carmen's long, polished fingernails plucked a tissue from the box and delicately dabbed at her eyes. Jenny waited as she opened her water bottle, sipped a mouthful, then replaced the cap before making eye contact.

'You send me home?'

Jenny frowned at the hopeful tone in the woman's question.

'Do you want to go home?'

Carmen frowned, as though the question was unclear.

'I like Australia, but…'

'You don't like your boss.'

Carmen nodded.

'He keeps my passport and he…' She faltered and reached for her tissue once more.

Jenny gave her a few moments, but when Carmen remained silent, she continued with her questions.

'Marj and Mateo said you were assaulted by your boss.' Carmen buried her face in her hands. 'Is your boss Terrence Sullivan?'

Carmen's thick, dark hair swayed as she shook her head from side to side. Her face remained hidden.

Jenny's hopes of holding Sullivan on assault charges were dwindling.

'If Sullivan didn't hurt you, who did Carmen?'

Another shake of the head told Jenny she needed to change the subject, for now.

'Do you know a woman called Katie?'

Carmen peeked over her fingertips.

'Sí.'

'You're not in any trouble. If you provide us with the information we need, you may be allowed to stay in the country as a witness.'

She hoped her words were true. If they didn't catch Maryam's killer, there would be nothing Jenny could do to help this woman.

She came here to work. To visit Australia, earn some money and travel the world. Someone here stole her liberty. Held her passport so she couldn't leave. Now, she appeared to also be a victim of sexual assault.

Mateo thought Sullivan was at fault. If it wasn't him, who was it?

'How do you know Katie?'

Carmen wiped at her tears with the now soggy tissue and sipped from her bottle of water again.

'Katie. She set up the club, train us to do cards right.'

'Did Tanya help too?'

Jenny was trying to piece together Tanya and Katie's relationship. They now knew Katie was using a false name. They were aware she left her husband. But how did she end up in the middle of the outback? How long was she in Coober Pedy and where was she before?

'Sí.' Carmen flicked her hands as though she were dealing cards. 'Tanya also teach.'

Jenny already suspected Tanya worked with Katie. But none of this explained how the body ended up in Tanya's car. Or why Katie was killed.

'How long have you been in Coober Pedy?'

Carmen frowned, as though she didn't understand.

'Coober Pedy is the name of this town Carmen. Do you know how long you've been here?'

Carmen counted on her fingers and Jenny wondered what the woman was doing.

'I don't know how you say… catorce meses.'

Jenny reached for her phone, opened the translation app, then realised she didn't know how to spell Spanish words. She passed her phone to Carmen.

'Can you type it in here?' She pointed to the Spanish side of the app.

Carmen nodded, typed and handed the phone back.

Jenny read the translation.

'Okay, so you've been in Coober Pedy for fourteen months, where were you before coming here?'

Carmen shrugged.

Jenny wondered why the woman was suddenly evasive but decided to circle back to the question later.

'Carmen, the man who hurt you, has he hurt any of the other women?'

Carmen reached for another tissue, sipped her water, then shook her head.

'When did you last see Katie?'

Carmen shrugged, but as she glanced up, her haunted expression made Jenny shiver.

Could she have witnessed Katie's murder?

'Carmen, there's only so much I can do to protect you from immigration and deportation. I need an excuse to make sure you stay in the country.'

Carmen's dark eyes found Jenny's. The glistening of tears was replaced by a steely determination.

'Leigh.' She spat the name out.

'Leigh Mundy assaulted you?'

Carmen nodded.

Jenny knew the guy was a leech the moment she met him, but sexual assault… She shook her own doubts away. Carmen was a victim. Maybe Katie was a victim of Leigh Mundy's unwanted sexual attention, and he killed her to stop her telling Ben.

Jenny was tired and she still needed to interview Sullivan. Carmen must have been as exhausted.

'Carmen, I need you to give me a written statement, and I'm afraid I'll need details.'

Carmen shook her head. The gesture travelled through her body until she was visibly shaking.

'But it can wait until later in the morning. I'll get you a room in the motel over the road. Have a shower. Get some sleep and we'll talk more soon.'

As Carmen glanced up, Jenny noticed a slow smile. Her skin tingled as a knock on the door made her jump.

O'Connell poked his head in.

'Next interview is ready. Nellie will show Ms Perez out.'

Chapter 34

Jenny's thoughts were scattered as she joined O'Connell in the interview room. Terrence Sullivan sat next to an unknown woman with broad shoulder pads that went out with the 80's. A sheen lingered over her heavy makeup. The overpowering scent of floral and musk perfume made Jenny's nose itch.

'Mr Sullivan, thank you for waiting.' Jenny dragged out the chair next to the recording equipment, allowing O'Connell to take the lead.

'Make this snappy constables. My client has been waiting here for hours and it's after 2am. A ridiculous time to be making a victim statement.'

'Senior.' O'Connell tapped his shoulder.

'What?' The woman's overplucked eyebrows creased.

'I'm Senior Constable O'Connell. This is Constable Williams.'

The lawyer sat back with a huff.

'I don't care who you are. It's an ungodly hour to be here and I have a mind to make a formal complaint.'

O'Connell lifted his hand.

'The only one holding up this interview now is you.'

The lawyer's top lip lifted in a snarl.

'Get on with it then.' She rolled her hand in a royal wave.

'Mr Sullivan. Can you explain why you have illegal workers operating your charity casino?'

Sullivan opened his mouth, but it was the lawyer who spoke.

'No comment.' She leant forward like a cat ready to pounce. 'Keep your questions to the incident we are here for.'

O'Connell tongued his teeth, swallowed and drew his shoulders back.

'Mr Sullivan. Do you know Omar Suleiman?'

Sullivan glanced at his lawyer who nodded for him to answer.

'No.'

'Do you know Maryam Suleiman, also known as Katie Montgomery?'

Sullivan and his lawyer exchanged a quiet conversation before the lawyer lifted her chin to O'Connell.

'My client is aware a woman named Katie Montgomery has worked with his charity casino events in the past.'

Illegal gambling events more like it. She wanted to ask him why he was operating a charity event in the middle of the outback, usually reserved for wealthy city high society.

Coober Pedy was a long way from his cushy HQ office with the fancy wellness centre and private members only bar.

But O'Connell was leading this interview. She forced herself to remain quiet, and calm.

'Can your client explain why Katie Montgomery's genuine passport, in her real name of Maryam Suleiman was found amongst documents of illegal workers also working for Mr Sullivan's charity event?'

Sullivan leant forward in his seat. The lawyer slapped her hand on his knee.

'Mr Sullivan is the Chair of a large organisation. His charity events are run as a not-for-profit and he has a team of staff who handle the hiring and firing. I fail to see what any of this has to do with the attack on his person.'

'Really?' The question left Jenny's lips before she could stop it.

O'Connell suppressed a grin. She accepted it as permission to carry on.

'Your client was attacked by the woman's husband.'

'Estranged' the lawyer corrected.

'So you do know who Omar Suleiman is?'

'I didn't. But I did my homework Constable. Unlike you, I'm not green around the gills.'

Sullivan laughed unnaturally. Jenny studied his body language. Their eyes met and she held his gaze. He broke it when his phone rang.

'We are in the middle…' she protested.

He ignored her, slipped the phone from his pocket and frowned at the screen.

'I need to take this. It's Mikey's nanny.'

Jenny forced herself to stay calm. It was after 2am and no surprise Sullivan's nanny was trying to determine why he was late home.

'Ruth. What's…' Sullivan jumped to his feet. 'When?'

O'Connell frowned. The lawyer turned in her seat to watch as Sullivan began to pace the crammed space.

'What do you mean you *don't know*?' A vein above his right eye began to pulse, making the eye twitch uncontrollably. 'Get Leigh and Dave on the phone. Grab my security team.'

'What's going…' The lawyer slid her chair back as Sullivan put his finger in the air to force her to silence.

'I'll be there in ten minutes.' He ended the call and shoved his phone into his pocket.

Rage contorted his features as he turned to face Jenny and O'Connell.

'While you idiots kept me here, my son was kidnapped! I want every police officer searching for him.' Sullivan pointed at O'Connell. 'Now!'

The senior constable rose to his feet smoothly, leant on the desk and lifted his finger like a handgun, pointing right at Sullivan's head.

'We have a murder case on our plate Mr Sullivan. I'll spare *one* constable to investigate but given you are in the middle of a custody battle over your son, my best guess is you'll find your son with his mother.'

Jenny gawked as O'Connell reached across her to the recording equipment.

'Interview ended at 2.37am.' He slapped the STOP button and turned to Jenny. 'Williams. Follow him to his place. I'll get Phillips to meet you there and take over. Then get yourself some sleep.

He strode from the room leaving Jenny to deal with the judgemental glares from Sullivan and his lawyer.

Chapter 35

Jenny reached for her mobile phone, hit the snooze on her alarm and rolled onto her back to stare at the pitch-black ceiling.

Living in a dugout was great for sleeping in, but it was hard when it came to finding the motivation to get up. Without a visible sunrise, her body-clock often refused to cooperate.

Last night was exhausting. Jenny only managed a few hours' sleep between worrying about Mikey and trying to link Sullivan to Maryam's murder. The headache creeping up the back of her neck grabbed her scalp like a vice.

The snooze gave way to a blaring buzzer, insisting she get up and shower. Phillips was no doubt getting an ear-bashing from Sullivan about the police's lack of cooperation and he was right. No one was trying too hard to find Mikey. The consensus was Tanya grabbed some personal items, took her child in the evening and was likely on her way out of town.

Twenty minutes later, Jenny parked outside Niko's café and smiled as she slammed the Dodge door and noticed the two old blokes sitting on the bench against the wall.

'Hey.' She jumped to the concrete veranda. 'Glad to see you doing better Bob.'

The old, retired miner grunted, shoved his pipe into his mouth and puffed like the stroke earlier in the week never happened. But Jenny noticed his free arm stayed limp at his side.

She glanced over as Ad relit his hand-rolled smoke, shoved it between his lips and grinned contently.

'Good to have you both back.' She opened the creaking screen door to a line of customers.

'Constable.' Niko whizzed by with his arm full of coffee cups. 'I've made your regular.'

Jenny followed him as he weaved his way to a table and lowered the cups.

'Can I grab a chicken pie?'

'Already on the way.' Niko rushed back to the busy counter.

Jenny turned to Sam and his best mate Mick. Seeing their contrite faces now reminded her of the first day she met them at the Coober Pedy hospital after a car accident.

It was the same day she literally bumped into Nick. Sam introduced his brother, but it was months before they became friends. Longer again before she broke down Nick Johnston's walls.

'Thanks for hanging around guys.'

'Thanks for not dobbing me into Nick,' Sam grinned.

'I hardly think attending a charity event would annoy your brother. Unless you knew it wasn't legal?'

Niko raced over with her pie, then disappeared as quickly. Jenny turned to Sam, taking in how his maturing physique made him resemble Nick more every time he visited from university. Except Sam could never keep his thoughts or emotions hidden like his older brother. He squirmed under her scrutinising gaze, lifted his coffee in both hands and hid behind it a moment.

Mick patted Sam's hunched shoulder.

'Just tell her mate.'

Jenny let her gaze fall on Mick, who wore the same thick Ned Kelly style beard he did when they met. It made him appear older than his twenty years.

'Tell me what?'

She glared at Sam, who chewed his lip, sipped his coffee once more, then swallowed hard.

'It's not the first event we've been to and well…' Sam glanced at Mick who nodded for him to go on. 'They kind of cash your chips in afterward if you know who to talk to.'

Jenny sipped her coffee and fought the nausea in her stomach as she digested what Sam was saying.

'So you buy in?'

Sam nodded.

'And where was the last event you attended?'

Sam scratched his new manscaped chin.

'There was one in February, upstairs in the Royal Mail. You know, where Tash's shop was?'

Jenny's head thudded. Was it her headache or Sam's news? She decided it was likely both. The Royal Mail Hotel and shopping complex was the same place Eric was camping rough and managed to inadvertently prevent Mikey's abduction. Zeigler's unpaid parking ticket popped into her head.

'And where did you first find out about these events?'

It was Mick who answered.

'At uni, during orientation week. There were a couple of engineering students we spoke to. They were going, and we tagged along. It's usually invitation only, for obvious reasons, but they vouched for us.'

Jenny forced herself to remain calm. Sam and Mick were barely twenty. She told herself they were naive country boys with no idea illegal workers were being exploited.

'Where was the event held?'

'Where they build the ships out at Osborne.' Mick answered again.

'In the shipyards?'

Sam nodded.

'Yeah, in the sheds there.'

Jenny needed to connect Sullivan and his goons to the shipyard at the time of the event.

'I need dates. But first, I need to know if you recognise any of the staff who worked at the Adelaide event, with those who were at the event last night?'

'Sure.' Sam finished his coffee, appearing more relaxed now. 'The girls at the tables were hot. Pretty hard to forget. They were all at the Adelaide event, and the manager dude.'

'Manager?'

'Yeah. Don't know his name, but he cashes out the chips or oversees the big, stocky guy doing it.'

Jenny was certain Sam was talking about Leigh and Dave, but she needed to be sure.

'Describe him.'

'He's got mean eyes, bit taller than you, with a tattoo running from his wrist to his neck.'

Leigh Mundy's rippling biceps filled her mind. Sam and Mick's testimony, together with Carmen and Marj's encounters with him should be enough to charge him with illegal gambling, and sexual assault, but they needed more than the CWU connection to charge Sullivan.

But none of this provided a motive for Maryam's murder. She needed to re-interview Carmen. Maybe she could help work out a motive.

But for now, she needed to set her future brother-in-law straight.

'I'll need those dates, and a statement.'

'You won't tell Nick?'

'Or my mum?' Mick sounded more worried than Sam, which was rare for the stocky, calm natured guy.

'I won't, but you will. This isn't about the gambling guys. Going to the casino for a fun night is one thing. Attending an illegal game is another.'

'It doesn't do anyone any harm if I lose some cash,' Sam pouted.

Jenny glared at the two bearded faces in front of her and realised those beards belied their immaturity.

'Illegal gambling operations don't turn over cash for fun. They launder it and they use vulnerable people like illegal immigrants, or desperately poor people to do the labour. They are up to their necks in drugs, prostitution and murder for hire.'

'That's all propaganda the government wants us to believe.'

Mick sat back and crossed his arms over his chest. His defensive stance was all wrong for him. In the two years she'd known him, he was always a chilled-out kind of guy. The voice of reason. Where was this coming from?

She studied his expression, drew a slow breath, then adjusted her position to face him square on.

'Where the hell did you hear that bull-crap?'

'They are taking our guns away and making us slaves to the system.'

Mick's words slapped Jenny in the face. She eyed Sam, who squirmed in his seat. Was he buying this ideology? When her uncle shot him, and nearly killed him, Sam was carrying a gun. It did him no good at all.

'In an ideal world, I'd agree with you Mick. But we live in a world where people reach for a loaded gun to solve an argument. Where the strong dominate the weaker and their guns are always bigger. I have a dead woman in the morgue to prove it, and this *harmless* gambling ring is connected.'

Mick lifted his chin and sniffed. Jenny bit her tongue, then pointed at Mick, then Sam.

'Breathe a word of that to anyone, and I'll arrest you.'

Chapter 36

Jenny was still seething over Mick's misinformed opinions as she strode into the station to find Gwen ringing the counter bell in quick, annoying bursts.

'Gwen. Can we help you?' Jenny lifted the counter passthrough.

'Where the hell is everyone? It's after lunch.' The newspaper editor's heels tapped out an impatient tune on the lino floor.

'Sleeping off a very long night I suspect.' Jenny scanned the office area to find it vacant. Two seconds later Phillips slid into the room, still pulling up his fly.

'Sorry. I was just…'

She lifted her hand.

'I've got this Phillips. How's Sarge going?'

'Fine!' She turned to find her boss entering with O'Connell one step behind. 'What do you want Gwen?'

'I can't believe you arrested Terry Sullivan.'

'We didn't.' Jenny corrected as O'Connell and Sarge rounded the counter.

'He was dragged in here and left in an interview room for hours. What was it then?'

'What's your interest in this Gwen?' Jenny knew the reporter was only ever interested in a story.

Her boss drew up alongside Jenny. 'Nothing to see here Gwen.' He waved the back of his hand dismissively. 'You'll get a statement when I'm ready.'

'I've been working on a story about Terry's charity work for over a year now. He's a community minded man, who gives freely of his time. You're so off beam on this one Mac.'

'Sergeant Mackenzie to you.' Her boss turned away. 'Get lost Gwen, before I find something to charge you with.'

Sergeant Mackenzie stormed toward his office. Jenny glanced at O'Connell who shrugged away the man's more than usual foul mood and approached the counter as Gwen continued her tirade.

'Terry is part of an important union that offers members job security and…'

'Gwen. I'm afraid your investigative journalism skills are waning in your old age.' O'Connell's expression was deadpan.

Gwen gaped. Jenny stifled a giggle. O'Connell waved for Jenny to step away from the counter and he'd handle his ex-wife.

'The CWU have been investigated for extortion, misappropriation of funds and last time I checked, they don't offer their workers diddly squat. They do, however, have a grossly overpaid management committee, with perks to shame even the worst budget rorting politicians.'

Gwen still gaped, speechless for the first time since Jenny met her. The idea of letting the woman remain silent was forgotten as something clicked in Jenny's head.

'You said you've been following Terry's charity events?'

O'Connell stepped back as Jenny slid in front of Gwen.

'Yes?' The reporter's eyes narrowed.

'Were you covering his event in Adelaide, at the Osborne shipyards?'

'Yes.' Another slow, cautious reply.

'So he was there, on the 30th November 2015.'

'Why?'

O'Connell stepped in close to the counter.

'Just answer the question Gwen. We'll confirm it anyway, but you might save hours of police resources.'

The reporter's eyes opened wide.

'What's in it for me?'

'You'll find out soon enough.'

Gwen studied O'Connell, reading every micromovement. After being married, and unaware her husband at the time was gay, she likely knew better now how to read him.

'He was there.' She answered Jenny's question, not taking her eyes from O'Connell.

Was O'Connell's coming out the reason she was such a hard person to deal with? Was it a broken heart or was she always the type to take advantage of every person and situation she found?

Jenny thanked Gwen as O'Connell turned and strode to his desk.

'I want an exclusive...' She waved her arm in an erratic circle. 'In whatever this turns out to be.'

'You'll know as soon as we do.' Jenny promised as Gwen tottered away on her bright red stilettos.

As soon as she disappeared, O'Connell turned on her.

'What was that all about?'

Nellie entered the foyer.

'What was what all about?'

The last thing Jenny wanted to do was get Sam or Mick in trouble, but illegal gambling and mistreatment of immigrant workers was nothing compared to Maryam's death.

'I have a statement here which confirms Leigh Mundy is heading up an illegal gambling operation behind the scenes of these so-called charity events. Gwen has now confirmed Sullivan attended at least one of those events in Adelaide.'

'There's no proof he knows what Mundy is up to.'

'No.' Jenny crossed to her locker, retrieved her utility-vest and pressed her backpack inside before locking it.

'But it does link him to our victim, because this statement also confirms Maryam and Carmen were working at both events.'

O'Connell pointed to Sergeant Mackenzie's office.

'We better brief the Boss.'

Jenny led a procession to Sergeant Mackenzie's door and knocked.

'Come!'

Jenny smiled at the short reply. She pressed the door open and entered to find her boss rubbing the outside of his sling.

O'Connell crossed to sit on the edge of Sergeant Mackenzie's desk with a smile.

'Seems Williams is having an influence on everyone.' O'Connell pointed to the sergeant's sling. 'When Omar was waving a bottle at Sullivan did you ask yourself, *What would Williams do?*'

Her boss failed to rise to O'Connell's banter.

'Let's debrief. Last night was a long one.'

'How is your arm Sarge?' Jenny noted his pale complexion and mood. 'Did Nev give you antibiotics?'

'Of course he gave me bloody antibiotics.' He picked up a whiteboard pen, then realised he couldn't write with his left hand. 'Get us up to speed Williams.'

He tossed the marker to her.

'Okay. Sam and Mick attended three illegal gambling events hosted by Terrence Sullivan under the guise of a charity event.'

She wrote details of all three events on the board.

'Sullivan attended them all, but we can only tie Leigh Mundy and Dave, his big burly offsider, to the illegal operations. Sam and Mick confirm they cashed out their chips with either Leigh or Dave at each event.'

'Do we bring them in?' Phillips hovered with Nellie by the office door. Both watching the counter.

'Not yet.' Sarge turned to Jenny. 'What did you get out of the illegal workers?'

O'Connell twisted toward the whiteboard on the corner of Sergeant Mackenzie's desk. 'Not much from the three Nellie and I interviewed. They were all too scared to say anything. We've handed them over to Immigration.'

'Carmen was more forthcoming.' Jenny wrote Carmen's name on the board next to the passport photos. 'She confirms Maryam, or Katie as she knew her, trained them on how to deal cards. Tanya was also involved. But more importantly, she claims Leigh Mundy sexually assaulted her.'

'Maybe we *should* bring Leigh Mundy in.' Sergeant Mackenzie turned to Jenny. 'Do we have Carmen Perez's statement yet?'

Jenny shook her head.

'She was too rattled last night. I got her a room at Marj's to clean up and get some rest. I'll take a full statement today. She confirmed her arrival in Australia was four years ago. That matches with immigration records. She said she came to Coober Pedy fourteen months ago. That tracks with Sam and Mick's timeline of illegal gambling events.'

Sarge rubbed his forearm and sighed.

'I can't believe we've had an illegal gambling ring operating under our noses for over a year?'

'*Right* under our noses.' Jenny wrote a location on the whiteboards. 'The February event was held around the corner at the Royal Mail before it was closed for renovation. If last night's crowd is any indication, I think they host smaller versions of this event around the district for the FIFO workers regularly.'

'I'll be.' Sarge attempted to cross his arms then swore. His face paled and Jenny wondered if he was taking pain-killers. She was about to ask when he carried on talking.

'Phillips, get on to the previous owner. Find out if he sold it because he was trying to avoid hosting these events, like Marj has been.'

'I doubt they'll admit it, but Sam has signed a statement.'

Jenny didn't mention how Mick refused to. Mick was a problem for another day.

'We'll keep Sam's statement close to our chest for now. These union thugs can be vicious bastards,' O'Connell suggested.

Heads nodded agreement.

Sarge turned to Nellie.

'Any luck finding Flynn?'

Nellie shook her head.

'I spoke with the Umoona community uncles and aunties, and he's been walkabout for a few days now.'

'Walkabout? He's only a kid. How…'

Nellie interrupted Sarge.

'He's an independent little bugger, but I know a few of his mates. I'll see if I can find him. But he called 000. He may have witnessed the murder too. He's probably hiding for a reason, and he won't be easy to find.'

Sergeant Mackenzie nodded.

'Run Leigh Mundy's known associates and financials. Get a statement from Perez. With Sam's statement, we should be able to bring him in for questioning, but I don't want to tip him off too early. We need to find out where Sullivan fits into this.'

'Sullivan is Mikey's father. According to Carmen, Tanya has been mixed up in the illegal gambling for a while.

She's the link to nailing Sullivan. Find Mikey, we find Tanya,' Jenny offered.

O'Connell pulled a pad and pen from his top pocket.

'I'll put out an Amber Alert.'

Sarge studied the whiteboard a moment, nodded at O'Connell then turned to Nellie.

'You and Phillips find Flynn. He could be the break we need to nail a killer.' He turned to Jenny. 'O'Connell can run Mundy's details. You get Carmen Perez back in here to sign off on what she told you.'

'On my way Sarge.'

Everyone filed out of the office. Jenny held back a moment for the room to empty.

'You okay Boss?'

He nodded. She didn't believe him.

'Are you taking pain medication?'

'It doesn't sit well with me.'

His expression made her think about his drinking problem after his daughter died. She wondered if maybe he'd become addicted to pain medication at the time.

'At least take some paracetamol. It works well and it isn't addictive.'

He scrutinised her a moment, then nodded curtly.

'Go find a killer Williams.'

'You got it.'

Chapter 37

Jenny entered the motel reception to find Marj balancing precariously on a short ladder. A Christmas banner with crinkled, gold foil flags printed with scratched bright-red letters spelling out Merry Christmas, jiggled and twisted in her hand.

'Hey Marj.' She rushed toward the ladder. 'What do you think you're doing up there?'

The motel owner's red lipstick smile matched the red on the flags perfectly.

'Now, what does it look like I'm doing?'

Jenny stepped back to study the banner.

'Maybe I can get you a few new decorations.'

Marj levelled a puzzled gaze at Jenny.

'Why?'

'Well.' Jenny ushered the motel owner from the ladder with a wave and reached for the sad string of colour. 'These are a little...' She pointed to the damaged lettering. 'A little worn out.'

Marj stepped back, arms across her ample bust. Jenny's stomach tumbled as Marj's expression grew melancholy.

'They are vintage though.' She tried to brighten her tone. Marj remained silent. 'I'm sorry. Are these sentimental?' She hurried down from the ladder.

'Oh, it's alright Luv. You're probably right.'

'No. I shouldn't have said anything.'

Marj ambled to the step ladder and plonked down on the top rung.

'These old things have been around since Jason and I took over the motel.'

Jenny's stomach tightened at the mention of Marj's partner, long passed from cancer.

'Then keep them up. What do I know?'

'No.' She reached up and yanked them from the bulkhead. 'You pick something up for me. It's time to embrace a new generation. Something trendy. What are you young folks doing with decorations now?'

Jenny racked her brain to answer. What did she know about Christmas decorations? Her grandmother decorated the tree with homemade items from the grandchildren, and her mum was so busy on the farm when she was a kid, they were lucky if the Christmas tree even went up.

If she followed the trends, it would be all gold and white or blue and silver or carefully curated colour schemes suitable for Instagram or *Home Beautiful* magazine covers.

'I don't think the new stuff would suit the place Marj. How about you and I go through your boxes and see what else we can find? If we can't put something together, I'll check out the op-shop Monday.'

'But Christmas is next Sunday. I'm late enough with the decorations.'

'Maybe I can help.' Nick's smooth voice made Jenny spin to find him leaning in the doorway.

A slow smile crossed his lips as he strolled toward her.

'I overheard your discussion. I've got a huge box of decorations that survived the fire because they were in the shed.'

'Nick. I wasn't sure you'd make it this weekend.' Jenny wrapped her arms around his neck and kissed his lips lightly. 'But I'm glad you did.'

Nick held her waist, returning the kiss, 'Me too,' he whispered, then glanced over Jenny's shoulder as Marj spoke.

'But the box is all the way back at William Creek Station.' Marj wasn't complaining, but Jenny could hear the concern in her voice.

'We can grab them.' Nat appeared in the doorway, Benji right behind him.

'I thought you two were already out at the property.' Jenny hugged them both.

'Heading there now.' Nat rubbed his temples. 'Hit the grog last night after all the commotion.'

'It was a very slow start today.' Benji finished for his brother.

'I see.' Jenny grinned, then turned to Nick. 'Is Ben back on the property?'

'He will be soon.' Nick finished pulling down the old decorations without needing the step ladder. 'I spoke to him this morning. He said something about dealing with a personal issue first.'

Jenny frowned, but Nat interrupted her thoughts.

'Give us a drop-point on Google maps and we'll be on the way. Mum and dad are already pissy about us being late.'

'It did give them another chance to grab coffee at Nikolic's café though,' Benji added with a grin.

'Can't do a drop-pin guys. There's no reception out there.' Jenny unlocked her phone screen and brought up the map. 'But I'll show you how many k's Nick's front gate is from the Oodnadatta, Coober Pedy Road intersection. You can't miss it. There's a faded sign over the gate. Even I didn't get lost the first time I drove out.'

Everyone chuckled. Jenny turned to see Marj regarding her with smiling eyes.

'What?' She wrapped her arm around the woman.

'I wish you could have Christmas day here.'

'Oh Marj. Why don't you come out to William Creek and join us?'

Nick wrapped his arm around Marj's other shoulder.

'Jen's right. We have plenty of room.' He squeezed her shoulder. 'Join us.'

Marj swallowed hard as her eyes glistened.

'I'd love to.'

Jenny patted her arm.

'It's done then.' She turned to her brothers. 'You two bring back some decorations. Sam is out there.' She glanced at Nick who nodded. 'He knows where they are and when you get there, can you ask Ben,' she grinned, 'the other Ben, to give me a call?'

Both brothers saluted. Jenny gaped a second before realising she was in uniform. It felt odd to be giving her older brothers orders.

'Speaking of work.' She waved a hand over her utility-vest. 'I have to find someone.' She turned back to Marj. 'Which room did you give Carmen?'

'Room 10. But she's not there.'

Jenny's stomach knotted as she recalled Carmen's odd expression when the interview ended.

'Where is she?'

'Little Flynn, you know the Aboriginal kid who hangs around the place?' Jenny nodded, not trusting herself to answer audibly. 'I saw them talking outside the restaurant and they went for a stroll.'

Goosebumps covered Jenny's arms. Flynn called 000. He gave the drop-sheet to a killer. Was he leading Carmen away to her death? Surely not knowingly.

'Which way did they go?'

She failed to hide the urgency in her voice.

Marj shook her head.

'No idea Luv.'

Jenny pecked Nick's cheek, then squeezed between her brothers.

'I have to go.' She waved over her head. 'I'll see you as soon as I can.'

Chapter 38

Sweat soaked Jenny's shirt below her utility-vest as she jogged over the road to the Police Station. All she could think about was if Flynn was deliberately luring Carmen into danger, or from it.

A black F-250 parked up in front of the station as Jenny arrived. Her chest tightened when the electric window lowered to reveal Sullivan's scowling face. Mundy stepped from the driver's seat. The stocky guy, with the broken nose opened the front passenger's side, got out, but kept his distance.

Sullivan's finger jabbed toward Jenny.

'What are you doing to locate my son?'

Mundy glared at her. She held his gaze a moment before turning to Sullivan.

'Mr Sullivan, we are working several cases right now. If you have a complaint, you'll need to take it up with my commanding officer.'

'Don't get smart with me. Where's Tanya?'

'I have no idea, but we have an Amber Alert out for Mikey.'

'Amber Alert! You need to find Tanya—she's got my son. I have custody and she's kidnapped him.'

Jenny hesitated a moment. It was everyone's assumption Tanya took her son, but Sullivan's tone was too sure.

'How do you know that?'

He nodded to Mundy who withdrew a USB memory stick from his pocket and held it out to Jenny.

'Because we have video of her and some bloke taking him from the Sullivan residence while we were at the charity gala.'

Jenny suppressed a smile.

'Is that what you call it?'

'What are you implying?' Sullivan's indignant expression threw Jenny.

From the corner of her eye, she noticed Mundy shift his weight from one foot to the other.

An idea manifested in Jenny's head. She reached for the rear passenger side door handle.

'Maybe you should come inside Mr Sullivan.'

Mundy blocked her access, barring her way with his chest puffed out.

'Mr Sullivan is a busy man. You have your evidence. Find Tanya Rothchild, arrest her and get Mikey back.'

Jenny lifted her chin at Mundy. Neither of them budged as they read one another. The vein below his tattooed neck pulsed. For a moment, Jenny wasn't sure if he was going to attack her or run.

'Mr Sullivan.' Jenny peered around the tattooed arm into Sullivan's confused eyes. 'I really think you should come inside. We have a development in a case and it's linked to you and your organisation.'

The passenger side door thudded into Mundy's back.

'Leigh, move your arse.'

The bodyguard, come union site manager bared his teeth, but no sound left his lips as he stepped back and yanked Sullivan's door wide.

Jenny led the way inside, unsure if Sullivan was complying to cover his arse, or to find out what the development in the case might mean for the CWU.

His bewildered expression at her inuendo seemed odd considering she witnessed him threatening Ben last night. She couldn't shake the idea Maryam's murder was linked to Sullivan, through Ben's past.

She opened the foyer door.

'Come through this way Mr Sullivan.' She lifted the passthrough.

O'Connell glanced up from his computer screen in confusion.

'Senior, can you show Mr Sullivan into an interview room?' O'Connell lifted an eyebrow which she ignored as she turned to Mundy.

'If you can wait out here.'

'I'm not…'

'Leigh, it's fine. Take a break. You and Dave can grab a coffee or something.'

Sergeant Mackenzie opened his door and observed the discussions from afar a moment, then strode across the room.

'Actually,' Sarge pointed to Mundy. 'I think we might have a few questions for you too mate.'

Mundy tensed.

'Do I need a lawyer?'

Sarge grinned, but the mirth didn't reach his eyes.

'I don't know. Do you?'

Phillips and Nellie chatted as they entered the foyer but stopped as the collection of confused faces greeted them.

'Phillips, just in time. Can you show Mr Mundy to Interview Room 1.' He pointed. 'Nellie, you take Mr Sullivan to Interview Room 2.'

'Hang on a minute. I only came here to put a rocket up your butts. I want my son back and his bitch of a mother behind bars. Now your constable here said you needed to explain some sort of link between my organisation and an ongoing case.'

Sullivan searched faces.

'I'm not going anywhere until someone explains what the hell is going on.'

'Neither am I.' Mundy picked up the same tone as his boss.

'I don't know what Constable Williams was planning to discuss with you Mr Sullivan, but you,' Sarge pointed at Mundy, 'aren't going anywhere.'

'You can't keep me here.' Mundy crossed his arms over his chest and splayed his legs like a nightclub bouncer.

Sarge puffed out his chest. He wasn't a tall man, but his broad bulk made Jenny think of a bull. Instead of butting into Mundy, her boss leant in closely and hissed.

'I can arrest you if you prefer.'

'For what?'

'For the murder of Katie Montgomery, also known to our team as Maryam Suleiman.'

Chapter 39

Jenny's head was spinning as everyone filed into Sarge's office. She sat on the edge of the seat in front of Sergeant Mackenzie's desk.

'What's going on?'

'I just got off the phone with McGregor when you rocked up with those bozos. What did you bring them in for anyway?'

'Sullivan bailed me up outside with evidence proving Tanya and a guy took Mikey from his house during the charity event. I alluded to the event not being on the up and up. Sullivan didn't bite. Mundy, on the other hand was nervous as hell.'

'So what was your plan?'

'I didn't have one.'

'Nothing new there,' O'Connell chuckled.

Jenny rolled her eyes and continued.

'I thought if I could get them apart, I could tell Sullivan we have Mundy on the hook for illegal gambling.'

Nellie grinned mischievously.

'You wanted to see his reaction.' Jenny nodded. 'I like it.'

'I don't.' Sergeant Mackenzie grumbled. 'I've told you before Williams. Run your theories by me before you go off half-cocked.'

Jenny thought about arguing with her boss but decided it wasn't worth the effort. He wouldn't understand. She could barely explain her decision. All she knew was the moment Leigh Mundy and his offsider stepped from the F250, her gut spoke, and her mouth followed the order.

'Yes Sarge.'

O'Connell gave her a quizzical glance. She ignored him.

'What did Penny say then?'

Sarge sucked a deep breath in, fiddled with his sling absently and referred to a note on his desk.

'McGregor found traces of tattoo-ink in the samples taken from Maryam's fingernails.'

'That's hardly reason to arrest Mundy. He's not the only guy with tattoos.' O'Connell shared what Jenny was thinking.

'Correct, but we know Carmen claims he sexually assaulted her. We have him on the illegal gambling. Maybe he assaulted Maryam, and it went wrong. Let's apply some pressure and see if he pops.'

'He's getting edgy. I think he's ready to lawyer up.' O'Connell rounded Sergeant Mackenzie's desk. 'Is there anything else in the lab results?'

Sarge passed the notes to O'Connell.

'Not that I garnered, but Leigh Mundy doesn't know that.' A wicked grin crossed his face.

'You think you can bluff him?' O'Connell sounded dubious.

Jenny reached into her pocket and retrieved the USB stick.

'We probably should follow up on this.'

Sergeant Mackenzie shoved the device into his laptop.

'I'll take a look in a minute. Where's Carmen Perez?'

'I was on my way back to explain when Sullivan arrived. Marj saw Carmen talking with Flynn, now she's gone for a walk with him.'

'A walk!'

'Yeah, I was worried about them. Thought maybe Flynn was luring her to a killer, but when I saw the F250 turn up, I realised she's safe for now. All the suspects are here.'

'As far as we know.' O'Connell's words made Jenny's stomach knot.

It was true. Without a motive, anyone could be their killer. Anyone except Ben and Omar.

'Sullivan used Mikey to keep Tanya quiet. The victim was found in Tanya's car. Sullivan knows more than he's telling us.

'Mundy is in this up to his eyeballs,' Sarge rubbed the back of his neck. 'but I agree, we'll start with Sullivan.'

'Can I interview him?' Jenny sounded desperate, even to her ears.

Sergeant Mackenzie adjusted his sling and rounded his desk.

'You and O'Connell can do the interviews.'

O'Connell followed the sergeant into the main office. Jenny, Phillips and Nellie followed right behind.

The foyer was quiet. Dave, the spare wheel of Sullivan's entourage, scanned his mobile phone screen. He glanced up but returned his attention to something on his phone as Sergeant Mackenzie gave orders.

'Phillips, you and Nellie find Flynn. If Carmen isn't with him, find out where she is and don't let him go until we know who he gave the bloody drop-sheet to. We need to pull these threads together.'

'On it Sarge.' Phillips crossed to his locker.

Nellie a step behind, 'I think Eric might know where to find him. I've tried everywhere else, but Flynn is close to his uncle.'

'Uncle?' Jenny turned as Nellie pulled her utility-vest out. 'Like real uncle or you know, everyone's uncle?'

'Eric is Flynn's real uncle.'

'But Eric is Nev's half-brother.' Jenny's mind raced. 'Does Eric have other brothers or sisters?

Nellie laughed. 'Probably.'

'What the hell does it matter!' Sarge puffed out his cheeks. 'Nellie, find the little bugger.'

'You got it Boss.' Nellie checked out her service weapon and joined Phillips in the foyer.

'Williams. Get in and interview our suspects.' Sergeant Mackenzie pointed toward the interview rooms, then turned toward his office.

Jenny gave Nellie a final wave and caught Dave's eye. Sullivan's bodyguard or whatever he was, rose to his feet and lifted his chin in her direction.

'I'll go get that coffee then.'

Sergeant Mackenzie reappeared in the main office, laptop in hand and answered the question before Jenny could.

'Yeah. Why not.'

She watched Dave glance over his shoulder as he left.

'When you're ready Williams.' O'Connell called down the hallway.

'I'm coming.' Jenny hurried towards him, wondering for the first time how Dave might fit into all of this.

Chapter 40

Cool air pumping from the ceiling vents and the sound of chair legs scraping on the lino floor were the only sounds to break the silence. Jenny lowered into the seat opposite Terrence Sullivan without a word.

The CWU boss studied O'Connell as he readied the recording equipment. Jenny noted the man's calm exterior. As his eyes scanned the four grey walls and landed on her, she sensed his trepidation.

'Do I need to call Ms Buchanan back in?'

Jenny reached for a notepad.

'You're only here as a courtesy Mr Sullivan.'

'A courtesy.' His tone was flat, his expression thoughtful.

Jenny gazed at his plucked and tinted eyebrows, clean shaved face, stylish clothing and manicured fingernails.

Everything about the union boss made a mockery of the trade union movement.

Jenny nodded to O'Connell, who hit the *record* button and gathered his own pad and pen.

'Yes, but we will be recording this interview, for our own records.'

Sullivan sat back, eyes alert as he pointed to the recording equipment.

'You've not cautioned me, let's get that on record.'

Jenny plastered a smile on her lips.

'Of course. Let's get the formalities out of the way.'

She introduced herself, O'Connell and Sullivan for the recording.

'Mr Sullivan. Are you aware Leigh Mundy has been using your *charity* events as a front for illegal gambling?'

'Bullshit!'

It was the reaction she expected.

'I have a witness statement and I'm sure we can gather more, stating they bought in and were paid out by Leigh Mundy.'

And Dave, she thought to herself. She needed to run his record.

Sullivan crossed his arms over his chest.

'News to me.'

Jenny pressed on, hoping to read something in Sullivan's expression.

'The CWU isn't exactly squeaky clean, Mr Sullivan. Are you sure you don't know anything about it?'

'If I were running an illegal gambling racket, it wouldn't be in some backwater, outback desert shit hole like Coober Pedy.' Sullivan leant over the desk with his finger pointing at Jenny's chest. O'Connell stiffened but Sullivan didn't appear to notice or care as he carried on.

'And there'd be no way any of the elite high rollers *I'd* invite would be giving a bush cop a statement.'

Sullivan was right. Jenny also noted he didn't bite at her accusations of union corruption.

'So Leigh Mundy is operating alone?'

'He sure as hell isn't operating with *my* approval. I doubt he's alone though.'

'How so?'

'Sweetheart, I...'

'You'll address Constable Williams appropriately, Mr Sullivan.' O'Connell's tone was relaxed, but the vein pulsing at his neck said otherwise.

Sullivan nodded in O'Connell's direction, then returned his attention to Jenny.

'Sorry Constable. But if Leigh were operating illegally, and that's a big *if*, because one statement means nothing if this goes to court…'

Sullivan let the thought linger. The underlying threat wasn't missed by Jenny or O'Connell.

'Go on, Mr Sullivan.'

The union boss sat back and crossed his arms over his chest once more.

'If Leigh is running an illegal game behind the scenes, he'll need to handle a lot of cash, and he'd need someone to help him with it.'

'Okay. So let's say we believe you're not involved.'

Jenny knew it was unlikely, considering Sullivan's ex helped train the croupiers. But all their proof pointed at Leigh Mundy.

'How about a show of good faith?'

Jenny held her breath as Sullivan's expression grew sceptical. When he remained silent, she pressed on.

'We'd like Leigh Mundy's full employment history, including which projects he's worked on and where they were located, for the past four years.'

Sullivan's crass laughter peeled out so abruptly Jenny nearly jumped.

'I'm a union leader. You seriously think I'll let you access his complete employment history without a warrant.' He rose from his seat. 'We are done here *Constable Williams*.' He rounded the desk.

Jenny didn't intercept him. She'd expected him to refuse.

'Any further questions can come through my lawyer, but be aware, Ms Buchanan will eat you for breakfast if you don't dot every bloody *i* before you call.'

The interview door slammed.

O'Connell ended the recording.

'That went well.'

'I thought so.'

'How do you figure?'

'He didn't offer to get Leigh a lawyer.'

'True. But does that mean he isn't involved, or he's ready to let Leigh take the fall?'

Jenny rose and slid her chair back under the table.

'A question we should probably ask Leigh Mundy.'

Jenny opened the door to exit the interview and jumped back from the raised fist aimed right at her head.

'Geez Boss.' She held a hand to her chest.

'Sorry. I was about to knock.'

O'Connell peered over Jenny's shoulder.

'What's up?'

'I just finished viewing the video footage as Sullivan stormed out. Williams, you need to see this.'

All three hurried back to the laptop on O'Connell's desk. Sergeant Mackenzie sat in the seat, while O'Connell and Jenny hung over his shoulder.

'Sullivan is right. Tanya grabbed Mikey but look…'

He pressed *play*. Two figures, one carrying Mikey exited the rear sliding door of Sullivan's accommodation. The swanky BnB was known to Jenny from an earlier case. When it came to lush and private options, the Zen Yoga Retreat was about as good as it got.

'He installed security cameras around his room?'

'I wondered about that. Called the Zen manager and she said he paid her to install them. Win win she said.'

'So was he expecting this kind of trouble?'

'That's not the point Williams.' He pointed to the second person. 'Does he look familiar?'

Jenny leant across her boss, being careful not to bump his wounded arm, and hit *rewind*.

'It can't be him. He said he hardly knew Tanya.'

'Then he lied.'

Jenny's stomach knotted. It wasn't the first time he'd lied to her face. But if she got her way, it would be the last.

'I'll call Nick, see if he knows if Ben is back at William Creek Station yet or not.' She pulled her mobile from her pocket with shaking fingers. 'This must have been the personal business he told Nick held him up in town.'

Jenny dialled Nick's number.

'Is helping Tanya linked to Maryam's death?' O'Connell asked the question Jenny dreaded to hear.

Ben's name written inside the car boot. The engagement ring, ripped from the victim's finger. Ben helping a woman he claims to hardly know. Sullivan's threat and the speed-dial judge with a link to the Foresight Mining CEO.

Pieces of the puzzle were slipping together.

'I think this is linked to Ben's past.'

The phone in Jenny's hand continued to ring.

O'Connell rubbed his chin.

'How? We know Sullivan isn't the illegal gambling ringleader. Is Ben?'

'I don't think so, but Sullivan threatened Ben.'

'Why are we only now hearing about this?' Sergeant Mackenzies' tone was foreboding.

'Hey Jen.' Nick sounded puffed. 'Nearly missed you.'

'Where are you?'

'At the gym. Figured you were busy and it's bloody hot, so an airconditioned gym seemed like the best option.'

'Yeah, sorry about being back at work.'

'It's okay. Do you reckon you'll be good to come to the station tonight? It's only a week until Christmas and I don't exactly know your family very well. Entertaining them alone is a bit awkward.'

Jenny didn't want to answer his question because he wasn't going to like the answer.

'I'll try, but Nick, I'm putting you on speaker. I'm with Sarge and O'Connell. We need to find Ben.'

'Why?'

'He's gotten himself into a bit of trouble again.'

'What's going on?'

Jenny didn't want to keep Nick in the dark.

'Nick, he's helped Tanya Rothchild kidnap Mikey from his father. We need to find him. Is he back at the station yet?'

'No, that's why I need to head back tonight.'

'Do you know where he is?'

Jenny sensed Nick's hesitation and hoped Nick wasn't an accessory to kidnapping.

'I guessed the personal stuff was to do with his fiancé's death, but not this. I'll find him Jenny. But helping Tanya might be Ben's idea of payback.'

'It could be, but you need to be careful. We still don't know where Tanya fits in our current case.'

'But you said yourself she was just in the wrong place at the wrong time.'

Jenny swallowed hard at the two men staring over the laptop on O'Connell's desk. They were going to be pissed off to know she was talking to Nick about an ongoing case, but finding Mikey and the body in the boot was a tough day.

'Things have changed. Please let me know as soon as you find him.'

Nick drew a breath loud enough for Jenny to hold her own.

'Okay. I'll call you as soon as I find him.'

Chapter 41

Jenny ended the call and shoved her phone in her pocket.

'Nick is going to see if he can find Ben. Hopefully Tanya and Mikey are still with him.'

O'Connell rounded the desk.

'What were you saying about Sullivan and Ben?'

'You saw Ben at Marj's.' O'Connell nodded. 'He said it was too late to stop him doing something stupid.' O'Connell nodded again. 'Kidnapping Mikey is likely the stupid thing, but before he stormed out, I saw Sullivan make a throat cut sign across his neck, aimed right at Ben.'

Sergeant Mackenzie pressed his laptop closed

'A threat to keep quiet?'

Jenny nodded.

'Seemed like it to me. Now he's helping Tanya take Mikey. He might want to make sure she's safe before he reveals why Maryam was killed.'

O'Connell passed a manila folder to Jenny.

'Until we find Ben, we won't know. Sarge can make sure Phillips and Nellie know to keep an eye out for Ben and Tanya. But right now, we have a prime suspect to interview.'

'Once Carmen makes her statement, we have Mundy for assault. We have enough to charge him with illegal gambling. Even if we get a DNA match from the skin cells, we still can't prove he killed Maryam. And why dump her in Tanya's car?'

O'Connell pointed down the hall.

'All very good questions we'll be sure to ask.'

Jenny followed O'Connell into the interview room to find Mundy laid back with his feet up on the table.

'What does a guy have to do to get a coffee in this place?'

'We reserve the coffee for the torture phase of our interview.'

Jenny kept her face deadpan. Mundy took a moment, then smiled as O'Connell laughed aloud.

'Funny girl.'

She shoved his feet down as she sat on the plastic chair opposite.

'You're looking calm for a man arrested in connection to murder.'

'I didn't kill anyone.' He lifted his hands in surrender. 'Innocent until proven guilty. Right?'

'We'll be recording this interview, we'll caution you, run through the formalities and then finish with some questions.'

'Go for it.'

Jenny opened the manila folder O'Connell gave her, introduced herself and O'Connell and finalised the procedures to ensure whatever Mundy told them would be admissible.

'We have evidence that you and Katie Montgomery, also known as Maryam Suleiman, had an altercation shortly before her death.'

Mundy leant forward.

'What evidence?'

Jenny was surprised he didn't immediately request a lawyer.

'Our forensic team retrieved your DNA from under her fingernails.'

Not strictly true, but Mundy didn't know that.

The union thug bit down on the inside of his cheek. His nostrils flared as he fell back in his chair with arms crossed.

'We argued. What about it?'

'Maryam is dead Mr Mundy. What was your argument about?'

'Work.'

'The illegal workers or the illegal gambling?'

Mundy baulked but recovered with a sly grin.

'Neither.'

'Then what was the argument about?'

Mundy dropped his hands into his lap with an exaggerated sigh.

'What's in it for me?'

'What?' Jenny glanced at O'Connell to see what she was missing. His expression was as confused as hers. 'You fought with the woman before she died. If you have information clearing you of any wrongdoing, that's your reward.'

'I've got more than that.'

Jenny's heartrate quickened.

'I want immunity from prosecution relating to the illegal workers, gambling and any stupid accessory charges you can throw my way.'

O'Connell leant across the desk.

'This better be good.'

'Oh, it's more than good.' The smug expression was back. 'I can give you a witness to Katie's murder.'

Jenny fought to remain composed. It couldn't be that easy.

'And why have you kept this information under wraps all this time?'

'Everyone needs a *get out of jail free* card from time to time.'

'We'll need more than that.'

O'Connell's words nearly floored her. What was more important than finding a killer?

Mundy seemed as surprised as Jenny.

'Who's funding the illegal gambling?'

'I can't give you what I don't know.'

'What do you mean, you don't know?' O'Connell shoved a lined pad in front of Mundy. 'Who provides the workers and fronts the money?'

Mundy sat back casually. Jenny's heart thudded in her chest. Did O'Connell just blow their chance at finding a killer for information on a gambling ring?

'I'll give you everything and more, if you get my immunity and a new identity.'

The deep, rich sound of O'Connell's laugh unnerved Jenny.

'Mate. There are only a handful of people on witness protection in Australia, and I doubt you have enough to join the list.'

Mundy pursed his lips, but he wasn't concerned. His expression was almost sadistic.

'I can give you a killer, a gambling ring and corporate extortion at the highest level.'

Jenny's skin tingled as goosebumps covered her arms.

'What kind of extortion?'

'The construction and mining industry kind.'

Jenny thought her head might explode as she tried to digest Mundy's information. O'Connell kept a cool head. The CWU weren't linked to mining, but Mundy said construction and mining. Was he confirming a link to Ben and the AFP case?

'Give us the witness, before someone else gets hurt. We'll discuss the rest if it pans out.'

Mundy barely contained a smirk.

'The little abbo kid.'

Jenny was too shocked to correct his politically incorrect language.

'How do you know Flynn witnessed the murder?' O'Connell pressed on, unphased.

'I don't, not for sure, but I know someone who's been trying to find him for days and I don't think it's so he can run another odd job for them.'

An inexplicable chill ran down Jenny's spine.

'Who?' Jenny's voice quivered. 'Who's looking for Flynn?'

'Immunity.' Mundy's expression reflected his power.

Jenny returned it with her own contempt.

'Flynn is with Carmen Perez right now. If anything happens to either of them because you kept vital information to yourself, your deal will be off the table, and we'll be adding manslaughter to your charges.'

Mundy's eyes widened. The chill returned but was quickly replaced by a slow throbbing, building at the back of Jenny's skull.

'Where does Carmen fit into all of this? Is she in danger too?'

'Immunity.'

O'Connell stormed to his feet.

'You heard the constable. Where does Carmen fit into this?'

Mundy rolled his lips, then licked them repeatedly.

'If Flynn is harmed...' Jenny repeated.

'*She's* the Boss. Carmen is the Boss.'

Jenny tried to hide her shock. Carmen was the victim. Her passport was held with the others. Her stomach tossed as she studied Mundy's expression and recalled Carmen's odd smile at the end of her interview.

'Like, boss of the gambling?' She needed clarity. She needed to know she didn't totally misjudge Carmen.

'She's the boss of everything.' The smirk on Mundy's face made it obvious he knew he'd shocked Jenny. Leaning forward, he pointed beyond the interview room walls. 'Follow her trail if you can find it.'

He scoffed as though the challenge was outside their skillset.

'All roads from Carmen lead right to the very top.'

Jenny shoved her chair back hard enough it hit the interview room door. On her feet, now she loomed over Mundy with every inch of her six-foot frame.

'And Tanya. What about Tanya?'

Mundy dropped back in his chair unphased.

'She's Sullivan's whore. Pure and simple.'

'But she knows who's in charge of the gambling ring. She trains the croupiers.'

Mundy crossed his arms.

'I'm done talking until that immunity agreement is signed, sealed and delivered.'

Jenny flung the door open before O'Connell could end the recording. She vaguely heard him wrapping things up as she ran down the hallway.

'What the hell?' Sergeant Mackenzie surged to his feet.

'We need to raise Nellie and Phillips on the UHF. Flynn is in danger, and I think I know where we'll find Ben and Tanya.'

Chapter 42

Sergeant Mackenzie surged to his feet and grimaced as he lifted his injured hand to halt Jenny's advance.

'Hey. Slow Down.' He met her in front of her locker. 'Talk to me.'

Jenny forced herself to take a deep breath.

'Carmen and Flynn were seen leaving the motel over an hour ago. Mundy told us Carmen is the ringleader, not Sullivan. And Flynn might know who killed Maryam.'

She flung the locker door open, scrambling around for her utility-vest, Taser and left the door hanging open as she rushed to clip her radio mic to her lapel.

'Mundy could be yanking your chain.'

Jenny shook her head.

'I don't think so. Tanya isn't talking, but she must know what's going on. I think she convinced Ben to help her get Mikey in exchange for what she knows.'

Jenny didn't wait for a reply. The more she considered Carmen's tears, the more she realised the woman played her. Vulnerable immigrant, at the mercy of the big bad guys. She fell right into it.

'Phillips, this is Coober Pedy station. Come in.'

As Jenny spoke into her mic, O'Connell marched Mundy into the hallway

'I'll get this one back into holding.'

Sergeant Mackenzie nodded as the Senior Constable disappeared down the hallway, then turned to the weapons safe on the back wall.

Unlocking it, he handed Jenny her service weapon, then retrieved an M4 rifle along with his own pistol. He shrugged out of his sling and tossed it onto O'Connell's desk before shouldering the rifle.

'Your hand's not better yet,' she protested.

'Better enough.'

Jenny nodded, then tried the radio again.

'Phillips…'

'Receiving you Coober Pedy Station. What's up?'

'Have you found our missing person?' Jenny checked her weapon and slipped it into the holster at her hip.

'Roger that. We are at the Royal now. Witness confirms he's inside.'

'Proceed with caution.' Jenny reached for O'Connell's vehicle keys and left the station without bothering to check to see her boss was right behind her.

The reply was delayed.

'Say again?' Phillips' tone conveyed confusion.

'Proceed with caution. Suspect is with our missing person.'

Another moment passed before his reply.

'Roger that.'

Jenny considered how to proceed, then pressed the lapel mic.

'We are one minute out and will approach from the East.'

'We'll give you five, then proceed from the West entrance.'

'Roger. And Phillips, keep an eye out for uninvited guests.' Jenny failed to still her nervous energy as Sergeant Mackenzie locked the station door and joined her in the Police Landcruiser.

'Let's go Williams.'

Jenny slammed the vehicle into drive and gunned the motor, kicking up dust in her wake.

'I can't believe she fooled me.'

'Get over it Williams. You're not infallible. It won't be the last time.'

Jenny glanced at her boss before turning into Wright Street. The Royal Mail hotel came into view on the corner of Paxton Street.

'This is where Mikey was left. The same place Sam attended an illegal gambling night, and Zeigler's parking fine was for the adjoining carpark. Are they still using this place?'

'Right around the corner from the station,' Sarge scoffed. 'A little ironic when you think about it.'

She parked the vehicle in front, knowing there was no way to approach the location unnoticed. The vacant land next door provided an unobstructed view from the disused motel and shops up and down the road in all directions.

'Who's the unexpected company?' Sarge checked his service weapon, then added a clip to the M4 and checked the mechanical safety was engaged.

'Ben.'

'Ben?'

'It's just a gut feeling.'

'The infamous Williams' gut.' Sarge tried to lighten the mood as they exited the vehicle.

'I hope we aren't too late. Flynn left with Carmen nearly two hours ago.'

'Can only do what we can do Williams.'

Sarge shouldered the rifle and cautiously approached the tall, chain-link fence surrounding the dormant work site. A printed banner, featuring the planned renovation, obscured their view beyond.

White spots dotted Jenny's vision. She forced herself to breathe as her boss reached a chained gate.

For a moment, her heart sank. Precious time would be lost going back to the vehicle and getting bolt-cutters or a battery powered angle grinder, and the noise would alert Carmen.

She breathed a sigh of relief as the chain slipped free to open a wide gap.

A long, rickety veranda stretched out beyond the barricade. Boarded-up shop windows and dry-rotted posts precariously held the upper storey balcony in place.

Sarge stalked along the covered concrete, stepping around gaping holes in the surface and cautiously assessed the danger.

Jenny repeatedly scanned their rear, above and past any gap in the window coverings until they reached double glass doors, lined with black builder's plastic. She knew the former entrance opened into a foyer, with a wide staircase rising through the centre.

Sweat broke out on her hands, but a chill ran through her body despite the heat. Sergeant Mackenzie retrieved the rifle from his shoulder, clicked the safety off and brought the weapon to his cheek.

She placed her hand on the left door handle and turned to her boss.

'Ready?' she whispered.

Sarge's head nodded over the butt of his rifle.

'Let's do this.'

Chapter 43

Jenny drew her weapon, tested the door was unlocked with a slight tug, then flung it open. Sergeant Mackenzie focussed through the rifle scope as he stalked into the foyer. Jenny entered a heartbeat behind, scanning over her pistol sight to the right of the foyer.

Her muscles tensed as she checked up the stairwell, to her right and down past the stairs to the derelict arcade beyond.

Checking to her left, she noticed Sergeant Mackenzie doing the same.

Neither spoke as they nodded the approach was clear. Jenny wondered how Carmen managed to get Maryam's body into the car boot on her own. If she had help and it wasn't Mundy, who was it?

She brushed the thought aside as she stepped onto the first stair rung. Her instincts screamed they were already too late.

If Carmen was mopping up loose ends, Flynn might already be dead. Were they going to find his lifeless body upstairs?

Glancing to her left, she saw the same stern expression on her boss's face. But she wasn't giving up. Nodding, she let Sarge lead the way. One careful step at a time, they ascended the chipped tiled staircase

As her head poked above the upper landing, she halted and scanned the area. An expansive room, full of broken timber, torn floorboards and hanging wire greeted them. With the demolition well underway, hiding places were limited.

Her dry mouth begged for water as she tried to swallow.

Sergeant Mackenzie advanced past the broken balustrading. She followed, carefully watching where she stepped on the damaged floorboards.

A vintage reception desk spread out across the entire foyer. Jenny recalled the former grand chandelier and worn rich-blue carpet. Gaping holes and exposed copper pipes replaced a wall of leather wrapped pigeonholes.

Jenny raised her weapon, held it out before her with both hands and stalked to the right side of the polished, ornately carved bench. The hairs on the back of her neck struggled to rise against the heavy sweat.

Sergeant Mackenzie approached from the other side. Jenny focussed over her weapon, picked her way with each step and tried not to hold her breath as she rounded the counter.

The crash of timber and breaking glass made her heart pound. She fought the urge to spin toward the sound. Instead, she focussed on clearing the bench first.

Her head throbbed. The tendons in her neck tensed. She stepped into the space beyond the counter and almost giggled with relief.

Her boss lifted his rifle barrel. Jenny turned to see Phillips and Nellie approaching from the rear external stairs.

'Clear your end guys,' she called out, 'but I think we are too late.' As the words left her lips, the gravity of them hit her hard.

'Let's check every corner.' Sergeant Mackenzie nodded to his left.

With the walls free of plasterboard or linings, it was clear there was no threat, but her boss was right. Everywhere needed to be checked. The thought of finding Flynn dead, shoved somewhere under demolition debris gripped her heart.

Fighting her emotions, she followed Sarge, preparing herself for the worst possible outcome. As they entered and cleared each room, hope bloomed in her chest. Flynn was a survivor. He roamed free throughout the harsh local desert country every day of his young life.

If anyone could escape danger, it was Flynn.

'Williams.' Sergeant Mackenzie halted, bent down over a pile of fabric and turned to Jenny.

One unsteady step at a time, she joined her boss to lean over his shoulder. Nausea swept through her stomach at the sight of the shiny red basketball jacket Flynn lived in, lying in a crumpled heap.

Sarge lifted the jacket with the muzzle of his rifle and let out a puff of air.

'He's been here, but he's gone now.'

'Thank God.' Jenny turned toward Phillips and Nellie as they approached from the other side of the vacant building site.

'I thought Eric said Flynn was in here.' She failed to keep the frustration from her voice.

Nellie holstered her pistol and lifted her hands in surrender.

'Hey. Don't shoot the messenger. He was outside, loaded up a bit as usual but he said he saw Flynn go inside.'

'Was that before or after his last blackout?'

'I get you're annoyed Jen. I'm pissed off too. Eric is bedding down in the carpark out back for the night. We can interview him again.'

'Okay ladies.' Sergeant Mackenzie lifted both hands like a boxing referee. 'Williams, you quiz Eric again. See if you can nail down a timeline. Take Phillips. Nellie, you're with me.'

Jenny swallowed her anger.

'We need to dig deep into Carmen's background.'

Sergeant Mackenzie rolled his eyes at her.

'Williams, I know you're upset you fell for Carmen's lies, but I've been doing this a while.'

'Sorry Boss.'

Sergeant Mackenzie nodded.

'You and Phillips handle Eric. Nellie, let's go. We'll run Perez and see if we can find Flynn.'

Sergeant Mackenzie scanned the faces of all three constables.

'Flynn is quick on his feet. He's all right team. I can feel it in my old bones.'

The comment lightened the mood. Even Jenny let herself laugh, but deep down, she hoped her boss was right.

Chapter 44

Jenny and Phillips picked their way down the rickety rear fire-exit stairs into the Royal Mail carpark. Beyond the pitted bitumen and faded lines, a worn timber fence gaped with human sized holes.

Ducking through, Jenny stepped into the rear dirt block as the sun cast its final glow on the horizon. Illuminated against the fading orange and purple light was a bundle of canvas, lying flat beyond the chain and timber boundary fence.

She waited for Phillips to join her before approaching Eric. He wasn't known for becoming violent, but it was wise to be cautious.

'Eric.' She stepped closer, Phillips strolled along beside her. 'You awake mate?'

The bundle of canvas heaved as Nev's half-brother rolled over with a groan.

'Bugger off.' A dark hand protruded from the swag and waved to reveal the lighter coloured skin of his palm. 'No more bloody...'

A heaving sound turned Jenny's stomach.

The moan that followed filled her with concern. Eric might have an alcohol problem, but she'd never seen him vomit in public before.

'You alright Eric?'

The unmistakable reek of cheap spirits wafted her way, but another smell followed as she reached for the torch on her utility-vest.

'Eric. Do you know where you are?'

Eric didn't respond as Jenny crouched down and reached for his arm, hanging limply outside the canvas swag. She recoiled as clammy, cool skin greeted her.

Jenny tried to still her own rising heartrate as she fumbled to locate Eric's pulse. Finally, an erratic beat pulsed in his wrist. She desperately tried to count them. Then turned to Phillips.

'Call an ambulance.'

'He's just drunk Jen.'

'No. Call the ambulance. I'll call Nev.'

Phillips reached for his lapel mic as Jenny dug into her pocket, retrieved her phone and dialled her roommate. It answered on the second ring.

'Jen. What's…'

'It's Eric.'

'Great!'

'No, Nev. It's serious. Is Eric diabetic?'

'Of course. Who isn't in his situation?'

'Nev. I've called an ambulance, but you might want to get out here. I think Eric is falling into diabetic shock.'

'Can you smell a sweet smell on his breath?' Nev's tone was suddenly all business.

'Yes.'

'Shit. It's not shock. He needs insulin. Where are you? I'll be there in five.'

'Out at the Royal Mail Hotel.'

Rustling fabric and keys jingling told her Nev was on the move.

'Jen.' His voice made her jump.

'Yeah.'

'Don't move him. You understand. Unless he stops breathing, *do not* move him. If the ambulance beats me there, tell them he's slipped into diabetic ketoacidosis.'

The call ended.

Jenny gaped at the phone screen, then turned to Phillips.

'Did you hear that?'

He nodded, barely visible in the fading light.

'Ambulance is on the way.' He reassured her.

She was torn between finding Flynn, staying with Eric and helping Nellie and the team figure out where Carmen could be when Eric spoke.

'Big white fella.'

Jenny hunkered down low to hear Eric's words.

'What big fella Eric?'

The ambulance siren filled the hot, still night air. Carpark dust lifted as Nev's ute slid to a halt seconds before the ambulance.

'I need fluids with an insulin infusion.' Nev called to the paramedics as he crossed the carpark and crouched down beside his brother. 'Thanks Jen. I've got him.'

The hoarse note of Nev's voice made her eyes sting with hot tears. As much as Eric and his vices annoyed Nev, they were brothers first.

'Come on Jenny.' Phillips dragged her to her feet. 'We've got to find Flynn.'

'Flynn?' Nev reached for the saline bag and cannula in the paramedics outstretched hand. 'Get me some light.' A high voltage spotlight fell over them. 'What about Flynn?'

'Don't worry Nev. Focus on Eric.' Jenny patted his shoulder. 'We'll find Flynn.'

'Hang on a sec.'

Nev expertly slid the cannula into Eric's arm, attached the bag of fluid, checked a syringe of insulin and injected it into the solution, then turned to Jenny.

'What's Flynn done?'

The urgency in Nev's voice confused her. Was it concern for Eric or something else? As Nev hoisted the bag up and waited for the paramedic to take hold, Jenny mulled over how much to share with Nev.

Nellie said Eric was Flynn's uncle. Was Nev also his uncle?

'He might be a witness in a case we're working on.'

Nev sighed with relief, then turned back to his patient with his stethoscope in hand.

'What's his BP?' He spoke to the paramedic using an automatic machine to take Eric's obs.

'200 over 120, but it's dropping.'

Nev drew a deep breath, then turned back to Jenny.

'I saw Flynn about an hour ago, when I came off shift at the hospital. He was with Nick's manager.'

'Ben?' Nev nodded. 'Where did you see them?'

'He was catching a lift out on the Flat Hill Road.'

Jenny turned to Phillips.

'That's West of here, right?'

'Yep. He must have headed out that way from here.'

Nev peered up from his patient.

'I figured Ben was giving him a lift to Umoona, on the way to William Creek Station.'

Jenny squeezed Nev's shoulder.

'Thanks Nev. At least we know he's safe with Ben.'

'Safe?' Nev pushed to his feet. 'What's going on?'

Jenny swallowed hard.

'The case Flynn might have witnessed is serious.'

Nev grabbed Jenny's arm and led her away from the paramedics, as they continued to monitor his brother.

'The body in the boot,' he hissed.

'We think so.'

Nev rubbed his hands down his face and blew out in frustration.

'Who is Flynn to you? Nellie said he was Eric's nephew.'

Nev's expression was difficult to see in the fading light, but everything about his stance made Jenny's stomach lurch.

'Flynn is my son.'

'He's what! Why the hell doesn't he live with you then?'

'It's a long story Jen.' He glanced back at Eric. 'I need to finish up here, but can you keep me in the loop? Find Ben, find Flynn. Make sure he's okay and when you find him, I'll be there to help you get a statement.'

Jenny rubbed the back of her neck. For nearly two years she and Nev lived in the same house. Not once did he allude to having a son.

'I'll call you when we get a hold of him, but Nev, he's still in danger. Ben has no reason to hurt Flynn, but the information Flynn has might make Ben do something stupid.'

If it hasn't already. Jenny kept the thought to herself.

'If you have any idea where they might be going, you need to let me know.'

Nev shook his head against what should have been a magnificent sunset.

'No idea. Like I said. I thought he'd go to Umoona.'

Jenny bit her tongue. She knew Nev was a player when she met him. His casual relationships came into focus on her first case in town. The fact he was a dad shouldn't surprise her.

Still, she thought he trusted her enough to share something so important. She reminded herself Nev's private life was his business.

'I'll keep you posted.'

'Thanks Jen. I mean it.' He squeezed her forearm. 'For Eric and Flynn.'

Jenny nodded. Nev let her arm go.

'Let's go.' Jenny strode toward the police vehicle. Phillips jogged to catch her.

'Where to?'

'Back to the station. I'll see if Nick managed to track Ben down. Maybe Sarge dug up some background on Carmen. If she murdered Maryam, someone must have helped her put the body in Tanya's boot.'

Jenny couldn't help wondering if she may have misjudged Tanya after all. She certainly missed the signs with Carmen. Ben picked Flynn up. Was he working with Carmen and Tanya or was he too now in danger?

Phillips unlocked the Police Landcruiser.

'She might have forced the victim into the boot, then killed her.'

It was possible. But the victim was bound hand and foot. Doing that inside the boot would have exposed Carmen to an attack. Jenny's instincts assured her Carmen needed an accomplice. Maybe more than one. She only hoped Tanya wasn't one of them.

Chapter 45

The headlights of the police Landcruiser caught a figure waiting outside the police station. Phillips barely drew the vehicle to a standstill before Jenny flung the door open and met Nick at the glass entry door.

'Hey. Did you find Ben?'

'No. But I fitted all the vehicles with GPS tracking in case of a break-down on the property. I've found the car, but not Ben.'

'Where?'

Phillips approached them.

'You two coming in?'

She nodded, then followed her partner, Nick close behind her.

'It was parked at Ted's Garage, but they were closed, so I'm not sure if he was having engine trouble or what was going on.'

'I'll get on to Jed, see if he booked the Troopy in for repairs. If he did, maybe Ben has a loan vehicle.'

'Jen.' Nick's tone sent a shiver down her spine.

She stopped in the foyer, allowing Phillips to carry on and turned to face her fiancé.

'What's up Nick?' she whispered, aware of the audience at her back.

Nick glanced over Jenny's shoulder and stepped in closer so as not to be overheard.

'Last time I spoke to Ben, he sounded wired. I think he's going to get himself in trouble.'

Jenny nodded.

'I almost guarantee it. You know him better than me after working with him for a year. But he said something the other day at Marj's that makes me think he hasn't managed to cut his ties with crime.'

Nick opened his mouth to profess Ben's innocence but she didn't let him.

'I know what you're thinking. He's likely tried to break free. But whoever has a hold on him isn't letting go. I think Katie was collateral damage.'

The engagement ring tossed in the boot of Tanya's car. Ben's name written on the inside of the boot with the victim's own hand, when in reality, she was dead before she was put in the boot.

And putting the body in Tanya's car, knowing she would discover it. It was a warning, to Tanya and Ben. She was sure of it now.

'Ben wants revenge, and I think he's willing to do anything to get it.'

'But he doesn't know who killed Katie any more than you do.'

Jenny rolled her lips. Nick read her expression.

'Do you know who killed her?'

Jenny shook her head.

'Not for sure. But we know Flynn likely witnessed the murder.'

'And Ben has him.'

'Williams!' Jenny spun at Sarge's tone. 'We've got leads to run.' He waved a piece of paper aloft. 'Phone records to request.'

'I'm sorry.' Jenny gripped Nick's arm. 'I need to get back to work. Are you staying tonight?'

A smile crept across Nick's face.

'I'll grab you all something to eat from Marj.'

Jenny leant in and kissed his cheek.

'Thanks. It's going to be another long night.'

'Williams!'

'Coming.' Jenny hurried across the foyer, rounded the counter and ripped the paper from Sergeant Mackenzie's fingers as O'Connell hung up from a call.

'That was Nev.'

Jenny suppressed a rush of guilt over how quickly she'd forgotten about Eric's health.

'How's Eric?'

O'Connell gave her a thumbs up.

'He's on the mend. Nev said thanks and he also wanted to let us know what Eric said when he came around.'

Jenny stopped typing.

'He was pretty out of it when I found him, but he did mumble something about a big white fella.'

O'Connell tapped his nose like she hit the mark, spot on.

'Not just any big fella. Eric said he heard a woman yelling out for someone to grab the kid.

'That makes sense. I wondered about an accomplice?' Jenny scanned the paper in her hand absently.

'Seems so. Eric said Flynn took off past him like a roo in a spotlight.' He grinned. 'Those were his exact words.'

'And there was someone with Carmen when she chased after Flynn?'

'Yep. Dave.'

'The same Dave who heard us talking here in the foyer?'

O'Connell nodded.

'Yep. He would have heard Flynn was with Carmen and knew Nellie and Phillips were on the way to find him.'

'He was on his phone in the foyer. He likely contacted Carmen. But she was with Flynn for over an hour before Dave heard us talking. If she was the killer, he would be dead already.'

'Maybe. Killing someone in anger is one thing. Killing Flynn would be premeditated. You need a cold heart and steely resolve for that.'

Sergeant Mackenzie scratched the back of his head with his uninjured hand.

'I want everything we can find on Carmen Perez and Dave,' the sergeant huffed. 'Does anyone bloody know his last name?'

Nellie waved with her back to the counter computer screen.

'I might be able to help there.'

Jenny abandoned the phone records and crossed to Nellie, O'Connell two steps behind.

'Who is he?'

Nellie pointed to the screen.

'I checked known associates of Leigh Mundy, nothing. So I dived into the construction union membership database.'

O'Connell tutted over Jenny's shoulder.

'You hacked it?'

Nellie laughed.

'Hell no. I wouldn't use a government computer to hack anything.' She pointed to a document on her screen. 'This is a copy of the committee minutes, leaked to a blogger friend of mine who investigates shonky corporate organisations.'

'And the CWU is about as shonky as they get.' Jenny pointed to the document. 'Is that what I think it is?'

'It is. Meet David Boyle. Member of the executive committee for the CWU.'

'Are you sure? We only have his first name and the thug hanging around Sullivan seems more like a bodyguard than a union leader.' O'Connell barely got the words out before the screen populated with dozens of images.

'I did a search on the internet. Took about 2 seconds to bring up images of the CWU membership committee.' Nellie pointed. 'This one is straight off the governance page on their website.'

'That's him.' Jenny crossed to her computer. 'I'll search for a police record.'

'Done!' Nellie hit *print* and the laser printer whirred under the counter. 'I also found he's unofficially affiliated with the Harlequin outlaw motorcycle gang.'

O'Connell lifted the piece of paper from the printer.

'And it keeps getting better and better.'

He passed it to Sergeant Mackenzie, who scanned the single sheet before casting his eyes to the ceiling.

'You've got to be kidding me.'

His frustrated tone made Jenny swallow hard before asking.

'What?'

Her boss rolled his shoulders and met Jenny's confused gaze.

'David Boyle did time with Ben Stokes in Paramatta.'

Jenny covered her mouth with her hand.

'I knew Ben was hiding something about his past.' Her palms grew sweaty.

'Are we sure Ben is after Flynn to find Maryam's killer? Or to help Boyle mop up a mess?

Chapter 46

Jenny grabbed the keys to the Landcruiser from behind O'Connell's desk and turned straight into Sergeant Mackenzie. Her boss crossed his arms over his chest, winced at his cut hand, but continued to bar her way with his broad shoulders.

'Where do you think you're going?'

'To find Flynn.'

'Don't be stupid Williams.'

O'Connell cleared his throat.

'What Sarge is saying, is you could drive around town all night and not find him.'

A thought popped into her head.

'We have a palm print from the donga where we found Maryam's floral top. We need to run it against Dave Boyle. If he has a record, we have his prints in the system.'

'It's too late to get McGregor now, but I'll put a request into the lab. Maybe the night team will get to it. But it will only prove he was connected to the workers, not our victim specifically.'

O'Connell was right. Jenny swallowed her frustration.

'Nick found the vehicle Ben was driving parked outside Ted's Garage. I need to call Jed to see if the car broke down and if Ben borrowed another vehicle.'

O'Connell pointed to Sergeant Mackenzie's office.

'Williams, grab the whiteboard out here. We need to work with what we do know.' He pointed to Phillips. 'Call Jed's after-hours tow number and find out if Ben has a loan vehicle.'

Phillips lifted the counter phone handset with a wave.

'On it.'

Jenny rolled the whiteboard out into the main office.

'I don't believe Ben is helping Carmen and Dave with this. When I spoke to him at Marj's, he said he wanted to take back control of his own life. He was done with the AFP, us, and his past. I think his past is directly connected to this gambling ring.'

Sergeant Mackenzie rubbed his chin, then nodded.

'He deliberately left us in the dark about how he met his fiancé and where she worked.'

Jenny nodded agreement.

'I think Ben knew Maryam before he moved here. He arrived a little over a year ago, around the same time we know the illegal gambling operation relocated here from Adelaide.' Jenny tried to piece things together in her head. 'I think Ben has been trying to get away from his past for a while. We can't ignore the link between Ben and Boyle and the Harlequins!'

'It's way outside our purview Williams.' Sergeant Mackenzie snatched the whiteboard marker from the rail. 'But we'll add the link. If it's relevant to the murder case, we'll be able to follow it up, but either way, the AFP need to be looped in on this now.'

'AFP aren't sharing much except to say the investigation has gone cold. Nick told me he was asked to get close to Ben. I hope he isn't so close he's missed something.'

'The AFP keeping everything compartmentalised is standard practice.' O'Connell turned to Nellie. 'I think we can push for a warrant to get Boyle's and Ben's phone records. Compare them to Tanya's once they come in.'

'They'll be using pay-as-you-go phones.' Nellie didn't hide the frustration from her voice.

'Probably right, but it's procedure. A shame we haven't found the victim's phone.' He turned to Jenny.

'Track down Maryam's financials and trace her known previous addresses since she left her husband. And go over the medical examiner's reports on our victim again. See if they've narrowed down a murder weapon.'

Jenny sat down at her computer and opened the postmortem file. A recent update caught her attention. She opened it and glanced up to O'Connell.

'Wooden fibres were found in the victim's face wound, but the lab is waiting on species.'

'That's something.' O'Connell returned to his own work as Phillips hung up the phone.

'Jed said he wasn't open this afternoon. He's waiting on a secure transport to take the VW away to Adelaide for evidence, then the cleaning crew need to pressure wash the place. According to him, it stinks too much for him to work in there.'

'I can attest to that,' Jenny agreed.

Her partner's brow was creased with worry.

'Should we do a drive by?'

Sergeant Mackenzie tapped his lip with the whiteboard marker in his left hand.

'What are you thinking?'

'With Tanya's car still impounded at Ted's Garage.'

A stone thudded into Jenny's stomach.

'You think Ben broke in to steal it?'

'Tanya probably has spare keys to it,' Phillips offered.

'Good call, Phillips.' Sergeant Mackenzie turned to the whiteboard and awkwardly circled the registration number for Tanya's vehicle. 'You do a drive by and see if it's still there. Call it in as soon as you get there.'

'Will do.'

Jenny tossed the keys she'd stashed in her pocket, to Phillips.

'Nice work.'

Her partner snatched the keys from the air and grinned.

'Let's see if it goes anywhere before we celebrate.'

Jenny returned her attention to scanning the autopsy report, confirming the possible wooden object could have been an axe handle, baseball bat or similar. There was nothing else helpful in the report.

She began checking Tanya's phone records again, letting her mind attempt to put the puzzle pieces together. If Ben knew Maryam before she came to Coober Pedy, he could have been the one to get her the job with Carmen's team. Did he know Carmen was in charge?

Not likely. The woman went to great lengths to blend in with all the other illegal workers. The passport in Zeigler's office. Working alongside the other women at the gambling tables.

But Ben did time with Dave Boyle. Sullivan appeared to have Judge Povich, the sister of the CEO of Foresight Mining, Jamie Povich, on speed-dial when he needed a favour.

Jenny reminded herself the CWU and Foresight Mining were the AFP's responsibility, but she couldn't let this all go. What affected Ben, affected Nick too.

Puffing out a frustrated breath, she began checking Maryam's driver's licence records for past addresses. Considering the woman changed her name, she wasn't expecting to find anything.

Her phone buzzed in her pocket.

She withdrew it and scanned the caller ID.

'Ben?'

Chapter 47

Jenny sensed everyone turn her way at the mention of Ben's name.

'Jenny. I'm sorry. I should have…' A high-pitched scream made Jenny's blood run cold. 'Where are you, Ben?'

The sound of grunting kicked Jenny's adrenalin into gear. She raced behind O'Connell's desk and grabbed his vehicle keys as muffled voices and the slap of flesh on flesh filtered down the line.

'Ben! Tell me where you are?'

The radio squelched behind O'Connell's desk.

'Coober Pedy Police. Come in.'

Jenny recognised her partner's voice over the crackling line as O'Connell dived for the radio mic.

Jenny blocked one ear, desperately trying to focus on Ben and the continuing grunts and moans.

Sergeant Mackenzie tapped her on the shoulder.

'Ted's Garage.' He hoicked his thumb in O'Connell's direction, then handed over her service weapon. 'Phillips is there.' He pointed to the phone in Jenny's hand.

'Hang on Ben. We're on the way.' She kept the phone line open as Sarge snatched the keys from her hand, shouldered the M4 he used earlier and strode from the station.

'What about me?' Nellie was on her feet, rushing for the lockers.

'Stay here. Listen out for the radio Constable.' O'Connell's tone was clear as he checked his own weapon out and followed Jenny through the foyer.

Jenny empathised with Nellie but understood O'Connell's orders. Nellie was less than six months out of training. A police stand-off was no place for a rookie.

They were going in with no idea who was armed, and with what. Was Ben a good guy, or a risk? He phoned her. Jenny's gut said he wasn't going to hurt anyone except the person who killed his fiancé.

'This is a mess.' Jenny slipped into the rear passenger's side as O'Connell accepted the keys from their boss. The siren began wailing before they left the parking spot and drove down the lane next to the station.

As the police Landcruiser turned from the laneway onto Malliotis Boulevard, Jenny caught sight of Nick through her side window. Turning, she watched him rush into the station, arms full of takeaway boxes from Marj's restaurant.

She pressed the phone back to her ear as the police vehicle slid sideways into Wright Street.

The line was dead.

'Phillips heard yelling when he arrived at the garage.' O'Connell kept his eyes on the road as he spoke. 'A quick peek inside, found Tanya, Ben, Flynn, Carmen and Dave all inside. He called right away.'

'That must have been when Ben called me.'

The vehicle tyres squealed. Sergeant Mackenzie reached for the handle above his door.

'What did he say?' His voice was eerily calm.

'Sorry, then a fight broke out.'

'Sorry, like I killed a girl or sorry I didn't call you earlier.'

'The latter, I think.'

Nervous energy vibrated through her body as O'Connell slid the Landcruiser around another corner. This wasn't the first time the Senior Constable drove like he stole it. But this time, her fingernails weren't gripping the seat. This time, she was leaning forward, urging him to go faster.

Phillips came into view below the strobing red and blue lights of his vehicle. O'Connell's high-beam fell on the rear barn doors, wide open to expose the cargo area. Phillips retrieved a rifle and slung it over his shoulder as O'Connell yanked the handbrake on.

Jenny was first out. Sarge and O'Connell seconds later. They converged on Phillips as one. He passed her a rifle.

'Dave has a pistol, not sure if Carmen is armed. Ben is out cold, and Tanya was screaming like a stuck pig until a minute ago. Then it all went quiet.'

'Our siren might have spooked them.' O'Connell refused a rifle. 'Is there a rear entrance?'

'Jed isn't here yet,' Phillips offered.

Jenny knew the garage well. More than a dozen times she'd spent hours in there with Penny, going over vehicles from various crime scenes. She recalled the big rig with human remains in the grill and stifled a shiver.

'I know there's a rear door, but it could be locked.'

'Get around back and check. Take Phillips,' Sarge ordered, then turned to O'Connell. 'You and me on the front door.'

O'Connell nodded, slipped his weapon from his utility belt and cautiously followed Sergeant Mackenzie. Jenny swallowed hard, unclipped the holster tab on her pistol, then positioned the rifle strap over her shoulder and hoisted the weapon into position.

A car pulled up behind the two police vehicles as her bosses moved into position. Red and blue police lights continued to strobe over the scene, revealing a figure rounding the bonnet of his Landcruiser ute.

'Stay there Nick. Please!'

She watched him cross his arms and lean against the bonnet. Then she turned to Phillips.

'Let's go.'

He nodded as she led the way past the closed roller doors and down the side of the high roofed shed. Two industrial bins pressed against the shed wall, leaving a narrow gap between them and the chain-link fence.

The tall boundary fence was well over Jenny's head and featured razor wire. There were no obvious holes or damage to allow escape.

She flicked a switch to turn on the tactical light at the side of the M4 and stalked into darkness. Her heartbeat hammered in her ears. The vein on her neck pulsed with every footfall.

Jenny reached the rear door and waited. A firm, quick tap on her shoulder from Phillips told her he was right behind her, and they were clear to proceed. Releasing her hand from the rifle trigger, she reached for the doorhandle and twisted.

Finding it unlocked, she whispered without turning to Phillips.

'On three.'

'Got it.'

'One. Two. Three.' She ripped the door open. Phillips rushed in. Jenny one step behind.

'Police. Stay where you are! Hands in the air!'

The bright shed lights ruined Jenny's night-vision for a split second. Her heart thudded in her chest. The front door burst open. Sergeant Mackenzie and O'Connell barged in screaming.

'Police! Put your hands up!'

Silence greeted them.

Chapter 48

Jenny dropped to her knee and scanned under the various vehicles parked in the mechanic bays.

Nothing. Nobody in sight.

She wondered how they slipped away, then shook her head. They couldn't have. They had to be in here somewhere. Armed and waiting.

Goosebumps tingled her skin as her stomach flip-flopped nervously.

Sergeant Mackenzie was first to move. Barrel raised, he crept toward a Nissan Navara on a car hoist. O'Connell circled the late model Isuzu truck in the adjoining shed bay.

Jenny rounded a vintage truck to find Ben, unconscious on the ground. Tanya's VW Passat a few metres away with the driver's side door hanging open.

'I've found Ben.'

She rushed to his side and checked for a pulse.

'He's alive!'

O'Connell joined her, then reached for his lapel mic.

'I'll call an ambulance.'

The sound of metal hitting concrete made Jenny spin on her haunches.

'Where did that come from?' She lifted the rifle to her cheek and cautiously rose.

Sergeant Mackenzie used his rifle barrel to point toward the back of the shed. Jenny stalked past the Isuzu truck. Sweat rolled down her forehead, stinging her eyes.

'Put the ambulance on standby.' O'Connell instructed down the radio mic, then lifted his own pistol and followed Jenny.

Phillips tracked wide, covering the space between the truck and where Ben lay unconscious.

Sergeant Mackenzie held back, rifle aimed and ready, then called.

'Boyle. Carmen. We know you've got Tanya and Flynn. You need to let them go and come out, with your hands up.'

A muffled squeal made Jenny drop to one knee and search below the truck. Her barrel swung from the differential, past the rear wheels, then back to the front wheels. She turned to O'Connell in confusion.

'I can't see anything.'

'Bloody little…' The harsh voice trailed off. A thud made Jenny spin back in time to see a flash of shiny red fabric scurrying out the other side of the Isuzu.

'It's Flynn.' She lowered her rifle and rounded the truck. 'Flynn, wait. It's the Police.' The figure whizzed past Phillips, who lunged but missed.

Flynn was out the rear door before Phillips could clip his rifle safety on.

'Damn.' He slung his rifle over his shoulder. 'I'll get him.'

Another scream dragged Jenny's attention back to the concrete below the truck. Wooden boards ran along what must have been an old mechanic's pit, boarded up years ago when the hoist was installed.

She pointed to the rough sawn timbers with the muzzle of her rifle. Sergeant Mackenzie frowned, then nodded he understood what she was seeing.

'Boyle, Carmen. We can do this the easy way, or the hard way.' Jenny stalked down the side of Isuzu truck, stopping at the front wheel. 'There are three fully armed police officers here. Give yourselves up before someone else dies.'

Jenny's heart thudded in her chest. Her palms were damp with sweat, but she didn't dare remove them from her weapon to wipe them.

O'Connell manoeuvred into position on one side of the truck. Sergeant Mackenzie held back to cover the exits.

'Let Tanya go, and come out with your hands in the air,' Jenny called.

Seconds passed. Jenny hoped her partner caught up to Flynn. Even if he did, would Flynn give them what they needed to put Maryam's murderer away for good?

A plank of wood on the pit wiggled beneath the Isuzu truck.

'Alright. We are coming out.' Carmen's voice sounded shaken as a hole appeared under the truck.

The plank of wood slid to one side, then another. Two raised hands appeared, then a head. Carmen crawled from the hole, then Tanya.

'Boyle!' O'Connell's tone made Jenny shiver. 'Don't make me come and get you.'

The sound of an ambulance siren peeled out beyond the shed.

Jenny shouldered her rifle, pulled her pistol from her waist belt and indicated with the barrel.

'Carmen, Tanya, on your knees, put your hands behind your head.'

O'Connell focussed his weapon beneath the truck as wide hands with thick fingers preceded Dave Boyle's head appearing from the mechanic's pit.

Jenny's stomach knotted.

'Where's Mikey?'

Tanya dropped to her knees without protest.

'Tanya.' Jenny waited. Tanya remained silent, refusing to make eye contact. Jenny reached for her right hand. 'I need to cuff you, until we know what's going on. But where's Mikey?'

Tanya's shoulders sagged and her limbs went limp as Jenny zipped the cuffs into place. Changing tack, she reached for her metal cuffs and crossed to Carmen.

'Where's Mikey?'

Carmen pressed her lips closed in a thin, fake smile. Jenny grabbed her arm, wrenched it down and behind her back. Carmen howled as Jenny cuffed the first wrist, then dragged her other hand behind her to secure the cuffs.

'Slowly,' O'Connell ordered as Dave's bulky frame crawled out from under the Isuzu. 'Keep your hands where I can see them,' he ordered again as Jenny pulled Carmen to her feet by her bound wrists.

Sarge stepped forward and relieved her of her prisoner as O'Connell secured cuffs on Dave. Jenny dropped to her hands and knees, pulled her torch from her utility-vest and scurried toward the edge of the pit with her weapon and the torch extended.

As her torch beam scanned the greasy pit walls, her heart sank.

'What have you done with Mikey?'

Her question was met with silence.

Chapter 49

Jenny crawled out from beneath the truck, opened the driver's side door and climbed into the cab. There was nowhere Mikey could hide inside. Jumping down she met Sergeant Mackenzie's concerned expression with one of her own.

O'Connell attempted to use his police-issue cuffs on Boyle's wrists but quickly realised the man's bulky forearms and giant hands were too large. Sarge tossed him a pair of zip-tie cuffs as he helped Mikey's mother to her feet.

Flashing lights strobed through the open doorway, silhouetting Phillips as he returned empty handed.

'Flynn is in the wind.'

Jenny continued to scan under the vehicles, and in every corner.

'I can't find Mikey Sarge.'

Boyle sneered at Jenny as O'Connell marched him toward the exit.

'We'll find him Williams.' He nodded toward Tanya. 'See what she knows.'

'Nothing. That's what she knows.' Boyle growled the words out as his eyes met Tanya's.

Mikey's mother dropped her head, eyes hitting the floor. All Jenny could see was the woman's scraggly blonde hair creating a wall of silence—one she was going to struggle to break through.

Phillips waited with Tanya until their other suspects were removed. Jenny hated the idea of treating her like a suspect, but there wasn't a choice. The woman was keeping secrets. Lots of them. From the moment they brought her in for questioning after the accident, she'd been evasive.

Now her son was missing *again*.

'Tanya!' Jenny approached. The woman continued to stare at her feet.

'Tanya. Look at me.' Jenny dipped low, hoping to catch her gaze. The wall of hair remained impenetrable. 'Where is Mikey? Is he back with his father?'

Still no reply. Jenny resisted the urge to grip Tanya's biceps and shake her.

'Tanya! Is he safe?' The panic in Jenny's voice was obvious.

Where was the feisty woman who bashed on Mrs Farrell's window?

Paramedics hurried into the garage, reminding Jenny Nick's farm manager was injured. Ben moaned from the ground, blood pouring from a slice to his forehead. At least he was conscious. Maybe now they'd get some answers.

She returned her attention to Tanya.

'We can help you, but only if you tell us everything you know.'

Tanya lifted her face to Jenny with an expression too difficult to read. They needed a miracle to get this woman talking.

'We'll give you some time to think, but if you know where Mikey is, tell me. I'll make sure he's safe.'

An emotion washed over Tanya's face. One Jenny could finally read. Until Mikey was safe, there was nothing coming out of Tanya's mouth.

Jenny waved for Phillips to take her away.

'I'll check on Ben and meet you out front shortly. Can you check on Nick for me?'

A relaxed grin crossed her partner's face.

'Do you think he stayed put?'

Jenny thought about the time Nick didn't wait for her to contact him on the radio. The day he was shot and nearly bled to death on Murphy's kitchen floor.

'I hope so.'

Phillips eased Tanya toward the exit as Jenny crossed the grease-stained concrete floor.

'How's he doing?'

The paramedic gave a curt nod.

'He's stable. In and out of consciousness. I think he'll have concussion, but we need to do x-rays to make sure he hasn't got a cracked skull.'

'Thanks. Ask the emergency team to let us know when he's cleared to talk to us.'

'You got it.'

The team lowered the gurney in preparation to transfer Ben, as Jenny turned to examine the scene.

She wasn't a forensic tech like Penny, but during her time in Coober Pedy, she'd spent many hours combing through crime scenes with her friend.

As she circled the VW Passat, all she could think about was how Ben sustained the head injury. Was it here? If so, then he was either slammed into a solid object like a pillar or one of the vehicles. Or he was struck by something?

Dropping down to her haunches, she studied underneath Tanya's vehicle. Finding nothing of interest, she straightened and circled the car, meticulously watching for anything out of the ordinary.

The concrete floor was stained with various colours. Likely oil, or automatic transmission fluid or any number of other motor vehicle type substances, but an odd shaped dark spot caught her eye.

Crouching down, she confirmed her suspicions. Rising, she followed the trail across the open space between the hoist and the truck over the pit. The droplets weren't large, supporting Jenny's theory they were likely from Ben's wounds.

The trail guided her toward the rear office. A flicker of hope filled her heart. Maybe Mikey was hiding here? In all the commotion, they didn't search this area. Why would they? All the suspects were accounted for.

Maybe Mikey hid in the office. A flurry of hope was washed away as she realised Tanya would have said something if Mikey was in the building. No one in their right mind would want a toddler to be left alone here.

One step at a time, she followed the blood drops to the office. The hair on her arms rose at a sound beyond the open door. Instinctively, she slipped her weapon from the holster.

The thud of each heartbeat rushed through her ears. Jenny reached the open doorway to find a shadow hovering beyond the obscured glass panel in the door.

'Police!' She lifted her gun toward it. 'Show yourself.'

No one spoke. No one came into view. Jenny lifted her lapel mic.

'This is Williams on scene. I have a code 20.'

She debated physically going to get her partner. The dark shadow pressed between the door and the wall, rustled, making the decision for her.

She was out of time. Whoever was hiding there could be armed. She could be in danger.

With both hands on her weapon, she kicked to shove the door hard against the wall, hoping to catch whoever was hiding behind it off guard. The rippled glass shattered as the door struck whatever was beyond.

Commotion broke out behind her as Phillips yelled for the paramedics to get down.

Her partner was behind her in seconds. Just in time to see the coat rack, shrouded with a full-length oilskin Driz-a-Bone poke out beyond the shattered glass.

Jenny shoved her pistol back into the holster as laughter peeled out behind her.

'You'll take a while to live this one down.' Phillips lowered his own weapon.

The coat rustled.

Phillips lifted his pistol once more and rounded the door. A ginger cat rubbed up against his leg and purred.

'That makes two of us.' Jenny pointed to the ground. 'I was following a blood trail. I think this is where Ben was hit.'

'Do we leave it for forensics?'

Jenny shook her head.

'No, we need to secure it first.' She retrieved her weapon and stepped over the blood and broken glass.

Phillips followed her.

The office was crammed with rusted, dirty filing cabinets, a long bench with a kettle covered in greasy fingerprints. The desk at the side of the room was piled high with invoices, mechanical instruction manuals and more than one mug with half drunk, congealed milk scum on top.

Phillips drew up behind her and gagged.

'That's foul.'

'Can't disagree with you there.'

Jenny holstered her weapon and rounded the desk to find more blood. This time it wasn't on the ground.

'I think we've found the weapon that struck Ben.'

Phillips joined her.

'Yeah, but there's too much blood on that cricket bat to be from Ben's injuries.'

Jenny nodded as she reached into her vest pocket for a pair of gloves.

'I think we might have found our murder weapon.'

'In Jed's office! You're not saying Jed did this?'

Jenny rolled her eyes at her partner.

'No. I think one of those four people out there.' Jenny pointed, then suddenly recalled the flash of red track pants, racing from the scene. 'Or…'

Phillips holstered his weapon with a smile.

'I know that look. What are you thinking?'

'I'm thinking no killer leaves a murder weapon, covered in blood, out in plain sight.'

'You're right. They would have cleaned it, then tossed it or burnt it.'

'Which means, someone took it before they got the chance.' Jenny reached for the bat, lifted it then turned toward the doorway. 'And I think I know who that someone is.'

Phillips followed her out.

'Flynn!'

'Exactly. Let's secure this evidence, then we need to find Flynn.'

Chapter 50

Phillips carried the carefully wrapped cricket bat into the police station. Jenny followed with a mix of energy and frustration. The lingering aroma of what was now a cold dinner, reminded her Nick was yet to return her text.

He was gone when she exited Ted's Garage. According to O'Connell and Sergeant Mackenzie, he was gone when they loaded their prisoners into the paddy wagon Nellie drove out to the scene.

'Hey.' Nellie glanced up from behind the counter, then stuffed spaghetti Bolognese into her mouth and spoke over it. 'Your pasta is in the fridge when you want to heat it up.'

'Thanks Nellie.' Jenny's appetite was gone. 'Where's Tanya?'

She was desperate to find Mikey. Despite the warm night, the boy was only a toddler. He might not freeze to death, but dehydration was a real fear.

Nellie pointed her pasta-loaded fork toward the interview rooms.

'In Interview Room 1.'

Jenny glanced at her phone once more to read her text message to Nick.

Where did you go?

Still no reply.

'Williams.' She turned to O'Connell with a frown. 'Get the bat off to forensics, pronto, then we need to take another run at Tanya.'

'She's not talking until we find Mikey. Did anyone see if Sullivan knows where he is? I'm really worried about him.'

O'Connell nodded.

'We did. He wasn't too happy we brought Tanya in without Mikey.'

Sergeant Mackenzie strode from his office.

'And he's throwing his weight around, threatening to call in a few favours and get us all sacked.'

Jenny passed O'Connell's desk on her way to her locker.

'Of course he is. Instead of being productive and spending his energy searching for his son, he's having a go at us.'

The Senior Constable's spaghetti was almost gone, but the aroma made her stomach growl aloud.

'You should eat.' O'Connell pointed down the hallway to the break room.

'I'm good.'

'Just eat, Williams. It's been a bloody long night.' O'Connell's smile softened his words.

'And it's not ending anytime soon.' Sergeant Mackenzie lifted the marker pen from the shelf below the whiteboard. 'Grab some food Williams. We're all tired, but no one is going home until we interview our suspects about the whereabouts of Mikey Rothchild.'

'What about the murder?'

'We need a forensic report on the cricket bat and more evidence before we consider questioning them about murder. Without Flynn's statement, we only have conjecture. Unless Ben and Tanya can shed some light on things.'

Jenny understood what the sergeant was saying. Boyle could easily claim he was chasing down Sullivan's son and his kidnappers.

Without Flynn or some real physical evidence, they had nothing concrete. Boyle would be out on bail by Monday.

'I also want a statement from Ben and Tanya about his attack, and Mikey's kidnapping. If Sullivan decides to press charges, they might both end up in prison.'

Jenny's stomach knotted.

'That's hardly fair.'

'But it's the reality Williams.'

'I know. I don't have to like it though.' Jenny glanced at the clock on the wall. 'I'll eat, but then I'm going on the hunt for Flynn. I'm not sure if he saw the murder, but if the cricket bat is our murder weapon, I believe Flynn is the reason it ended up in Jed's office.'

O'Connell tossed the takeaway container in the bin.

'Let's see what the lab says first.'

'Should Jed be on our suspect list?' Phillips joined the conversation. 'He's lived in town as long as me.'

Jenny thought about the greasy haired local. Jed wasn't too bright. He was a little creepy at times, but she didn't believe he was a criminal mastermind.

'We should rule him out. Does he have a criminal record or links to any of our suspects?'

'Nope.' Nellie tapped her screen. 'He does have an outstanding speeding fine though.' She grinned.

'Let's leave the speculation for now Williams.' O'Connell pointed toward the break room once more. 'Food.'

'Excuse me!'

Everyone turned to identify the voice coming from the front counter. Sergeant Mackenzie rushed to turn the whiteboard around as Nellie abandoned the stool and attempted to block the woman's view.

It was after 11pm and the lawyer, peering around Nellie for a last second view of the whiteboard, appeared to have been woken from sleep.

'I'd like to see my client.'

Nellie turned to seek guidance. Jenny joined the new constable and studied Sullivan's lawyer a moment before recalling her name.

'It's been a busy night Ms Buchanan.' Jenny's tone was mildly sarcastic.

The woman's chest rose as she reset her shoulders and lifted her button nose into the air.

'My client is David Boyle. I represent all CWU members, and he is currently being detained without charge. I'd like to see him now.'

Jenny wondered how the lawyer knew Boyle was in holding. Then recalled the fact an ambulance, two police Landcruisers and a paddy wagon with lights and sirens likely woke half the town.

Still, she needed clarification. The timing was odd.

'How do you know he hasn't been charged?'

The lawyer's smile failed to reach her hazel eyes.

'Because if you'd charged him, he would have called me himself.'

This woman reminded Jenny of Samantha Hayes—the lawyer who was now doing time for her part in the murder of Melinda Smart. Hayes was connected to the Harlequin outlaw bikie gang. Maybe this lawyer was too. Boyle certainly was.

'O'Connell, show Boyle's lawyer through to Interview Room 2.' Sergeant Mackenzie opened the passthrough to Jenny's right. 'Phillips, bring him up from holding.'

'You got it.' Phillips disappeared past Sergeant Mackenzie's office toward the holding cells.'

'Jenny!'

She turned as she recognised Nick's voice. But it was Flynn who caught her attention. Nick coaxed the walkabout kid by the scruff of his shirt into the foyer.

'Flynn.' Jenny rounded the counter. 'Where the hell have you been? Why did you run off?'

Flynn's smile widened and his dark eyes sparkled with mischief, but his sense of humour evaporated when his eyes landed on something behind Jenny.

He backed up into Nick, then attempted to dart around the grazier, but Nick was expecting the move.

'No you don't little guy.'

Flynn squirmed, then wailed at the top of his lungs.

'Hey bub.' Nellie joined Jenny. 'Flynn. Nick's not going to hurt you mate.'

Flynn scratched at Nick's hands. Jenny turned back to the counter in search of Flynn's distress. She eyed the lawyer's grim expression but realised quickly the cause of Flynn's fear. Behind Ms Buchanan, being led down the hallway in handcuffs, was a broad, angry figure and he was staring daggers at the struggling Aboriginal kid who was desperate to make his escape.

Chapter 51

Jenny was shovelling the last mouthful of her pasta into her mouth when Nev rushed into the foyer.

'Where is he?'

'He's safe Nev.'

The comment was true. Sergeant Mackenzie formally charged David Boyle with Maryam's death. His lawyer ranted for a full ten minutes but left shortly before Nev arrived.

For now, Flynn was safe, but unless they got him talking, holding Boyle was going to be impossible.

'Can I see him?' Nev's usually calm manner was replaced with a contorted expression and breathlessness.

Jenny tossed her rubbish in the bin and lifted the passthrough to let Nev in.

'Absolutely. And convince him to talk while you're at it. Nellie tried. But he's being stubborn. We can only keep him safe if we get the evidence to keep our suspect in a cell.'

Nev licked his lips as his brow furrowed.

'I'll do my best, but Flynn and I aren't exactly best friends.'

That went without saying. The kid was a juvenile delinquent. According to Nellie, even the Elders at the Umoona Community were struggling to decide what to do with him.

'Nellie and I'll be in there with you, but we believe he knows who killed our victim and he's avoided us and hampered our investigation at every turn.'

'He's just a kid.' Nev sounded defensive.

'Yeah. A very clever one. But Nev,' Jenny gripped her friend's arm, preventing him from racing down the hallway to the interview rooms, 'the guy who killed Ben's fiancé is connected. Flynn is in danger if we can't keep him locked away. We need to know everything he knows.'

'If the guy is that connected, Flynn will be in danger no matter what.'

Nev was smart. Jenny should have known better than to think he would miss that fact.

'I can't go into details, but if we have enough to bury this guy, there is a very good chance the AFP will roll the suspect for more information relating to other criminal activities.'

Nev rolled his shoulders and nodded.

'Let's give it a go.'

Jenny opened the interview room door to a wave of cool air. Nellie sat across from Flynn with coloured pencils and paper strewn between them.

'Hey bub.' Nev rounded the table, slid out the chair and nervously sat. His dark brown eyes focussed intently as he leant toward Flynn.

'You doing okay?'

Flynn shrugged and kept his eyes on the red pencil moving back and forth over his picture.

Worry lines spread across Nev's face.

'I'm sorry I didn't know you were in a bind until Jenny told me earlier today.'

Another shrug.

Jenny puzzled over Nev's uneasy posture and absent smile. Now father and son were side by side, she could see the resemblance and wondered again why he never mentioned he was a dad.

'Hey Flynn. I know you're probably tired.' Jenny passed a packet of cheese snacks across the table. 'Are you hungry?'

Flynn's eyes narrowed at the offering. He was only ten. Was he old enough to fully understand the gravity of what he'd witnessed?

Jenny thought about her own childhood and what she remembered when she was ten. Probably not. But it was her job to get the information without scaring the kid. She wondered if they should be calling in a child psychologist but dismissed the idea.

The window to hold Boyle was closing and they needed to know where Mikey was being kept before something horrible happened.

Thinking of the toddler gave her an idea of a safe, neutral place to start her interview.

'Do you know where Mikey is?'

Flynn stopped scratching his pencil on the paper and lifted his eyes to Jenny's. A frown knitted his thick eyebrows together.

'The little boy who was with Ben when he picked you up.'

Flynn went back to colouring the picture of Michael Jordon reaching for a slam dunk.

'Flynn, he's not quite two, and he's very scared by now. He was with his mum, but now he isn't and the police need to find him.'

Flynn worked the bright red pencil over the Nike shoes on the cartoon figure's feet.

'Hey bub. You don't want anything to happen to Mikey mate.' Nev glanced at Jenny as he spoke. 'I know his mum will be really worried about him.'

Flynn lifted his chin and glared at Nev. That look cut Nev deeply. Flynn was challenging his father with a question. *Did Nev ever worry about him?*

Flynn returned his attention to colouring-in. Nev placed his hand on Flynn's forearm to make him stop.

'I get why you're angry. I've been busy with work but…' Nev let go of Flynn's arm and scratched his forehead as though searching for words. His eyes fell on Nellie.

She shook her head. A silent conversation passed between them. Jenny tried to comprehend it but failed.

'No excuse. I get it. But this little boy's mum wants him home safe mate. Tell Jenny what you know about Mikey. Before something terrible happens to him.'

Flynn swapped pencils for another colour and for a moment, Jenny thought he was going to continue ignoring Nev. His answer surprised her.

'*His* dad picked him up.'

Nev frowned. Jenny wasn't sure if the expression was the message or the tone it was delivered in.

'Flynn. How do you know his dad picked him up?'

'A fancy big black F-250 took him. Heard 'em talk'n to Tanya.'

'What did they say?'

'Said he was gone for good if she didn't keep her mouth shut.'

'Did you see the man in the F-250?'

Flynn nodded.

'I'll get a photo.'

Jenny rose as her mobile buzzed in her pocket. She checked the caller ID and wondered why Marj was calling her so late.

'I'll be right back.'

She left the interview room, raced to her workstation to get a photo of Terry Sullivan printed and answered the call as she got there.

'Marj. Thought you'd be in bed.'

'I'm not that old Luv. You remember I put my feelers out to see if there was another bar in town, or anything weird going on, before all the trouble with the union guys came knocking.'

'I do. What have you found?'

'Tracey, from the Underground Motel gave me a call. Seems there was a late check-in tonight.'

A late check-in didn't seem worth a call at this hour, but Marj never missed details.

'You think it's related to the Union thing?'

'I know it is. After everything went sideways Friday night, I got the warning out to everyone. The guest who checked in was a single woman with a toddler.'

Jenny's pulse kicked up a notch.

'And you'll never guess who paid for the room.'

'Terry Sullivan.'

'I knew you'd guess. Just love saying that,' Marj chuckled.

'Thanks Marj. I owe you one.'

'No Luv. If you can get these guys out of Coober Pedy and if possible, behind bars, I'll rest a lot easier at night.'

Marj's tone made Jenny's blood run cold.

'Marj. You said Sullivan didn't exactly give you a choice with the charity event. Did he, or one of his boys threaten you?'

'It was that Leigh Mundy fella, but Sullivan knew what was going on.'

'Thanks Marj. We'll have this wrapped up very soon.'

Chapter 52

Tanya beamed as she hugged Mikey to her chest. The little boy showed his blue teddy to his mother and chatted in his own language.

Jenny slid a takeaway coffee cup toward Tanya.

'Thank you,' Tanya whispered and Jenny knew it wasn't for the drink.

Her heart ached, but this little reunion was going to be short-lived if Tanya didn't cooperate.

'Don't thank me yet.' Jenny sipped her caramel latte. Wishing she'd asked for a double shot.

Tanya glanced up with a creased brow, then lifted her nose in the air.

'I know there's a price. But I'm willing to pay it.'

Jenny nodded for Nellie to start the recording equipment and went through the formalities.

'What can you tell us about Maryam Suleiman's murder and the illegal gambling activities in Coober Pedy?'

'Only what I know.'

Jenny sipped her coffee, savouring the sweetness. She let the flavour wash over her, aware this entire interview would snatch her serenity away any moment.

'Let's start with how Maryam Suleiman's or Katie Montgomery as you knew her, how her body ended up in your car.'

'I don't know exactly. I picked my car up from the wreckers and I was on the way back when I crashed.'

'Why did you go to the wreckers?'

Tanya's expression grew confused.

'To pick up my car.'

It was early Sunday morning, and Jenny was tireder than she could ever remember. Either she was missing something, or Tanya wasn't the brightest.

'Tanya, how did your car end up at the wreckers?'

'Oh. Sorry. Katie was at my house Monday night. Ben gave her the engagement ring on Friday, but she didn't wear it at work over the weekend. Kept it hidden so the bosses wouldn't find it. Only a few of us girls knew she was engaged.'

Jenny had a theory about why the engagement was kept secret, but now wasn't the right time to pursue it.

'We were celebrating with a few drinks and then she took a call.'

'She had a mobile phone?'

'Yeah. She got super upset. Said she needed to go, but I'd picked her up and I was too drunk to drive. Third strike and all, so I gave her my keys.'

'What time was that?'

'No idea.'

'You said you picked her up. Where from?'

Tanya stroked Mikey's thick dark hair absently.

'Carmen's place.'

'So Carmen was Katie's friend?' Jenny's theory was coming together in her head.

'Sure. Carmen, Katie and me got together sometimes. We kept our distance from most of the workers because they came and went and we didn't want to know too much.'

'You knew they were illegal?'

Tanya shrugged.

'Not for sure, but I reckon Carmen did. She worked for Boyle way before I met Terry and Katie joined after me.'

'Katie started in Adelaide, right?'

'Yes.'

'Did you ever meet Ben in Adelaide?'

Tanya frowned.

'No. Katie met Ben here.'

'You're sure?' Tanya nodded. 'Who introduced them?'

Ideas were forming in Jenny's head faster than she could process them on the lack of sleep and food.

'Carmen I think.'

Ben's connection to Boyle and the mining company extortion made it clear he likely knew what Carmen and Boyle were up to in town. Was it all linked to the federal police investigation?

She shook the thought aside. Her jurisdiction was the murder. She needed to focus.

'Did Carmen know they were engaged?'

'Yes.' Tanya's tone turned sorrowful. 'She was one of us. We thought… Katie told us over the weekend.'

'Was Carmen celebrating with you?'

Tanya shook her head.

'Please answer for the recording.'

'No.'

'Why did you leave it until Wednesday afternoon to pick up your car?'

Tanya passed a piece of cheese to Mikey, lifted her coffee, sipped and pushed it far enough away the boy couldn't accidentally knock it.

'Because I didn't know where it was until Carmen told me to pick it up from the wreckers.'

'Do you know who called Katie and what it was about?'

'No idea.'

'Do you know where Katie's phone is?'

Tanya's features relaxed as she nodded.

'After you told me she was dead, I found the phone at my place. She must have dropped it when she took off. She was pretty rattled.'

'Is it still there?'

'Yep.'

The chances of the call to Katie's mobile being traceable were slim, but it was worth pursuing.

'Okay. I'll send an officer over to retrieve it. That's all we need for now. But the AFP are going to want to talk to you about other parts of the operation.'

'I'm not talking to any feds until my ex loses custody and all access to Mikey. I want a restraining order.'

'Do you have evidence linking him to the illegal gambling?'

'None. He flies in, indulges himself at the tables, then flies right out.'

Jenny rose.

'The AFP will likely subpoena you Tanya, but I'll see what I can do.'

Jenny meant what she said. Tanya needed a break. She hoped she could pull it off.

For now, she needed the last pieces of evidence to charge not only Boyle, but Carmen with murder.

Her phone started ringing as she left the interview room.

'You're up early on a Sunday. Thought you had weekends off.'

'Funny.' Penny's voice perked Jenny up. 'I got called in because someone put an urgent rush on a handprint match and a murder weapon.'

'And.'

'The shed print matches Boyle. We also have a partial for him on the bat.'

'Nothing on Carmen?'

'No physical evidence linking her to the murder scene or the victim's remains.'

'Damn. I'll need to get Boyle to implicate Carmen somehow.'

'Not my department. Gotta go, but I'll see you Sunday.'

'Sunday?'

'Yes, next Sunday. It's Christmas and Tim and I are joining the Johnston family Christmas.'

'Since when?'

'Since Nick invited us and I managed to get the shift off.'

'That's awesome. See you then.' Jenny hung up. She was finally going to be able to have some time with Penny and it wouldn't involve a murder or some other forensic investigation.

'You done Williams?'

'We are Sarge. Nellie is heading over to Tanya's place. Apparently, the victim's phone has been there all this time.'

'Would have been nice to have known that earlier.'

'Agreed. I just got off the phone to Penny. We have enough to formally charge Boyle with Maryam's murder.'

'In that case, all our suspects are in custody, so we'll start interviews Monday at 7am. It will give us time to analyse the victim's phone and get some rest. We can come back with fresh eyes.'

'Are we arresting Sullivan?'

Sergeant Mackenzie shook his head.

'Nothing on him at this stage. He picked up his son from one of his security team who found the kidnappers.'

'But he ranted at us. Went to great lengths to let us believe Mikey was still missing. Then stashed him away in the Underground Motel with his nanny.'

'He was probably trying to distance himself from whatever Carmen and Boyle had planned for Tanya and Ben.'

'You really think so?'

Her boss shrugged.

'I already told you Williams. You can't solve them all.'

Chapter 53

Jenny's eyes flew open in complete darkness. She struggled to rise beneath a heavy weight on her chest. Sweat drenched her body. Something shifted in the darkness. She jumped to her feet before recalling she was in her dugout bedroom with Nick.

'Jen. You alright?' Nick's husky voice was barely audible over her beating heart.

'Yeah.'

'Were you dreaming?'

She shook her head before realising he couldn't see her.

'Sort of. I woke up disorientated, and your arm was over my chest.'

'Come back to bed.'

She heard him pat the sheets.

'I'm wide awake now. I need coffee.'

Nick groaned. The sound of fabric told her he was getting out of bed. Reaching in the darkness, she clicked the bedside lamp on and saw Nick pick up his watch.

'What time is it?'

He tightened the wristband and turned the dial over to read it.

'5. I better get back to the farm.'

'And I need to get ready to nail a murderer.'

'I like my job better. Cattle don't shoot at you.'

'I thought you were enjoying the AFP private investigation stuff.'

'Not as much fun as I thought.'

Jenny wanted to warn Nick to be careful. This latest case with the CWU and illegal gambling was now linked to Jamie Povich, the CEO of Foresight Mining through Sullivan and his relationship with Judge Temperance Povich.

The threats against local landowners started around the same time the highway work commenced. The same time Ben arrived in town.

It wasn't a coincidence. Was Boyle behind it from the beginning? Was Sullivan pulling his strings, or was Carmen?

It would all be out of her hands soon. Once the murder charges were laid, the Australian Federal Police would take over. Jenny didn't like the idea of not knowing if Nick was still in danger.

'Have you heard from Ben? Is he cleared to leave hospital?' Jenny said.

'Not yet. I'll call past the hospital this morning. Then I'll meet you at Niko's for coffee.'

Ben needed to answer questions before heading back to William Creek. She was tempted to remind Nick. But didn't.

'Sounds good.'

Half an hour later, Jenny drove her Dodge from the dugout into town. Ted's Garage came into view, reminding Jenny of Saturday night. She slowed down on the way past, noticing two cameras mounted on the corners of the shed.

Flynn said Sullivan picked Mikey up from the garage. Sullivan claimed he knew nothing about Boyle or Carmen's activities. A smile crept across her lips as she dialled Ted's Garage after-hours number.

Jenny entered the interview room two hours later with a second caramel latte in hand.

'Mr Sullivan. Thanks for coming in so early.' Jenny nodded to Ms Buchanan, dropped into her seat opposite Sullivan and made a show of savouring her coffee.

The CWU official relaxed back and nodded for his lawyer to lead the conversation.

'What is this about Constable? I have two other clients here and my day is full enough without this.'

'I understand.' Jenny passed O'Connell his cappuccino and nodded she was ready to start the interview. 'I assure you we aren't wasting your time. It's important we get this interview out the way before we start the next two.'

Sullivan leant forward.

'Why?'

His lawyer shook her head and tutted.

'Why didn't you advise the police that Mikey was safe with your nanny Saturday night?'

'No comment.' Ms Buchanan answered for Sullivan.

'You wasted valuable police resources.' Jenny reached for the tablet O'Connell held up for her. 'But I think we understand why.'

'Get to the point Constable or we are leaving.'

The lawyer lifted her briefcase to her lap, to emphasise her point.

'I'm afraid your client won't be going anywhere today, Ms Buchanan.' Jenny pressed *play* on the tablet and turned it to face them.

Sullivan glanced at the screen. Then realisation hit him. He knew exactly what his lawyer was about to see.

'This footage clearly shows when Mr Sullivan collected his son from Mr Boyle and Ms Perez. He was fully aware that Ben Stokes' life might well be in danger.'

The CCTV recording clearly showed Sullivan rounding the F-250 to take Mikey from Carmen while David Boyle held Ben in a headlock.

'That proves nothing. Ben Stokes aided Tanya Rothchild in the kidnapping of my client's son. Reasonable force was needed to extract the child.'

'Firstly, Mr Boyle is not a law enforcement officer or a licensed private investigator or even a qualified security guard.

298

He should have called the police if he knew the whereabouts of a missing child under an Amber Alert.'

The lawyer huffed.

'No comment.'

'Tanya Rothchild will testify Mr Sullivan threatened to permanently take custody of her child if she didn't keep quiet about the illegal activities being conducted by David Boyle and Carmen Perez.'

That wasn't exactly what Tanya agreed to do, but if this interview went well, Jenny was sure Tanya would cooperate fully.

'It is her understanding the attack on her and the attempted kidnapping of her son was undertaken at her ex-partner's request.'

'Hearsay.'

'I disagree.' Jenny prodded the tablet. 'This video speaks to collusion.'

Ms Buchanan shoved the tablet toward Jenny and leant in to whisper to her client. Jenny knew the video wasn't enough to get Sullivan locked up, at least not for long, but in the right hands, it could draw a spotlight on Sullivan and add fuel to the AFP case against the CWU.

'What do you want?'

'It's not what *we* want that matters.'

The lawyer's eyes narrowed.

'I don't understand.' She glanced from O'Connell to Jenny.

Sullivan sat forward with a sneer.

'I think I do.' He nodded for Jenny to go on.

'Tanya Rothchild requires you to cease custody proceedings now and in the future.'

Sullivan fell back in his chair and crossed his arms. Chewed his lip a moment, then crooked his finger so his lawyer would draw closer.

Their conversation was hushed, but short. Ms Buchanan's expression was sour, but she finally nodded to her client.

'So if my client signs the paperwork, Ms Rothchild stops making up stories implicating my client in any wrongdoing. And you take any, and all charges relating to illegal gambling, illegal workers and the murder of Maryam Suleiman off the table?'

'Exactly.'

Chapter 54

Jenny barely contained her excitement as she compiled Tanya's statement. She wouldn't implicate Sullivan as her part of the agreement, but she certainly gave more than enough evidence to make sure Boyle and Carmen went away for the attack on Ben. She would further testify to overhearing them discuss silencing Flynn for good.

Her evidence, together with the police statements and Flynn's account would see neither of them walk free today.

'Williams.' Sergeant Mackenzie called from his office doorway. 'Where are we at with the murder charges?'

He waved her into his office. O'Connell joined them.

'The physical evidence against Boyle is damning. A partial fingerprint was on the weapon. Penny has matched the blood to Ben and Maryam. His handprint was found where the victim's top was recovered.'

'Anything to link Carmen to the murder?'

'Nothing yet. Flynn took the bat, because he wanted it. He didn't realise it was used to kill anyone. He only got scared of Carmen and Dave Boyle when they started chasing him.'

'So Tanya didn't witness the murder. Neither did Flynn. All we have is the victim's last phone call. Any luck tracing the number?'

'It was a pay-as-you-go and we haven't found one amongst Carmen or David Boyle's possessions. We've also checked CCTV footage of the newsagency it was purchased at. Nothing.'

'Damn'

All eyes scanned the whiteboard, hoping something would jump out at them.

'Do we sweat Boyle?' O'Connell waved a folder in his hand. 'Maybe he can tell us where he or Carmen were staying?

If Carmen made the call, he might be willing to let her take the fall?'

Jenny considered O'Connell's words.

'I think I saw Mundy dealing drugs at Marj's bar. He claimed Carmen was the boss of everything. We know Boyle has links to the Harlequins. Maybe we offer him a deal?'

Sergeant Mackenzie shook his head.

'No way. No one rolls over on the Outlaw Bikies and walks away. Boyle isn't talking. We need more evidence.'

Jenny scanned the whiteboard photos again. She opened the printed copy of the postmortem once more and scanned the details, then glanced back up at the photos, stopping when she saw the ring photo.

Frowning, she rescanned the victim's injuries again. Then glanced up once more and focussed in on the photo of Ben's name, written in blood.

The ring…

The name…

An earlier theory rolled around her head. She checked the injury report one more time. She was right. Maryam was dead when Ben's name was written in the boot. She scanned the rest of the report. Right again. The engagement ring was forcibly ripped from the victim's hand.

'Do we have Ben's statement yet?'

'No and we won't get it,' Sarge huffed.

'What?'

'The AFP have closed in. I'm not sure how they found out what we were investigating?'

'If I had to guess I'd say Ben.'

Sarge frowned. 'Ben?'

'It's just a feeling. Something Nick said.'

'Either way. We can't talk to him until after the AFP have. And even then, we can only ask him about Maryam's death. What are you thinking?'

'I think Ben's been involved with these guys from the start. Not necessarily by choice. His connection to Boyle. Povich being the CEO and her sister the judge.'

'We agree on that. What's the point?'

'Sarge.' Jenny turned the postmortem results around to show her boss. 'These injuries suggest Maryam was dead before she was dumped into the boot. Her hands were bound so tightly, I don't see how she wrote Ben's name on the boot lining.'

'You think the killer wrote Ben's name?'

'Yes and I think they ripped Maryam's engagement ring off her finger in anger. She was a bargaining chip to keep Ben in line. Maybe she was ordered to seduce him. I'm sure she wasn't supposed to fall in love and get married.'

'But the DNA on the ring and the blood have already been run.'

'I need to call Penny. I've got an idea.'

'Get on with it then.'

Jenny slipped her mobile from her pocket and dialled her friend's phone directly.

'Hey.'

'Hey yourself. I'd ask how your weekend was, but I know you were working.' Sergeant Mackenzie gave her a wind-up signal. 'Sorry to put the pressure on, but has the DNA come back on the bottle and tissue?'

Sergeant Mackenzie glanced at O'Connell who shrugged he didn't know what Jenny was referring to. Everything was so busy, she forgot to tell them she asked Nellie to collect Carmen's bottle and tissue when she cleaned up the interview room.

'It has. What do you need?'

'Great. Can you run it against the engagement ring and Ben's name, written in blood in the boot?'

'Whoever wrote Ben's name, likely wore gloves.'

'Maybe. It's always bugged me why Maryam's ring was thrown into the boot with her body. The autopsy report indicated tissue damage consistent with the ring being torn from the victim while she was alive. That's something you do in anger.'

'Without gloves. Nice one. I'll run a comparison now.'

Keys clicked as Penny sought out the results. Jenny ignored the quizzical expression from her bosses and busied herself collating photos and evidence ready to interview Boyle.

'Bingo!' Penny's excitement filtered down the phone.

'So which is it?'

'On the ring. Nothing on the bloodied name.'

'Thanks Penny. You've made my day.'

'Actually, I think I might have made your year.'

'Big call.'

'Sending you a file and I'll let you be the judge.'

Penny hung up before Jenny could ask any further questions.

'Penny is sending a file through. Something big by the sound of it, but Carmen Perez's DNA was most definitely on the victim's ring.'

'She might be able to explain that away. Didn't you say she was one of the few people who knew Maryam was engaged?'

'Yes, but Tanya never said she let anyone handle the ring and she didn't wear it when she was at work.'

'Still, see what McGregor is sending through. I think you'll need more than DNA on the victim's ring.'

Jenny trudged from Sergeant Mackenzie's office, dropped into her office chair and opened the file Penny sent her.

Butterflies fought with nausea as she read the details. It seemed that there was so much more to Carmen Perez they didn't realise.

Chapter 55

Jenny hit *print*, rushed to the printer and grabbed the warm sheet. Turning, she jogged to Sergeant Mackenzie's office, where O'Connell and her boss still studied the whiteboard.

'Carmen's DNA is a familial match to a cold-case involving drugs and organised crime. And her last name isn't Perez.'

Sergeant Mackenzie rolled his eyes.

'Great. The AFP are probably already on their way.'

Her boss was right. They needed to act fast.

'Nellie!' she called over her shoulder.

Sergeant Mackenzie opened his mouth as Nellie's head appeared in the doorway.

'What's up?'

'Do you know anything about a cold-case involving the death of Emelio Lopez?'

'Do I ever. His wife and child were brutally slain, and he was found with his tongue cut out and his balls…'

'Okay. We get it Nellie.' Sergeant Mackenzie waved his hand at the former cold-case blogger. 'What's this got to do with Perez?'

'Lopez was the familial match.'

O'Connell whistled.

Sarge grunted.

'How familial?'

Jenny smiled.

'Like brother and sister kind of familial.'

'Finally, some leverage.' Sergeant Mackenzie pointed to Nellie.

'You seem to have the background on this one. How far will Ms Perez go to keep her identity hidden?'

Nellie's white teeth filled her face.

'All the way. Lopez's murder was a retribution killing. The kind requiring the torture and agonising death of the entire family.'

'Good. You two, take this one.'

Nellie's brown eyes widened.

'Me?'

'You know the case. You take the lead.'

Nellie fist-pumped the air and jumped up and down before smoothing her uniform and pressing her lips together.

'Ready?' Jenny patted the newest team member on the shoulder.

'Damn right. Let's do this.'

Ten minutes later Jenny readied the recording equipment, then nodded for Nellie to go ahead.

The woman sitting across from them no longer resembled the trembling victim Jenny interviewed Friday night. How easily she'd been fooled.

Maybe she was faking it again now. Maybe the smug look on her face was another role she knew how to play.

Nellie cleared her throat and readied a pad and pen.

'Ms Perez. I'm Constable Miller, I believe you know Constable Williams.'

Carmen sneered at the young constable.

'Where's my lawyer?'

Nellie smiled so genuinely Carmen appeared confused.

'You mean Ms Buchanan?'

'Yes.' Carmen's tone was wary.

Nellie's smile widened.

'Oh, she won't be able to help you. Sorry.'

Jenny knew Nellie was playing a role of her own. The blogger was smart, determined and well versed in the Lopez case. She also knew exactly why Ms Buchanan couldn't assist Carmen right now.

A deep crease almost joined Carmen's thick black eyebrows together.

'Why not?'

'Ms Buchanan is brokering a deal and assisting Mr Boyle to unburden himself.'

Carmen threw herself back into the seat.

'Rubbish.'

Jenny noticed Carmen's tight-fitting dress, accentuated her curves and wondered when she'd changed. And why? Was she expecting Phillips or some other admiring male to interview her?

Neither Nellie nor Jenny was going to be impressed with her eyelash flutter.

'No. Really.' Nellie's tone was sweet. 'You see we had a bit of evidence against Mr Boyle, but he said he was following *your* orders.'

'That's ridiculous.'

'Well, I guess time will tell. Maybe you have something you'd like to share. Something to disprove Mr Boyle's claims?'

'You said yourself all the evidence points to Boyle. Him saying otherwise won't hold up in court.'

Nellie lifted her thick eyebrows at Jenny.

'Wow. Who needs a lawyer? Looks like you've got it all covered. Except…'

Nellie fiddled with a folder on the table, opened it, showed something to Jenny who nodded, then closed the file and placed her hand firmly on top.

'What's going on?'

'Good question.' Nellie's smile was back. 'You see when you were in here, lying about Leigh Mundy assaulting you and putting on all those tears, Constable Williams asked me to collect a few things when you left.'

Carmen frowned, then her expression contorted.

'Now you get it. You gave us your DNA and we found it on the victim's ring. The ring you tore from her finger because you were annoyed she was engaged to Ben.'

'I want a lawyer.'

'Ms Buchanan is busy.'

'I want a public defender.'

'You're an illegal visa overstayer Ms Perez. I can request an immigration lawyer for you, but that might take a while.'

Perez crossed her arms over her exposed cleavage.

'I'll wait.'

'That's your right of course, but we've been asked to make a statement to the press…' Nellie glanced at Jenny. This time she waved her hand indicating she wanted Jenny to finish her sentence.

The drama was right up Nellie's alley. Jenny suppressed a smile.

'What Constable Miller is saying is that when we make that statement, we'll be forced to advise the media of your real name, Ms Lopez.'

The colour drained from Carmen's face.

'You can't.' she choked on the words.

'We can and we will.' Nellie resumed the interview. 'Unless you help us out.'

Carmen's eyes narrowed. She remained silent, weighing up her options. Jenny was impressed when Nellie let the silence linger.

'What do you want?' Carmen spat the words out.

'If you didn't kill Maryam, you won't mind telling us where your burner phone is?'

Carmen's tongue slid along her teeth.

'I don't have one, but… Boyle does.'

Jenny knew that was unlikely, but she remained quiet as Nellie continued.

'Where will we find it?'

Nellie shoved a pad of paper toward Carmen, then held the pen against the page, ready for Carmen to take it in her hand.

'Write down the address.'

'If I do, will Boyle's deal be cancelled?'

'Ms Perez. You'll be charged with accessory to murder. But the judge will consider your cooperation with police.'

As Carmen scribbled the address down, Jenny tried to ignore the niggling feeling they were being played again. She heard Sergeant Mackenzie's words in her head once more.

You can't solve them all.

Carmen would be charged with attempted murder, false imprisonment, assault, accessory to murder and if Jenny knew anything about the AFP, she'd likely endure hours of questioning.

Nellie snatched the pad from Carmen and jumped to her feet.

'Thank you for your cooperation.'

Nellie hurried from the interview room. Jenny spoke into the recording.

'Interview ended. 12.43.' She clicked the recording equipment off.

'I've been meaning to ask you, off the record.' Carmen licked her lips. 'What does Ben Stokes have to do with Boyle and Foresight Mining?'

Carmen opened her mouth but stopped when someone cleared their throat behind Jenny. She turned to see a blue clad

AFP officer with ash blonde hair and a crooked nose shake his head.

'No more questions Constable. We'll be taking Ms Lopez from here.'

'Can I see your credentials and paperwork?'

She eyed the automatic pistol strapped to his thigh as he reached into the side pocket of his pants and retrieved a folded sheet of paper.

'I'm Senior Sergeant Ray Black.' He handed her the paperwork. 'I've heard good things about you Constable Williams.'

'You were quick.'

'I was in the area.'

Jenny nodded understanding. She was face to face with Nick's AFP liaison. Was he here to speak with Ben? She opened the paperwork.

'Your boss has already checked it.'

'I'm sure he has.' Jenny read the details, hoping to pick up a clue as to whether Carmen was being taken because of who she was, or what she knew about Ben, Boyle, Sullivan and everything the men were linked to.

She sighed as she read Boyle's name on the orders. These murder charges would be used to turn them against the organisations further up the chain.

Senior Sergeant Black held his hand out.

'Are we good?'

Jenny slapped the paperwork into his hand.

'As good as we can be.'

The officer's eyes softened as he regarded her a moment.

'They won't be breathing fresh air any time soon. You have my word.'

Jenny nodded, allowing herself a slight smile.

Senior Sergeant Black brushed past her on his way to Perez, then turned.

'Nick's right about you Constable Williams. You are going places. I'll be seeing you.'

Chapter 56

Expansive, arid flat land reached out toward the distant escarpment. A heat haze shimmered over the ochre rock, jarring against the clear blue sky. Jenny's mind drifted back to her first visit to William Creek Station.

She shivered as a tingle brought goosebumps to her skin. The day's hot dry breeze was replaced with the memory of a cool wind funnelling through a limestone and ochre chasm, where native art and stretching gums wrapped around her soul and brought a smile to her lips.

Corellas circled overhead, landing on the parched native pea bushes bordering the long dead lawn. Their squawking call drifted on the hot breeze.

'Dinner is ready.' Nick wrapped his arms around her waist and kissed her exposed shoulder.

Jenny wondered if she should tell Nick about her visit to the Fergusson farm earlier in the week. The CFS report confirmed arson. Mr Fergusson revealed a mining company was sniffing around his property, but this time it wasn't Povich or Foresight.

Was it all a coincidence?

Ben's statement was confiscated by Senior Sergeant Black and the AFP before Jenny could read it, but the AFP officer assured her Ben was not a threat to Nick or anyone else out at William Creek.

She hoped he was right.

Nick squeezed her waist, then let go and reached for her hand.

'Are you coming in?'

'Of course.'

She let him lead her through the glass doors, into the open kitchen dining area. The aroma of roast lamb and seafood carried her toward the buzz of jovial voices and Christmas carols playing quietly in the background.

'Jenny.' Her mum opened her arms and drew her into a hug. She then lifted the ostentatious Christmas-themed tablecloth with a smile.

'This must be Nat's handywork?'

Jenny laughed at the pallets stacked on sawhorses with old livestock sale signs laid on top.

'Great way to extend the seating.' She hugged her mother again and turned as Marj hurried toward the table with a platter loaded precariously high with prawns.

'Thanks for getting these Marj.'

Marj lowered the platter carefully to the table.

'My pleasure Luv. Least I could do was bring a little something.'

Jenny hugged her mum away from home, caught her real mum's wink, and embraced a wave of emotion. As she scanned along the table extending all the way from the dining area into the living space, hot tears stung her eyes. She didn't fight them.

Benji sat next to her dad, Nellie was next to him, leaning in and laughing with her flirty eyes. Nev and Flynn sat opposite, reading jokes with silly smiles.

The snap of a Christmas cracker drew her eyes to the far end. Tanya unfolded the paper hat and placed it on Mikey's head.

The toddler grabbed it away and tossed it to the ground with distaste.

The room erupted in laughter. Mikey spun to the audience with a grin. Tanya reached down, retrieved the hat and slipped it back on his head. Half a second later, he ripped it free, whipped his head around and waited for another round of laughter from his adoring fans.

Jenny was still giggling when she chose a seat between Penny and Tanya, promising herself there would be no shop talk on Christmas Day. But that didn't stop her mind wandering.

Carmen Perez and David Boyle were in jail. Leigh Mundy was granted his immunity, but Jenny knew he was going to earn it. The AFP were pumping him for information about Carmen Perez's side gig of supplying him with drugs to sell to the FIFO workers.

She wondered if the AFP would turn Dave Boyle or Carmen against the CWU or Foresight Mining. There was no doubt this was all connected. Jenny still didn't have all the pieces yet.

Penny jabbed her in the ribs.

'Where's your head girl?'

She gave Penny a one-armed hug, lifted her wine and drained the glass, then noticed Tanya's non-alcoholic ginger beer.

Leaning toward Penny, she whispered. 'Maybe we should have gone alcohol free?'

Tanya overheard.

'No way.' She adjusted Mikey on her lap. 'My drinking problem is mine to sort out. But thanks for helping me get a decent job. It's going to help a lot.'

Jenny glanced along the table to see Marj deep in conversation with her mum. She turned back to Tanya.

'Cleaning for Marj isn't easy work, but I admit I was a bit worried it might not be ideal for you. The bar is right there. Will it be too much temptation?'

Tanya stroked Mikey's hair and passed him his blue knitted teddy before meeting Jenny's eyes.

'Temptation is everywhere.' She nodded toward Marj as the motel owner reached for a prawn. 'Marj is a good sponsor and without the custody issues, or work stress, I think I'll be able to cope better.'

Jenny caught Marj's smile and quick nod. The woman was a solid rock for Jenny. With her on side, Tanya's chances of making life-changing choices were much better than most.

'Hey everyone, sorry I'm late. Trudy wouldn't let me get away.'

Ben's voice made Jenny's stomach tighten. Nick pulled out a chair opposite her, sat, then waved for Ben to join them as he topped up Jenny's wine glass.

The farm manager made eye contact with her and offered a genuine smile.

'Hey Jenny. This looks amazing.'

He nodded to Penny who nodded back.

Jenny forced herself to put work out of her head. Nick assured her Ben was now working with him to assist the AFP, but the longer the federal investigation went on, the edgier Jenny got.

Sam delivered another tray of prawns to the table squeezed in opposite Jenny's brothers and joined their banter good naturedly.

Platters and bowls of aromatic food made the rounds as conversation rippled around the table. Jenny absorbed the hum and fought the burn of tears at the back of her eyes. Nick's foot tapped her leg beneath the table. She rubbed her bare foot up his calf and nodded.

He lifted up his glass.

'Hey everyone. Can we get your attention? Jenny has…'

'You're pregnant!' her mother blurted out.

The table erupted in nervous giggles. Penny side-eyed her. Jenny shook her head vigorously, then scowled at her mother.

'No mum.' She composed herself. 'But we've set a date for the wedding.'

'Finally!' Marj threw her hands in the air and smiled past her bright red lipstick.

'September the 23rd,' Jenny offered.

'But that's next year,' her mum complained.

'A week away is next year mum,' Nat pointed out.

Her mother pouted.

'You know what I mean. Why so long?' She glared at Nat. 'I want more grandchildren.'

Jenny felt for her brother. Nat explained earlier that day about his pending divorce. She used the opportunity to warn him not to make his kids a bargaining chip between him and his ex-wife.

He assured her it wasn't an issue because Kimberley had full custody, and he was taking the opportunity to travel.

Her mum's pout was warranted. Under the circumstances, access to her grandchildren was going to be severely limited. She only hoped Nat didn't regret his decision later.

Her dad lifted his glass.

'September sounds wonderful Bub. At least we don't have to come back to this stinking heat in February or something.'

'I'll drink to that.' Nat lifted his glass. 'Cheers and congrats little sis.'

'Thanks Nat.'

She caught Benji's eye. He lifted his glass and nodded, then returned his attention to Nellie at his side.

Maybe her brother was going to be back in Coober Pedy sooner rather than later.

Penny nudged her shoulder.

'16th of September it is then.'

'No, 23rd.'

'No. 16th for the hen's night. Adelaide. No arguments.'

Jenny rolled her eyes to the ceiling as Nellie hooted.

'Hell yeah. I'm in.'

'Okay. Okay. Adelaide it is.' Jenny caught Nick's blue eyes smiling at her and reached across to tap her glass against his.

'I can't wait for you to be Mrs Johnston.'

'Who said she's dropping her last name?' Penny tapped her glass to Jenny's

'I did,' Jenny admitted. 'But not professionally. I'll still be plain old Constable Jenny Williams.'

Marj roared with laughter.

'Oh, Luv, there's never been anything plain about you and there never will be.'

****

Join Jenny when her bachelorette party celebration goes horribly wrong in *Her Stolen Bones* available in 2026

Can't wait for another *Opal Fields* story? Then join Detective Dawn Grave who you met in *Her Covered Bones,* when she's dragged away from Coober Pedy for family business. *Grave Regret,* book one in the *Dawn Grave Crime* series takes readers to the wet tropics to discover Dawn's dark past. Available at your favourite bookstore or on my website www.fionatarr.com

Stay up to date with my author world by joining my readers club. You'll receive a free deleted scene from book 1 in the Opal Fields series and learn a little bit about me along the way.

Join my readers club on my website www.fionatarr.com

Thank You!

I hope you enjoyed reading the *Her Stowed Bones*.

If you did, why not tell your friends, or better still, leave a review with your favourite retailer or on my website www.fionatarr.com, so others can make an informed decision about buying into the series.

If you leave a review, I'd love to see a copy, but most of all, I'd like to thank you for reading my stories. You're awesome, really! Without you, I'd be a lot less motivated to get in front of my computer screen and dream up these crazy crime/mystery adventures. Without you, I'd have never bothered to publish. Thanks!

Maybe you've read the new Dawn Grave series and still want more. You might like to see what happens when Jenny takes that detective job in the city. Jenny joins the *Foxy Mysteries series* team in book 2, as Jack Cunningham's new partner. So if you don't mind skipping the 'how she got to Adelaide' bit (I'll be answer this in a brand new series in late 2026), and enjoy a little sizzle with your mysteries, why not check out the entire Foxy Mysteries Collection. All my books can be found on my website at https://fionatarr.com/pages/books

Don't want to miss out on any new releases, but don't do email lists? Then follow me on Amazon or Bookbub or find me on Facebook or Instagram

Books by Fiona Tarr

Opal Fields
Her Buried Bones
Her Broken Bones
Her Scorched Bones
Her Hidden Bones
Her Lonely Bones
Her Covered Bones
Her Lost Bones
Her Stowed Bones
Her Stolen Bones

Dawn Grave
Grave Doubt – an exclusive novella available to my readers club members.
Grave Regret
Grave Intent
Grave Mistake
Grave Secret
Grave Catch

Foxy Mysteries
Death Beneath the Covers
Presumed Missing
Deadly Deceit
Twisted Vendetta
Dead Cold

The Priestess Chronicles
Call of the Druids
Relic Seeker
Shiloh Rising

The Eternal Realm
The Jericho Prophecy
Delilah and the Dark God
Reign of Retribution

Covenant of Grace
Destiny of Kings
Seed of Hope
Legacy of Power
Heir of Vengeance
The Ehud Dagger - Prequel